Koi brings out his fishing hooks, and a bottle of black ink he still has left over from his tenth birthday. It is precious to him. He has not unscrewed the lid in years. I hold back my scream while he carves the word *fearless* into my forearm.

"Now you have a tattoo that isn't from the Initiative," he says. I watch as he puts ink on the wound, and wraps my arm with cloth. "You have to do what it takes to make it home," he whispers. "You can never end up like her."

Nothing matters but these people, on this boat.

Nothing matters but staying alive.

I will be fearless.

D0401322

THE
MURDER
COMPLEX

LINDSAY CUMMINGS

DISCARD

GREENWILLOW BOOKS
An Imprint of HarperCollins*Publishers*

SANTA CLARA PUBLIC LIBRARY
2635 Homestead Road
Santa Clara, CA 95051

This book is a work of fiction. References to real people, events, establishments, organizations, or locales are intended only to provide a sense of authenticity, and are used to advance the fictional narrative. All other characters, and all incidents and dialogue, are drawn from the author's imagination and are not to be construed as real.

The Murder Complex

Copyright © 2014 by Lindsay Cummings

First hardcover edition, 2014. First Greenwillow paperback, 2015.

All rights reserved. No part of this book may be used or reproduced in any manner whatsoever without written permission except in the case of brief quotations embodied in critical articles and reviews. Printed in the United States of America. For information address HarperCollins Children's Books, a division of HarperCollins Publishers, 195 Broadway, New York, NY 10007.
www.epicreads.com

The text of this book is set in 11-point Adobe Garamond
Book design by Paul Zakris

Library of Congress Cataloging-in-Publication Data

Cummings, Lindsay.
The Murder Complex / Lindsay Cummings.
pages cm
"Greenwillow Books."
Summary: In a world where the murder rate is higher than the birth rate, fifteen-year-old Meadow, trained by her father to kill and survive in any situation, falls in love with Zephyr, a government assassin.
ISBN 978-0-06-222000-4 (hardcover)—ISBN 978-0-06-222001-1 (pbk.)
[1. Murder—Fiction. 2. Violence—Fiction. 3. Survival—Fiction.
4. Love—Fiction. 5. Science fiction. 6. Youths' writings.] I. Title.
PZ7.C91466Mu 2014   [Fic]—dc23   2014005186

15 16 17 18 19 CG/RRDH 10 9 8 7 6 5 4 3 2 1
First Edition

 GREENWILLOW BOOKS

To Don Cummings, my dad, who is the reason I write.
I love you.

Welcome to the Murder Complex.
You cannot see us. You cannot feel us.
But we are here.
And we control your every move.

CHAPTER I

MEADOW

It is the key to survival, the key to life. My father's old dagger.

"Peri!" I call out over the waves to my little sister. An old can bobs up and down in the water, mesmerizing me for a moment. Beyond the Shallows, the sea is packed with boats. Some of them are still afloat, with their masts stretching like arms to the sky. Others are half-submerged, shipwrecked and covered with moss.

Among the boats are other things. Old tires, half of a rusted car, plastic. A body lies facedown in the waves, her hair spread out like seaweed.

Behind me, in the city, the Night Siren wails. It starts

low, then whoops higher and back down again. Everyone on the beach hurries into the shadows, knowing all too well what happens when the sun goes down.

It isn't safe anymore. I call out to Peri again. "It's time to go!"

She holds up a tiny hand and gives me the signal: two grubby little fingers held high above her head.

Two minutes. It is always two more minutes with her.

The sun is sinking, a massive orange ball melting into the sea. It sets fire to the sky, and everything is dancing in colors. Reds, oranges, yellows. It reminds me of blood, it reminds me of my mother.

Peri comes running up to me, kicking a spray of sand behind her. "I found a periwinkle!" she squeaks, sounding like a startled seagull. "Like me!"

"Yeah? Let's see it." I cast a glance over my shoulder, at the few people who still litter the beach, before kneeling down to her level. Peri's big gray eyes, the color of sea foam, widen as she places the tiny shell in my outstretched palm. It's twisty and fat, with a sharp point at the top. A mollusk sticks out. Though it has barely enough meat for anyone to eat, I'm still tempted to shove it into my pocket. But somehow the Initiative would find out. As sure as the tide comes and goes, the

Initiative will always discover our secrets.

"It's a good one," I say, smiling down at her. "But we can't keep it."

The thick black numbers tattooed onto her forehead crease in frustration. 72050. Peri's Catalogue Number, just one number different from mine. Our barcodes show the Initiative where we are, *who* we are, every moment of our lives. As Peri grows, it will grow, and it will never fade or wrinkle because of the healing nanites we all have in our blood.

"Tell you what." I point the tip of my dagger toward the shell. "We'll mark it. That way, next time you find it, you'll remember." I etch a small heart into the side of the shell. It's crooked, and hardly legible. I drop the mollusk on the sand, let the waves take it away. Peri smiles triumphantly. She's a miniature version of me. Silver hair that hangs in loose curls to her waist. Like our mother's.

"Okay, time to go." She grabs my hand and tows me along the sand, humming the tune to an old lullaby under her breath. Soft, so no one but the two of us can hear it. Peri knows the value of silence in the Shallows.

At the far end of the beach, a jetty of large rocks juts out into the ocean. Waves crash on the rocks, and we get soaked, but it doesn't matter. The heat of the summer clings to me like fog.

Peri goes first, clambering on hands and feet up the jetty and over to the other side. I climb down after her and my breath catches in my throat.

Pirates.

They'll do anything for extra Creds. The Initiative pays them to guard the shore and take care of minor problems, as well as find and report the citizens who break the four Commandments of the Shallows.

Commandment One: Honor the Initiative.

Commandment Two: Thou shalt not attempt to cross the Perimeter.

Commandment Three: Honor the Silent Hour.

Commandment Four: Thou shalt not harbor useful items from the days Before.

"Pay up," one of the Pirates says. He stands from his spot by a blazing campfire. They are cooking fish.

We could never afford an entire fish. Whatever we gather is sent to the Rations Department, and mixed and pureed with other nutrient-rich foods for distribution.

"We don't want any trouble tonight," I say. I press Peri closer to my side. "We just want to get to our boat."

The Pirate laughs, and the two men with him join

in. They are all covered in tattoos. One of them has an Initiative tattoo—an open, unblinking eye—on his neck, just below his chin. "You want to go to sea, little girl, you gotta pay."

My hand finds the dagger on my thigh. There are only three of them. If I were alone, I could end this at once. But Peri tugs on my shirt, and I see the fear in her eyes. I cannot risk her safety. Not now, when the Dark Time is so close. And I have nothing to give the Pirates, nothing to buy us passage.

But Peri does.

She wears a pair of too-large tennis shoes, and the laces are still intact. Something like that is precious, and it kills me that I will be the one to take them from her.

"I'll give you the laces," I tell the Pirates, pointing at Peri's feet. "Then you'll let us go."

The largest man lets out a whistle. His breath is rotten. "I'm feeling generous tonight, little girl. Next time, you better come prepared. Understood?"

I nod my head. "Next time you might not get away with your life."

He thinks it's a joke.

I stoop to untie the laces. Peri frowns, but does not cry. She's strong, my little sister.

The Pirates snatch the laces and go back to their fish, laughing. Peri and I pass safely and run down the beach. We yank the palm fronds and seaweed from our boat. It is a tiny dinghy, large enough for only two people. I quickly untie the line, push the boat into the waves, and we leave the shore behind.

"Meadow? Will we eat tonight?" Peri asks me as I row, weaving through the maze of waste and litter. The wind blows her hair back from her face, and I notice how her cheekbones stick out, how her eyes are slightly sunken. She's losing more weight.

"Yes." I nod, looking away. The way she's studying me, as if I am the only thing in the world worth loving, makes my heart fill with guilt. If she only knew what I do to make sure she can eat. To make sure that all of us survive.

Two miles from shore, I stop and stare out at the black sea, feeling my shoulders burn from the effort of rowing. The dinghy bumps up against our houseboat. It is quiet here, a still night, the waves lapping the boat, the same way they always have. When my mother was murdered, I thought the world would end with her. But it goes on.

CHAPTER 2

ZEPHYR

A number is a stupid thing to fear.

57809. Each time I see that one I shiver.

45860. I spin away, face flushed, fingers trembling.

23412. Guilt. Hatred. Anguish. I want to turn around and bang my head against a brick wall until it bleeds, until I black out and leave the world behind.

Wards shouldn't have feelings. Especially the boys. We should be tough, able to fend for ourselves. At least, that's what the Initiative tells us.

It's stupid to fear a number.

But I do.

I do.

CHAPTER 3

MEADOW

Every night, I stay awake for as long as I can to keep my nightmares at bay. I stand on the deck. The sea is blacker than the sky, and even though I can barely see the waves rising and falling in the moonlight, I feel the motion beneath my feet. A gentle lull that makes me feel safe. The other boats around us slosh and groan at their moorings. There used to be others living on the boats.

But everyone has either been killed or disappeared. Now it is just my family that survives in the sea.

In the distance, I can see the lights of the Perimeter— the massive black wall that surrounds the Shallows.

My father tells me there was a war that tore the country

apart, and everyone left alive got the Plague. It turns your insides to mush. You die in an instant, and everyone close enough to see it happen dies, too.

Every so often, the top edge of the Perimeter blinks blue, then purple, and back again. The Pulse. The lights send a message to the Pin that is implanted in our arms, at birth. When it gets the message, the Pin releases nanites. They eat away at the impurities in our bodies, fixing our cells, like sand fleas cleaning the sand. Because of it, we are all healthy. Because of the Pulse, death by an illness or disease is no longer something to fear. The Plague cannot harm us here. Commandment Two is for our safety.

And that is the only reason why we stay.

I start to turn, ready to head back inside. Peri will be having her own nightmares by now. But before I do, something stops me.

I think I hear footsteps.

"Peri?"

Something hits me, hard, and the air is knocked from my lungs. I tumble overboard, crashing into the black sea.

Someone has me. We are sinking to the bottom of the ocean, fast, the moonlight overhead slowly fading.

I can't breathe, I can't think. I am going to drown.

Count to three. Relax your mind. Now survive. My father's words ring clearly in my head, and I obey.

My fist connects with human flesh, and I hear a low groan through the water. I reach back and grab the handle of my dagger, open my eyes, and thrust it toward my attacker. The blade connects, just as I feel three hard squeezes on my arm. The signal in my family, when we are ready to give up. I recoil, pulling the dagger away. I'm going to pay for this one.

I kick to the surface and suck in the cool summer air as my brother surfaces beside me.

"What the hell, Meadow?!" Koi rages, both of us sputtering salt water. "Dad!" he screams, and our father's face appears over the railing. He tosses the rope ladder down to us, and we swim toward it in the moonlight.

"Damn it!" Koi groans as he hobbles up the ladder and flops onto the deck like a dying fish. He lies on his back and gulps in air. Silver tendrils of hair frame his scarred face. "How many times have I told you? Leave . . . the dagger . . ." Groan. "On the boat . . ." Groan. "When we're sparring!"

I pull myself up the ladder and squat down beside my brother. He gives me the one-fingered salute and I wince at the small pool of blood gathering on the deck beneath his thigh. Blood doesn't bother me, most of the time. The nanites repair our wounds at a rapid rate. They leave scars behind, signs of our strength. But seeing my brother's blood makes my head spin. The thought of *me* being the one to end Koi's life makes me want to retch.

"You snuck up on me!" I whine. But despite the blood, I can't help but smile. Koi's wins tally three for every one of mine. "Here, let me help. . . ."

"No, I'm fine," Koi growls. The wound is already closing. "It isn't even that bad." He grimaces and swats my hand away. His scars are like hundreds of tiny teeth marks up and down his arms. Mine aren't as bad—only a few nicks here and there— but I wish I had more. Scars are trophies in the Shallows. They show we know how to cheat death.

"Nice work, Meadow." My father grins up at me. He turns the crank on a big, rusted wheel positioned on the bow of the boat. Down aft is a housing unit that holds a coil of barbed wire. Chains connected to the wheel release a thick strand of barbed wire from the housing unit. The wire snakes around the railing of our boat, its points sharp as knives. No one can ever be too safe. "You're getting better. I think you're ready."

"Really?" I try not to let my voice squeak with

excitement. Tomorrow is my birthday. Sixteen years old, and it cannot come fast enough. It is June, the sixth month of the year, when two special trains will run through the Shallows—the Red and the Blue Train. If I make it on, I will have my placement test, and if everything goes well, finally, a real paying job. That will mean more food and water rations for my family.

"Yes, really." My father motions for us to join him inside. We saunter in after him, and he lights a candle once we close the doors and shutters. I think I smell lilies, my mother's favorite flower. But the scented candles are long gone.

Across the room, I can see Peri sprawled on her mattress, arms and legs spread wide as if she's just collapsed after a long, exhausting run.

"Are you nervous?" Koi pulls up an old wooden chair and swings it around so he's sitting on it backward, arms spread casually across the rounded top.

"No," I lie, because I don't want Koi to think I'm weak. "Tell me how to get on the train."

He chuckles under his breath. "I've already told you, Meadow. A thousand times. Just keep your head down. Don't draw attention to yourself. You'll be fine."

I cast a sideways glance at my father, and he confirms

Koi's words with a silent nod. Our rations bag lies open on the table. My father's earnings for the week. I use my dagger to slice off a piece of bread from one of the loaves. It crumbles in my fingers when I lift it to my mouth, but I don't complain. We have learned to be thankful for what little we can get our hands on.

"What if I don't make it on?" I cast a glance at Koi. "Just tell me again. *Please*."

His eyes hold mine for a second, and he smiles. It is something Koi and Peri do often—a rare thing in the Shallows. "You'll make it on. You do what I've told you to do. Everyone else is going to scramble for the first train. It's a bloodbath, trust me, so you'll stay back and *wait*. You get on the second train, and instead of going for the cabin, climb right onto the top of it."

He made it on the train, three years ago. But he failed his placement test.

He hates himself for it. Every day I see it in his eyes.

"You'll get on the train," Koi says again. He reaches forward and places his hand on top of mine. It is something my mother used to do. "You're strong. When you make it to the test, you'll pass."

We are quiet for a while. My brother takes out an old piece of driftwood and starts to carve. I hear the scratching of his knife, the steadiness of his breathing. His carvings are always so real, like little snapshots of life, and I silently thank the world for not taking this little piece of happiness away from him. Tonight, his carving is of my father, cleaning his fishing hooks after the day's work. Sometimes I feel like I could just sit here forever and watch Koi. It is a simple thing, putting the tip of a blade to wood. But the end result is always something beautiful.

"Why didn't you pass the test, Koi?" I've asked him before. He's never told me the reason. He has always changed the subject, or gone back to whatever he was doing without a word.

But tonight, he sighs and sets his knife down.

"You remember your training?" Koi asks.

My father walks in and sets a pot of boiled water on the small table. I scoop my hands into the pot, take a mouthful, and let the warm water trickle down my throat. My father leaves without a word, and a few moments later, I hear the rumble of a storm overhead. "We've practiced survival for years," Koi says. "And what does Dad always tell us?"

I look over at Peri. "Kill or be killed," I whisper.

Koi nods his head. He picks up his knife again, and his

knuckles turn white. "When you get into that room, and you *will*, Meadow," he says, when he sees me open my mouth to protest, "there will be you and someone else. They'll test you with questions. The results will be inconclusive. They always are."

He flips the driftwood over and starts on another carving. "I failed, because I wasn't strong enough." His marks become rough. I think I see my mother's face, but he slams his knife into the tabletop and throws the driftwood aside before I get a close look. "The only reason I made it back is because I'm a coward. I fought my way out of that room so the boy up against me could live."

"Just because you didn't kill anyone doesn't make you a coward," I say. "It makes you good." Koi is brave because he still knows how to love, and how to be soft, in a world full of hate.

But me . . . I would kill for my family, even for a single loaf of bread.

"Only one of you will leave that room alive, and with a *job*, Meadow. And it will be you. *You* will do what I wasn't strong enough to do."

We stare at each. "Kill or be killed," he says. He goes back to his carving, silent and calm and so different from me.

Because suddenly I know what Koi is trying to tell me.

I am a killer, trained by my father, and I always have been. I stand up and grab the driftwood. Peri will want to keep this one.

"I'm sorry for what I am," I sigh, as I crawl in bed next to her. She rolls over and I feel her hot breath on my cheek.

Tonight, I am safe.

In the city, safety is a thing of the past. The murder rate has risen to 300 deaths a month and anyone could be next. My mother was.

Tomorrow, I will kill so that it will not be me.

CHAPTER 4

ZEPHYR

"Clean up that mess, 72348! What do you think this is, day care? Get moving, Ward!"

The Crime and Trauma Scene Decontamination officer is somewhat of a prick. And not just a regular one. He's a new prick, fresh on the job . . . the worst kind, with brand-new slacks, ironed and washed, probably by his mother, paid for by his wealthy Initiative father.

He's a grade-A bloodsucker. Leeches are protected by a Version 2.0 Pin. The CTSDs seem to age slower than us, and not a single one of them has a wrinkle or scar that shows.

I shove my sponge into the bucket of bleach and wring

it out, the thick scent wafting through my nostrils. The familiar wave of nausea rushes through me. Talan is glaring at me as she digs out the Pin from the victim's lifeless arm, nothing but a pair of flimsy latex gloves between her and number 34570's tendons. The Leech officer comes over and Talan places the Pin in the lockbox. The nanites will be recycled for the next person unlucky enough to be born into the Shallows.

If you ask me, Leeches deserve a bloody death and a shallow grave.

Talan leans over another body, this one with a bludgeoned head. She rolls her baby blues. I chuckle under my breath. I can almost hear her gravelly voice whining, "Oh . . . my . . . GOD . . . Zephyr . . . *Ohmigod*. It's not as bad for you. You're a GUY. I'm seriously considering prostitution over this."

I flash her a toothy grin and set to work scrubbing the bloodstained pavement. Talan's not all that bad looking. She's got sort of a sexy, mysterious look to her; curvy, in a good way, with electric eyes and long dark hair that reaches her slim waist. She'd get rations if she became one of *those* girls, sure, but she wouldn't last long. Nothing in the Shallows ever does.

A finger of hot sweat slides down my spine. Scrubbing

under the Florida sun is hard work. Today is Sunday. Collection day, the worst day of the week. It's a day of mourning and reflection.

I take a shovel and slide it beneath a body. All across the city's cracked pavement, there are bodies. Dead ones. Some days old, some only hours. There are bodies covered in flies, in birds that peck out lunch or steal strands of hair to weave into a nest. But the worst part is the blood. Dried, crusted rivers of it, stuck to the city's streets like glue. The metallic scent is choking, and when the heat rises from the tar and the sun shines down so strong it's like we are under one giant magnifying glass, the blood begins to bubble. When it's boiled for too long it begins to burn.

It's my job to clean the stuff up. All the Wards are assigned jobs that no one else wants to do. Like trash duty; hauling piles of it to the Graveyard, a big mountain of garbage on the edge of the city where the street gangs will most likely slit your throat. There's shoe shining, for the Leeches. Uniform washing.

It's all a bunch of useless skitz, but we've got to do it. *Commandment One: Honor the Initiative.* Every week, on Sunday, I show up and scan in. I scrub and clean and gag and lose my lunch twice. I sit in a sea of flies and try

19

not to think about the day I found Talan's daughter lying crooked on the pavement.

The worst part is that Arden was still breathing, lying there soaked in her own blood. The cuts were so deep, even the nanites couldn't staunch the flow. I watched Talan scoop her up and try to take her away for help, but a Leech held a rifle to her head. One of those big ones, with bullets that would blast a hole through her skull. "Finish her," he said. "Do the job right."

I did it instead.

I couldn't let Talan be the one to do it.

But that's the price we pay for being Wards. We're all pawns, orphans with no other choice. We'll do anything to survive, and the Leeches make sure it stays that way.

The bell sounds. It's time for lunch break. All around me, the Wards move as one, like a vast migration, toward the Rations Hall. The building is short and squatty, an old elementary school salvaged from the days before the world went to hell. In the corner, a massive hole in the wall is patched with blue tarps. Probably from an old air strike before the Perimeter went up. The original Survivors say it's better in here. They say even the trees died from the Plague, and the birds all fell right out of the sky. My theory is that the world's awful no matter where you go.

"Make it quick. We've got a city to keep clean here, Wards," the Leech barks. Beside me, I can hear Talan huff. We enter the hall and the stench of old meat hits us. Hot. Stifling. Strong enough to ruin anyone's appetite, but we're so fluxing starved it doesn't matter.

I follow Talan into the line. The Leech officer standing here is tall and grossly overweight. Like a wrecking ball. He watches while we scan our Catalogue Numbers, and barks at us to pick up the pace. I glance at the screens showing images of what we're allowed to eat today. A clump of some meatlike substance. I think of it as refried cat. One glass of recycled water. A woman with hair as short as a man's hands us our bags of rations through a small hole in the glass barrier. We take it without complaining. If we didn't, we'd be punished.

Some people, sometimes, are punished to death.

"This is bullskitz," Talan says as we find a spot at a table. She shoves a handful of meat into her mouth. "The Leeches cut our rations *again*."

I look down at my small allotment. "Stars, Talan. You're right."

"That word's never going to catch on," she says.

I shrug. "If I want the word to catch on, it'll catch on. They're practically gods, you know."

"You're *seeing* stars, if you ask me. Did I accidentally hit you in the head with a shovel out there?" She finishes her plate in record time.

Every day it seems like we get less. More for the Leeches to eat. Their towering complex is gated, surrounded by armed guards. Some days I think about reaching through the iron bars and plucking an apple from the tree that stands just out of reach. But then I'd be another body for Talan to scoop up, and as much as she drives me crazy, I can't let her go through any more of this life alone. She's the closest thing I have to family.

"God, I'd do anything to be fat," Talan says. "Wouldn't you? Think about it, Zephyr. Just imagine being so full you wouldn't be able to breathe."

I keep my mouth shut. The Leeches might not care about our well-being, but they do listen to everything we say.

I'm convinced they watch me the closest. As I eat, I can feel their eyes boring into my back. Sometimes I imagine they know me. *Really* know me, the way that not even my mom or dad did. I shovel my food into my mouth and let it slide down my throat. It tastes of dirt and earthworms.

"Oh, you've *got* to be kidding me," Talan growls. She stands and I look up.

The Leeches have gathered across the room. They take turns using their short black whips, lashing someone. I wince.

Those who step out of line pay for it. The jagged scars on my back are proof.

"We spend our lives committing ourselves to your safety," a Leech barks. Everyone goes quiet and every head turns to look at him.

"We devote our lives to making this world a better place! We command you to obey us, because we want to keep you from pain!" he shouts. He's tall, dark-haired, and lean-faced. Axel Worth. The Head Officer of the Wards. "And this is how you repay us?"

Two Leeches haul the bloodied man up to his feet. Blood drips from his nostrils. "This man stole extra rations," Officer Worth says. "This man spat in the face of our authority. He spat in *your* faces."

Talan huffs beside me. "Can we finish eating now?"

I stomp on her foot beneath the table to silence her.

"Do you know what we do to those that disobey?" Worth yells.

No one answers. He scans the crowd, passes right over me, and I look away. I don't draw attention to myself. That's why I'm still alive, and Talan should take a lesson

23

from me before she gets a rifle butt slammed in her face.

"We end them!"

Worth pulls out a pistol. I don't look away as he levels it and squeezes the trigger. Blood splatters against the glass barrier and drips slowly down, like rain on a windowpane.

No one moves. No one gasps, or shouts, or cries, because we've all seen it before.

"What. An. *Idiot*," Talan says to me.

"I was thinking the same thing," I say, and we finish our meals. They leave the body on the floor.

After lunch, the Wards will pick it up.

CHAPTER 5

MEADOW

I make it to the train tracks right on time.

There is a hiss and a puff, and in the distance, I can see the Red train coming first, hurtling toward me. The tracks skirt the town for the most part, bordering the beach and marshes. But right in the center of the Shallows, by the Rations Hall, the train runs along the street.

The people desperate enough to try for a spot on one of the trains start to crowd around the tracks like locusts. Some push and shove, while others just stand there and try to scream their way to the front. The ground starts to vibrate, and when the Red train slows to an almost-stop, the fighting begins.

Everyone is unforgiving and deadly, and I stay far away.

I wait until the Blue train comes, just like Koi told me to. It is no better than the Red, and I stand back and watch as citizens tear at each other like wild animals.

The last car glides past me, a rusted metal box with a ladder on the back for maintenance. There are already others doing what I am about to do. Soon there will be no more spots left on top. I run, pushing myself onto the balls of my feet, dodging left then right. I spread my arms and leap.

My hands grasp a rung and I hold on tight, legs dangling, swinging dangerously close to a man stretching to yank me off. I kick him, hard, right in the face, and scramble up the ladder as he grabs at the air.

The top of the train is covered in seagull waste, but it keeps the metal from getting too hot. I haul myself up onto my stomach and lie there with the others, heaving for air. The boy closest to me looks away the second I glare at him. He will not be a threat today.

At some point the tracks will fork. One train will go east, toward the Perimeter. The other will go west, past the Graveyard, toward the Initiative Headquarters. I hope that I have made the right choice.

If only Koi could see me now. I smile, and watch as the buildings recede. Thousands of tents litter the surrounding marshlands. Homes for Wards of the State. Sometimes I imagine that if I were a Ward, things would be easier. If I didn't have Peri or Koi to take care of, I could live free. I could do whatever I wanted, when I wanted, and if I died, I would not leave anyone behind.

But my brother and sister are the little piece of happiness I can call my own in this world. I can never lose them.

The Graveyard stands like a ghostly mountain range in the distance, piles of trash stretching to the sky. Four steam towers drop a constant fog over the Graveyard, working in vain to conceal the stench. Seagulls swoop down, picking at the piles.

Everyone in the Shallows knows to avoid the Graveyard at all costs. The Pirates are not the only dangerous gang out there. The Gravers are by far the worst. As the train barrels past, I start edging my way toward the back of the car, ready to leap if I have to. But the Blue train stays true to course, racing in the direction I want it to go. I watch as the Red train fades into the distance. I wonder if the people inside and clinging to the roof will find a better life. It's possible their lives will end today.

No one who chooses the Perimeter train ever comes back.

The Initiative Headquarters is the only building in the Shallows that's not crumbling. Its walls are made of titanium, nearly as thick as the Perimeter itself, and when I look closely, I can see security cameras along the top. The symbol of the Initiative is painted on the walls, a giant, all-seeing eye.

The train rolls to a stop and everyone piles out, the kids my age rushing for the gates at the front of the building. The older people, the ones who made the wrong train choice, run for the marshes, hoping to get lost in the undergrowth before they are shot.

Half of us entering this building will not come back out. Not alive, at least.

I look at the scarred girl standing beside me. I wish I had a pair of heels like the ones she is wearing. They are red, shiny, and pointed at the toe. She wears them with pride, as if she's killed someone for those shoes. Her scars tell me that she probably did. I stand 5'4" in my mother's old leather boots. They are cracked and worn, and suddenly I feel hopeless.

An Initiative officer approaches me, Catalogue Scanner in hand. He holds the scanner up to my forehead and it reads my number out loud. "72049. Meadow Woodson."

His eyebrows lift for a fraction of a second. "Woodson?" he asks me. "You got a brother?"

I sigh. Not now. "Does it matter?" I say, and clap a hand to my mouth. My mother's seashell charm dangles from my wrist, silver and bright under the hot sun. I expect him to correct me with a slap across the face. My other hand slides around my back, where my father's dagger is concealed. But the officer only studies me for a moment, a smile on his lips, and then he turns and moves farther down the hastily assembled line.

Inside the building, the ceiling fans churn above my head. Another Initiative officer sends the boys left, the girls right. We are ushered toward a waiting room. The second I walk in I wish I could turn around and go right back out. The walls shine and shimmer under the lights, and black Pins, from floor to ceiling, fill every square inch of space. Each one belonged to a citizen. The nanites have been removed, recycled for someone else. But the Pins bear our catalog numbers. Each Pin represents someone who maybe came to this building in hopes of a job, who stood in the middle of this floor and probably had the same thoughts I am having now.

Finally, we are led down a long white hallway, into a room too small for our group. We all pile onto couches and chairs. Some sit on the floor, others stand, and two girls get in a fight over a spot by the front of the room. They are both removed by the Initiative Officer.

Another girl breaks Commandment Four: *Thou shalt not harbor useful items from the days Before.* She shifts, and something small falls from her pocket: a coin. The girl is removed with the other two. I wonder if they have families at home who will starve because of their foolishness.

I end up on a wide leather couch that sticks to the backs of my thighs. Beside me is the girl with the red heels. We are so close together our legs touch. She is rough-looking, with a jagged scar running down the side of her face.

"Nice." I nod at her scar with a grin.

"You, too," she says, appraising the tiny scars that dot my arms.

We sit in silence for a while as girls are called into the testing room in pairs. Soon the room is so hot there is sweat dripping down my neck. After what feels like hours, there is no one left but the two of us.

"Looks like we're next." She turns to me. "You don't stand a chance."

"We'll see who comes out of there with a job." I keep my hands still in my lap. They are covered in sweat, and I want to rub it away, but I don't. "In case you had any doubt . . . it'll be me."

She shrugs, and then the door in front of us swings open. An evaluator with a large NoteScreen calls out our names. We stand together and follow him.

I gasp in shock as we walk through the door. It feels like I've been dunked into a pool of cold water. Air conditioning—who knows how much energy they are burning to keep this place cool today? I can hear the girl gasp as well.

Cameras line the walls of this room. We step forward and sit side by side in metal chairs. There is one evaluator, one work badge on the table beside him. That badge will go to the winning candidate. I cast a sideways glance at the scarred girl. She glares back, and I wonder when I will have to kill her.

"Woodson?" The Evaluator stands. His brown hair is greased back, like he's just spread a spoonful of oil all over it.

I smooth my palms over my denim shorts. The fabric is worn and tattered, and I feel so unprepared, so underdressed, so small. The room could swallow me whole. "Yes," I stammer. "Sir."

He stares at me. "Stand up."

I shove off my chair and swallow my nerves as he steps forward, examining me. "You're puny," he says, looking me up and down, and I grit my teeth.

Hold your tongue, Meadow.

It would be easy to kill him, to slip my fingers around his neck and stare straight into his eyes while he takes his last breath. Instead I dig my fingernails into my palms.

He looks at his NoteScreen. He licks his lips. "Your mother," he says, his voice full of acid. "Lark Woodson."

"You knew her?"

He taps something onto his screen. We are not supposed to speak unless directed to.

"We know everyone. Even the insignificant ones." I do not look away as he appraises me. "She teach you anything . . . worthwhile?"

"Of course she did. Did *yours*?"

"Mine taught me how to distinguish the worthy from the . . ." He looks me up and down. "Not. Have you broken any of the four Commandments, citizen?

"No. I honor the Initiative."

"You're a worthless liar."

He has no proof. This man does not know me. I should show him what I'm really about. But then I think of Peri's face. I owe her this, so I say what my father told me to say. "I'm strong. I know how to cook. I practically raised my little sister. I'll work hard if you allow me to. I'll take anything you have to offer. My family needs this."

He sighs and taps his NoteScreen. His face puckers up in disgust. "That's what they all say, girl."

When my competition stands, she looks like a soldier, proud and strong, despite the red heels, and the sundress that sways around her hips. The Evaluator questions her, asks about her mother and father, too. But there is no bitterness in his tone. Nothing he says makes *her* seem unworthy of his time. He seems pleased with all of her answers. They are solid and she does not speak out of line.

I sit still and keep my head high, though my heart is humming in my chest. I know I have already failed. It is impossible for me to win against this girl.

The Evaluator leaves, taking my opponent with him.

A woman comes in, dressed in crisp whites that make her pale skin seem even paler. She says nothing, just pokes a needle into my arm and takes my blood. She checks my vision, and even though I already know I am not color-blind, like Koi, I feel my body relax when she says my eyes are fine. She tests my hearing, my reaction times. She makes me walk in a straight line, stand on one foot, and then the other. I watch her face the whole time, trying to see if I have failed this as well, but she gives nothing away, only scribbles her notes onto a handheld screen, lips pursed. She is a wall as thick as the Perimeter.

I do not feel human. I feel like a rat trapped inside a maze.

Next is the paper exam. I answer questions about my skills, like fishing, and sewing, and how best to clean an infected wound. There is a list of jobs that I might receive, if I pass: hauling trash to the Graveyard, hospital duty, working in the Rations Hall, fishing, like my father. The worst job is assisting an Initiative member. I answer as best I can, and thank my mother for teaching me how to read and write. When I reach a question that asks me what my biggest weakness is, I leave the spot blank.

A man comes in and sits in front of me. He has blue eyes that should remind me of the sea, but he looks ill, and it makes my stomach feel all wrong. "Do you understand why you are here today?" He asks.

I clear my throat. "For an opportunity," I say, "to provide for my family."

"You have a father. A fisherman. You have a brother who is twenty-one, and a sister who is seven. Your mother is dead."

"Yes," I say. "Sir."

"Why do you think you deserve to have a job? You already have someone to provide for your family. Your father gets a bag of rations per week, just like the other families. If he works hard enough, and earns enough Creds, we gift him the opportunity to purchase other, less necessary items, to keep you comfortable. Are you greedy?"

I look down at my feet. "Because it is not enough," I say. I want to say more. I want to scream at him, to make him understand how horrible it is to see the way Peri's clothes swallow her thin frame, and the way Koi's face falls whenever he looks at her.

He leans back in his chair and laughs, a short bark like a dog. "The Initiative provides you with plenty."

"There are four of us, sir," I say. "We live on rations that provide for two. We have a child. She's growing fast, every day. She needs more."

"Then you should learn to ration better," he says. "Your father should work harder and earn more." He leans back, puts his hand to his temple. "Would you ever steal from the Initiative, Miss Woodson?"

The question takes me off guard. I feel my heart start to beat faster, harder. "I'm not stupid enough to try," I say, but the real truth is that yes, I would steal, if I had to. To keep Peri alive, I would even kill this man right now with my bare hands if I had to.

"Fair enough," he shrugs. "A final question." He leans forward. "Are you willing to fight for what you want?"

I look down at my hands. There is still blood under my fingernails from last night's fight with Koi. "Yes," I say. "I will always fight for what I want."

The man smiles for the first time. "Good," he says. He scribbles a note onto his pad. "Very good."

He stands up and heads for the door, and I am alone. There is a clock on the wall, an old-fashioned kind, that *tick-tick-tick*s at a constant rhythm, and after a while, it feels like my heart is beating in time with it. I am covered in sweat.

Finally, the door opens, and my opponent walks in. She has a smug look on her face, like she has already won.

My heart sinks. "Congratulations," I say to her, but she shakes her head.

"I thought you got it," she says. Her mouth hangs half-open. I see she is missing one of her teeth.

The door swings open again. We both whirl around. The Evaluator walks into the room. He has a silver work badge in his hand and a sickening smile on his face. "The test was inconclusive. You are both fine candidates."

"So what the hell does that mean?" the girl asks him. Her pleasant charade is up. "We both get a job?"

I hear Koi's voice.

Only one of you will leave that room alive.

You will do what I wasn't strong enough to do.

The Evaluator holds the badge between two fingertips, a dangling prize. "The Initiative wants someone for the Rations Department. Someone able to take care of themselves. Citizens get testy there, as you may well know." He lets the badge drop to the floor. I want to grab it, press it to my chest, never let it go. "A pity," he says, "that only one of you will work for us. But that's part of the fun, wouldn't you agree?" He laughs and rocks back and forth on the balls of his feet.

"The badge holder should report next door for further processing." With that, he turns around and leaves the room.

There is a moment of silence. The girl and I just sit there and stare at each other.

The girl looks at the badge, then back at me. Her eyes are as wide as oyster shells, and I see the pieces clicking together in her mind.

One badge. One job. One person will get those rations.

One person will leave this room alive.

I stand up a second before she does and dive for the badge. She collapses on top of me and we are one tangled mess, nails clawing, fists pounding, fighting for what we both so desperately need. She is fast, but she isn't trained like me. She tries to hold me down, and her punches are uneven, her arms as stiff as pieces of wood. I throw her off into the wall. Her head slams against it, and for a moment she looks dazed. She stands up and rushes for me. I side-step her and watch her tumble back to the ground, already out of breath and sloppy.

I'm guessing there is no way this girl got those scars from real fights. She probably marked herself to look stronger to enemies. It's clever, but a sign of true weakness. Part of me wants to stop fighting her. She never even stood a chance against me.

You will do what I wasn't strong enough to do.

Kill or be killed.

There is no other choice. She grabs the badge, and I grab her by the shoulders and slam her face into the floor.

"Give it to me!" I yell. She tries to twist around. I take an arm and twist it behind her back, like a broken bird's wing. "You won't win," I say, but she just keeps on writhing, screaming like an animal.

"So kill me!" she yells. "Kill me and you'll be just like them!"

I raise my hand and scream, feel my fist pound into her skull, right over her temple. Her body goes slack.

I take the badge from her hand. Then I turn for the door.

There is no handle. I can't get out.

I bang on the door. "I have the badge!" I yell. "Let me out!"

Nothing. There is a groan from behind me. The girl's eyes start to flutter open.

Only one of you will leave that room alive.

"She's done!" I yell to the door. I look up at the cameras. I hold up the badge. *"I'm* done!"

Nothing. I slump down against the wall and wait. Time is slow. I can hear people walking by outside the door, hear screams from somewhere, and I know that someone else is doing what I have yet to do.

It's obvious. The Initiative won't let me out until I do what they want. I take a deep breath. This is what my father trained me to do. This is what I have to do.

Sometimes we have to give up little pieces of our humanity so that we can keep living.

I grab the dagger from my waistband and walk over

to the girl. Her face is bloodied and bruised. I hold the dagger right above her heart.

Her eyes flutter open. They look right into mine.

Blue. Peri's favorite color.

"Do it," she says through tears. "I want to die. Do it. *Please.* We don't have a choice."

"It'll be quick," I whisper.

Then I drive the dagger right into her heart.

CHAPTER 6

ZEPHYR

By the time Collection duty is finished, we've filled three carts. Every week, there seems to be more. The carts are solar-powered, geared to help us bear the weight of the corpses. After we deliver them to the Leech Building, Talan takes to the streets with me. In the daytime, it's safest to walk in the alleyways, away from the crowds. But in the evenings, when the Dark Time is near, everyone walks right in the middle of the street, soaking up the last seconds of light before the darkness settles in.

"Ten years of knowing you, and you still do the same thing every night. It's boring," Talan says. Her arm is locked in the crook of mine, her head against my shoulder. "Come home with me instead. I'll teach you how to braid my hair."

I roll my eyes. "That sounds great and all, Talan, but I'd rather someone stick a knife in my throat."

"Suit yourself."

We end up standing in front of the doors of the Catalogue Dome. It's open every night at dusk, during the Silent Hour. It's the same thing we always do, and we stand here frozen, unable to go inside. Every so often, the old automatic doors slide open, creaking from years of overuse. A rush of stale air hits me, and for a moment, I think I might step in.

"Just go, Zephyr." Talan shoves me in the back. "Girls are so not attracted to pansies."

I turn around and see her there, hands on her hips. She's got full lips that are always set in a permanent pout. Even though we're both seventeen, she looks older, in a good way. I reach out and loop a finger around her belt. "Who says I need a girl when I've got you?" I pull her toward me and bury my face in her neck, sweeping her long hair aside.

"Holy skitz, you're coming on to me." She gapes at me, half-amused, half-flattered, and pushes me back.

"Come on," I joke. "You know you want this." I pose like I'm one of those ridiculous model guys that Talan and I found pictures of in an old pre-Fall magazine. Talan laughs so hard she almost cries.

"Stop!" she says, clutching her stomach.

We both stop laughing when the Night Siren goes off.

"All right," Talan says, as soon as the ringing dies away. "Grow a pair, and get in there." Her arm sweeps the doors open, ushering me in. I know she won't come with me. Seeing her daughter's picture will only remind her that Arden's death is something she cannot erase. It's not her fault Arden wandered off during Cleanup. It's *their* fault she got lost in the crowds, *their* fault that no one would help us search for her during our shift. Arden's blood is on the Leeches' bloodsucking hands. But Talan blames herself, and nothing I say will ever change that.

"I'll see you tomorrow, Zeph." She turns and strides down the street. I envy her strength, her fearlessness, but part of me thinks it's just because she wants to die so she can be with Arden again.

"Be safe!" I call out after her. She flips me the bird, and I smile as I watch her walk into the darkness. Talan always makes me happy, but the feeling goes away when I hear a creaking somewhere in the dark. I shiver and step into the Catalogue Dome.

Commandment Three: Honor the Silent Hour.

My breath catches in my throat. I stagger back. It is a virtual graveyard. All around me, lining the black walls of the Dome, are the numbers and portraits of deceased citizens. They're all staring at me.

Hallways lead away from the main lobby, and I set off toward the 17000 hall. My first victim's memorial is there.

Some faces leap out at me as I walk, letting my fingertips trail the smooth black walls. 17530. I picked up her corpse last week. I remember her number, because Talan made fun of her orange lipstick. "Like cat vomit," she said.

The Dome is quiet. My footsteps are the only sound I can hear besides my nervous breathing. There are hundreds of other mourners here, so many that the halls are completely lined with people on their knees, silently saying their good-byes.

I keep walking with my head down, dreading the moment when I look into his eyes.

But there he is. 17907. I sit cross-legged on the floor in front of his screen, a small black rectangle that flickers sadly when I place my palm on its warm surface.

Michael Kans. Husband. Father of three. Fisherman. Death during the Dark Time.

Brutally and undeservingly murdered by Zephyr James, is what it should say.

Michael's face is kind and wrinkled, his smile huge. Crow's feet pucker the skin around his eyes, and I wonder what made him smile so big when the picture was taken. Maybe it was his child, making a funny face. Maybe he was thinking of his wife. She was probably beautiful. I'm sure he loved her.

I rock on the floor in front of his plaque, not caring who sees me. Michael reminds me of my father. Someone who never deserved to die. "I'm sorry," I whisper through ragged breaths. I woke with his blood on my hands, his mangled body at my feet, and fragments of a memory I didn't want to piece together. His screams. My hands, strangling his throat. My heart, steady and sure while I made his stop beating for good. I don't know why or when I did it. But I know I did.

It's the same for all of them. "I'm so sorry."

I go down my list of numbers, visiting each memorial to pay my respects, begging myself to just *remember*.

I'm not a murderer. I couldn't ever be. It isn't possible, not Zephyr James. Not the poor, pathetic Ward who scrubs the blood off the streets each week, who gives his rations to the children in the Reserve, and looks after careless, wild, broken Talan, trying to keep her safe. Not Zephyr James. He isn't a murderer.

But he is. I am.

CHAPTER 7
MEADOW

I have never seen a man cry.

My father never does. Not even when Peri fell off of the houseboat and almost drowned. Not even when my mother died. At least, not in front of me.

No. I have never seen a man cry.

But right now, lying on the floor beside my mother's plaque in the Catalogue Dome, a boy is sobbing. I've heard mourning in the streets, deep moans and agonizing screams of fury, but the boy's cries are soft. I take an awkward step toward him, but stop. It could be a trap, and suddenly his weakness disgusts me.

"I'm sorry," he says, through his sobs. He's facedown

now on the tile floor, his fingertips touching the image of an elderly olive-skinned woman. I wonder briefly how she died, but then I see it. She was murdered, of course, like the thousands and thousands of others in this building. "I'm so sorry," the boy whispers again.

"Sorry for what?" The words are out of my mouth before I can stop them. They are entirely too loud.

The boy stops moving, stops breathing. I slide my dagger out, let it hang ready at my side. This is stupid, against everything my father has ever taught me. I turn around to leave. I'd only wanted to share my triumph with my mother, to show her the badge tucked securely in my pocket. But before I can take another step, I see it. The mark of a Ward, a thick black X tattooed onto the back of his neck. The woman on the plaque could be his aunt. His grandmother. His mother, even. And now he is alone.

Wards have nothing. They matter to no one. To the Initiative, they are nothing. They may as well be invisible.

I'm clutching lilies in my other fist. I got them on my way back from the city, thinking to give them to my mother. They're feeling prickly, and suddenly I know they aren't meant for my mother's memorial. Not today, at least.

I tiptoe forward. His T-shirt clings to his back. Strong

muscles like Koi's peek through.

I stop, stoop down, and place the flowers on the floor, the crushed white petals just touching his fingertips.

"I'm sorry, too," I whisper, so softly I can hardly even hear my own voice, and then I turn and run. I leave him there, alone, on the tear-soaked floors of the Catalogue Dome.

CHAPTER 8

ZEPHYR

I run the entire way home to beat the darkness.

I lose myself in the pumping of my legs, the hammering of my heart. I'm all body, and no mind. It feels good to be nothing, and even better to do something.

The train tracks lead out of the city, so I follow them. A long time ago, the city was bigger. But then there was a month straight of rain that softened the ground, and a sinkhole swallowed half of the Shallows. I stay as far from the Pit as I can, circling around it until I reach the marshlands that make up the Ward Reserve.

I slow down once I reach the gates. An old catalogue scanner sticks out of the warped metal, low enough that

I have to stoop down to place my forehead against it. There's a click and the gates slide open.

Thousands of patched white tents stretch before me, swaying in the wind like little ghosts. Pools of muddy water make the ground look like it's some puzzle with missing pieces, the water so dark that sometimes I like to pretend there's no bottom to it, and I could just fall into one of the pools and sink forever.

The scattered trees grow low to the ground, with thick branches that stretch out like skeletal arms, and every so often, my feet disappear in the mud, and I have to stop to pull myself out.

A few crackling fires light up the night. "Hey Zephyr," a little boy calls to me. Thomas, I think, but there are so many kids I can hardly remember their names. "I caught a squirrel. I broke its neck with my bare hands."

His face is covered in filth. There's no one to teach him how to take care of himself. But he looks proud beneath all the mess, and he grins at me like I'm the nicest person in the world.

"Clean yourself up tonight, okay?" I say, laughing. "And good job on the squirrel!" He nods, and I pat him on the shoulder as I pass by. Others smile and wave as I walk between the tents. Most are younger than me, but some are adults who have managed to survive. I break up a fight between a girl and a boy, wrestling over a loaf of moldering bread.

Talan's patchwork tent sits directly across from mine. My heart speeds up like it always does when I peer inside to make sure she's made it home safe. It settles when I see her, curled up in her blanket.

"Talan?" I whisper.

"I'm home, Father," she says, waving me away.

When I make it to my tent, I fall asleep not a second after my head hits the hard ground.

I spend the rest of the night waking to my own screams. Nightmares happen to all of us, but mine are full of faces and numbers.

When I'm finally too afraid to go back to sleep, I roll over in my sleeping bag and peel back the plastic flap that hangs in the doorway of my tent. The stars are out tonight. But the stars aren't what I want to see right now.

It's the moon. The moon that reminds me of the moon-lit girl.

My moonlit girl. She's the cure to my nightmares, the one thing that helps me feel safe when I can't even trust my own dreams to harbor me.

I close one eye and hold my thumb up, so that it covers

the silver orb that hangs in the sky. I open that eye and close the other and there it is again, just like that. Always waiting for me.

I imagine a life full of happiness. A life of safety, and eating three meals a day that leave me feeling full. There aren't many things I want.

But stars, I *want* the moonlit girl.

Someday, I'll meet her. She must be real, not just my imaginary protector. I feel her, strongly, like she's lying right next to me, and today, in the Dome, someone left me flowers. It's stupid, but for a minute I pretend it was her, like she saw my pain and wanted to make it better. I can almost imagine her voice, whispering in my ear, telling me everything will get better.

But tonight, I'm alone. I close my eyes.

Finally, I dream of something different.

I dream of a meadow full of crushed white flowers.

CHAPTER 9
MEADOW

My dagger shines bright silver. I imagine there are stains deep in the steel, the color of crimson from the blood of the girl with the red heels.

I fasten it to the sheath on my thigh before I leap from the train. I run the rest of the way down an empty alley that heads to the beach.

What scares me is I don't feel bad for what I have done. I did it to survive. Not for myself, but for Peri.

Tonight the beach is packed with people. I move quickly across the sand. I try to ignore a woman who asks me for food. Her teeth are rotting so badly she should pull them out. She reaches for me.

"Get back!" I yell, and the woman stumbles away.

Tonight, the dinghy is gone, probably out to sea with someone else, so I dive into the waves and start the swim, navigating my way through the wrecks and fields of floating garbage. By the time the houseboat finally comes into view, the Night Siren has gone off, warning me that the Dark Time is nearly here.

Moonlight shines down on the boat, illuminating the deck. Peri is there waiting for me, her white nightgown and silver curls dancing in the wind. So many nights my mother would be here waiting. It was her favorite spot, and she would stare out at the shore, watching the world fade away with the light. Looking exactly the way my younger sister does now. I dive deep and release the escape hatch, then surface and climb the ladder to the deck.

"Meadow!" Peri scampers over to me and buries her face in my stomach and I wrap my arms around her. She's skinnier, even more so than yesterday, if that is even possible. I press her closer to me. "Did you get it? Did you get the job?" she asks.

My father and Koi emerge from the cabin and watch me with tired eyes. My father has been working all day. Fishing off the docks, like most Shallows men do. It is a good job, and if he reaches his quota by the end of the year, he gets to bring home an actual fish for us to eat. Sometimes, we even get to go to the marketplace and buy extra clothing, a box of matches, a bundle of dried meat. But those things cost far too many Creds, and we don't indulge ourselves often.

Koi has spent the day guarding the boat, and more importantly, guarding Peri. "Well?" he asks. "What happened?"

"See for yourself." I smile. I place my badge into Peri's small hands.

"You're so badass!" she says, and I am so shocked that I laugh before I scold her. Her smile is different tonight. She is missing a tooth.

I stoop down to her side and run my hands through her curls. "You lost another tooth," I say to her. "You know what that means, right?"

"Koi says all my teeth will fall out and I'll look like a fish."

I glare at Koi, and he stifles a laugh. "You're just growing up," I say, "that's all. Soon you'll be as big as me!" I tickle her, right above her hips, the same place Koi used to tickle me.

Peri's laugh is sweet, like music. She falls to the deck of the boat, clutching her stomach, and for a second, I just kneel there beside her, wishing I could stop time.

Soon, my father will begin her training. I don't want to think about what my father will do to her, how he will harden her soft edges. How someday, she will be faced with a choice: kill or be killed.

I know Peri will be strong enough to survive. She's smart, and she can swim fast. She even knows how to read. I taught her with the *History of the Shallows* book. She knows how to take care of herself, too. But thinking of her being out on the streets makes me feel sick. So instead, I commit this moment to memory, the smile on her face, her laughter.

"All right, quiet down," Koi says. I plant a kiss on Peri's cheek. She giggles and wipes it off.

"Your mother would be proud, Meadow." My father is standing behind me, watching me, I'm sure. I don't know why I feel so empty at the mention of her. I don't know why I feel so dead inside.

I should be proud. But Koi is staring at me like I am dripping with someone else's blood. We all know what happened in that room today.

"Did she suffer?" he whispers to me. I shake my head. *No.*

His eyes meet mine, just for a moment, before he

whispers something under his breath. "You did what you had to do." Then he walks away and down the ladder to the engine room.

"Let's go talk in private for a moment, shall we?" My father places his calloused hand on my shoulder, and I flinch. His touch means the slice of a knife, a sudden spar, a jarring slam to the floor. His touch means training. It never means fatherly affection.

We settle down on the bow of the boat, both of us cross-legged, facing each other. The engine rumbles beneath us as Koi starts it up, and then our houseboat begins to move across the surface of the ocean in silence. Tonight, the sea is glass.

"There's something you should know," my father begins, his voice cracking strangely.

"All right." I nod, unsure of what else to say.

"It's about your mother. What do you remember about her, Meadow?"

My eyes close and there she is. Tall, brilliant, hair the color of the moon, the color of the seashell charm she gave me the last night I ever saw her.

She was an engineer, always the one to fix our boat when something went haywire. And she could sing. Oh, she could sing, and at night, when I sleep, when I dream of her, I hear her voice. It is beautiful, like a bird singing its summer song, like the sound of rushing water over smooth pebbles, or wind tickling the set of seashell chimes I made for her birthday years ago.

"She was perfect." It's all I can say because the tears have begun spilling down my face. They drop onto the deck and splatter, hot and sticky in the night air.

"She wasn't perfect," my father whispers.

My head pops up. "How can you say that?"

"I didn't mean it like that." He sighs, squeezing the bridge of his nose with filthy fingertips. "What I mean is . . . to you, to your brother and sister, she was wonderful. But Meadow, you have to understand. Your mother was a dangerous woman."

A sad laugh flies from my lips. Dangerous? My mother could defend herself, sure. We all can, thanks to him. But dangerous? For the last months she was with us, I watched her strength fade, as she refused to train, and her happiness wither away.

My father continues. "You know that the Initiative is all-controlling. That we no longer have the freedom to make choices because of them. Water—it isn't ours to drink anymore. The fish I catch—I can't bring them home to my family to eat unless I earn the right. Human lives—they are no longer precious the way they should be. We aren't precious, Meadow. We are numbers to them. That is it. Nothing more."

"I know all that. What does this have to do with Mom?" I'm getting frustrated, breathing too hard.

"You wear a number close to hers on your forehead. We all do. Similar ones. Recognizable ones."

"So?"

"So keep this in mind. You are of age, with a job in the city. Tomorrow you will get a Cred Orb. It will track your work hours, the rations you earn, and the Initiative will be watching you now, closer than they ever have. Things *will* change. You must *always*, always be ready to defend yourself."

He's not making any sense. I feel like I've just been smacked in the head with a two-by-four, and everything is confusing, buzzing around me like a horsefly. Why would they want to watch me? I am no one. My mother was no one. We are all no one, but I don't have time to think it through, because suddenly a flash of silver catches my eye. My father lunges at me with his knife, silent and deadly. Faster than I've ever seen anyone move before.

I stand and leap high and sideways, over the edge of the boat. The barbed wire clips me as I go.

I hit the water and it sprays into my nostrils. I kick toward the surface, and burst through the waves in time to see my father shaking his head in the moonlight.

"Damn it!" I scream, furious he caught me off guard. "What was that for?"

"It was a lesson," he calls down to me. "Swim to shore and come back tomorrow. You need practice surviving the Dark Time alone."

He turns and disappears into the cabin.

An hour later I drag my aching body onto shore. The warm sand has never felt better than it does now, pressed up against my cheek. I allow myself a moment to catch my breath, then head for the trees. I pick the tallest one and start to climb. And as I make my way up silently, branch by branch, I can't help but wonder if my father's words were true. I loved my mother. But did I really know her? I think of the way she was always on guard, always alert, almost like a predator.

Like me.

My bracelet catches on a tree branch, and I stop for a moment. The moonlight illuminates the smooth silver. A strange, swirling pattern is etched onto the back of the charm, lines overlapping each other in all directions. My mother never told me what the pattern meant. I think of the countless hours she spent in the closet beside the engine room of our boat, behind a locked door. It was the one place we could never go, the one part of our home that was off-limits. I remember the way her eyes were always glazed over when she emerged. The way she would paddle away from the houseboat and disappear for hours. When she returned in the middle of the night, she would kiss us all and sing to us, but tears would leak from the corners of her eyes.

My mother had secrets of her own. Like everyone does in the Shallows.

"You can't escape destiny, Meadow," she whispered into my ear the last night I saw her.

I look at the swirling pattern etched on the charm bracelet she gave to me.

The wind blows, and I shiver, even though it is full of summery warmth.

I'll find out what my father was talking about.

I'll find out who killed my mother.

And when I do, slowly, painfully, I will take them from the earth.

CHAPTER 10

ZEPHYR

The cracked concrete and run-down buildings of the city are nothing like the salt marshes, where everything is rumored to drip blood, and the nights are filled with the moans of the dying Wards it's reserved for. Of course none of that's true.

But we like to keep people thinking it is. There are colors in the marshes. Browns and greens, and sounds that aren't born of mankind. No one bothers us there. It's the only bit of freedom we get from the Leeches.

Work on Mondays starts early, before dawn. Talan walks beside me, and together, we push a second large cart full of mangled bodies and twisted, blackened limbs into the Leech building. Our footsteps echo eerily. Only the security lights remain on.

"I could eat five bags of rations right now." Talan is chattering away, as usual, completely ignoring the corpses flopping around as our cart hits a bump on the floor. "Actually, I could eat one of these guys!" She flicks the corner of the tarp and I get a whiff of death. That guy died only hours before he was collected.

"Flux, Talan. That's disgusting. Just shut up and push."

We reach the door of the Furnace Room, and I can already feel the heat. Sometimes I feel like I'm just going to sweat forever. Just an eternal drip, drip, dripping down my back. I lean my forehead against the scanner, a long black rectangle that stretches from the floor to the ceiling. The door click-whirrs open, and Talan and I push the cart inside.

The roar of the furnace is like rushing water, or the engine of a Leech boat starting up. After years of working together, Talan and I have a routine. I scan the foreheads of the dead with a portable scanner, attached by a cord to the wall. Talan holds back her puke as we lift the bodies, together, and throw them into the furnace. It's loud, and I can't hear what Talan is babbling on about. Thank the stars. Because I'm not in the mood to listen to her anyway.

All I want to do is think about *her*. The girl in my dreams.

It sounds stupid, like a fairy tale, or some sort of romantic sob story Talan would pick up if she had the Creds. But every night, the girl is there, silver hair hanging in waves to her waist like liquid moonlight, gray eyes the color of the ocean when a storm is about to roll in.

She isn't beautiful. She's different, rigid and untouchable, sort of like she's carved out of stone. She keeps me sane when nothing else can. It's like she holds me to the ground, like gravity, except much stronger. She protects me from the faceless people who haunt me each night and every waking moment.

There's twelve of them. Twelve numbers. Twelve human beings.

I killed them all with my own hands.

CHAPTER II

MEADOW

When I was younger, my mother showed me photographs of something she used to go to— a baseball game. She told me her mother held her close the entire time so she wouldn't get lost in the crushing sea of people crowding the stadium. She was worried she'd get separated from her, get pushed and shoved so far away that she'd never see her mother again.

I remember the fear that gripped my heart as I looked at the photograph. "It's like the Shallows," I said to her. "I'm going to lose you, aren't I?"

"You'll never lose me, Meadow." My mother smiled down at me.

I believed her then.

Everywhere I turn in the city, there's another face. Another Catalogue Number, another hot, sweaty body pressed up against mine. It is stifling. If I stumbled over and fell, I'd disappear, and no one would know or care.

"Watch it!" A man scowls down at me as I trample over his feet. I don't get the chance to apologize before he's engulfed by the crowd.

In the distance, I can see the Catalogue Building, a monstrous black dome that seems to scrape the underside of the clouds. It's the only city building that isn't covered in filth and grime and tattered posters that claim "Murder Is Madness, Stay Safe with the Initiative."

I pass the apartment building where we used to live. I was three when the Initiative took over, and I do not remember much. I remember pain, when my Catalogue Number was tattooed onto my forehead. I remember sobbing myself to sleep, and my mother opening the windows of my bedroom to let the night air soothe me. Now those windows are boarded up with planks of old salvaged wood. A rusted tricycle sits at the bottom of the steps. An elderly man and his wife pass me, carrying their belongings. Probably trying to cross the

Perimeter, as many do, thinking safety is just a short trip and a life's worth of credits away. Maybe even thinking that life is still the same out there.

I consider telling them to turn around and go home. They are breaking Commandment Two: *Thou shalt not attempt to cross the Perimeter.*

I consider telling them that if they get too close, the Pulse will send out a shock wave and paralyze them. They probably know all that. They probably know the risks. They probably don't care anymore.

I fork left when I come to the Library.

My father brought me to the Library, only once, when we had enough Creds to get inside. He pulled an old book from the shelves and brushed off the dust. I remember the way the dust tickled my nose as it danced through the air. My father held the book out to me. It was heavy in my arms, like an anchor.

"Take it, Meadow," he said. "Take it and run."

So I did. I walked past the scanners, head held high, silver curls brushed back from my eyes so I could see where I was going.

I didn't know the alarms would go off when I walked out the doors. And then they began to chase me. The Initiative security guards, from out of nowhere.

My father didn't come to my aid. He looked away, as if he didn't know me.

I made it home on my own before dark with the *History of the Shallows* still clutched in my hands. I am strong because of my father. I know I don't need anyone to survive.

So now, when three Landers, members of a street gang, approach me in the back alley behind the Library, knives drawn, the silver barrel of a gun pointed at my heart, I know I am ready.

"Hey, baby." The first man's voice is raspy, like an old smoker's. He eyes my work badge with the desperate hunger of a starving man. "You don't look old enough to work. Why don't I take that off your hands for you?"

"You could sell that sucker for a hundred Creds, boss," the man with the gun says.

"Make it two hundred when we sell it right back to the Initiative," the third laughs.

"It's going to cost you more than Creds to take this from me," I say as they close in on me. I can smell human waste and the scent of stale alcohol. The first Lander reaches me, places his hand on my breast, while the second one steps behind me, so close I can almost imagine his chest moving with each inhale. I know what they plan to do.

How they got a gun, I am not sure. Guns are scarce. My father owns a gun like this one, from before the Perimeter went up. It is hidden under the floorboards of our houseboat. Seeing one now helps me focus.

I take the badge from around my neck and let it drop to the street.

The first one is easy, like choking a child. He collapses to the concrete and I rip the gun from his fingers.

The second lunges at me, but I'm too fast. I dodge his blade and find the handle of my dagger. I sink the blade into his chest without hesitation. He crumples to the ground and I shatter his nose with the heel of my boot.

The streets are so crowded that no one hears me shoot the third.

CHAPTER 12

ZEPHYR

The bottom of the body cart is stained a deep crimson.

After we burn the last corpse, Talan and I push the cart to the storage room and park it with the others. Tonight, a cleansing system in the ceiling of the room will remove the blood from all of them.

But the dead will still be dead. Nothing can ever change that.

"There's an old building over on South that's full of crap," Talan says. I hold the door open for her, but she shrugs past me and opens the other one. Always independent. Never taking help from anyone. "Feel like playing maid for a few hours? Making some extra Creds?"

"Nah, but there's a one-eyed prostitute over on Fifth," I say. "Lend me some Creds?"

"You're such a ChumHead." Talan shoves my shoulder. "If you're going to visit a prostitute, then I should get to *be* one."

"No deal. No deal at all."

We step over a man sleeping in the street, and Talan steals the hat right off his head. "Still thinking about that kid, huh?"

She knows me too well.

Not a boy I murdered. Not a victim.

But just a Ward, and a new one, at that.

Eight years old. Missing a tooth, with deep brown hair the same color as mine. He showed up last week with a Leech officer, a fresh X tattooed on the back of his neck. The boy's face was stained with tears, and I don't know if he's stopped crying since.

"It's like watching my life on replay," I say to Talan. She looks good in the ball cap, but it'll only make her a target for someone else. Everyone wants what isn't theirs to have. I take it from her head and toss it into the gutter. She groans, but this is a game we play often. Soon she'll steal something else.

Eventually, she might get caught doing it, and then

she'll be another person for the Leeches to shoot in the head. Live target practice. "What's that word they use? Kleptomaniac?"

"It's called borrowing," Talan corrects me. "Not stealing."

If a Sellout saw Talan stealing, they'd take her right to the Leeches for a nice payday. When Sellouts catch Wards breaking a Commandment, they earn out big, because the Leeches can't see *everything* that goes on. Most of it. But they don't always see all of it.

"Actually, I *do* feel like cleaning out that building."

"Hell, no," Talan says. She grabs my arm and pulls me to a stop. Turns to face me, her blue eyes set in a cold glare. "I'm not doing a job so you can give your Creds to some random orphan." She puts her hand on her hip. Something that Arden used to do. "If that boy's father hadn't died, his son wouldn't be in the Reserve right now. It's not up to you to fix this problem."

"Someone has to do it."

"You don't have to take care of everyone," Talan says. "People die. Kids become Wards, and the world's a big pile of skitz, but so what? There's nothing you can do about it."

She puts her arm around my waist and tows me along.

The train rattles past, shaking the ground beneath our feet. We go by the Graveyard, where the loony-headed citizens all go, the ones driven crazy by the Shallows. There's a couple of towers between the trash mountains that are constantly spilling out steam, so the whole thing looks like some creepy ghost hangout.

"Maybe you're right about helping people," I say, stepping over a plastic bag that dances away with the wind, "but if it makes me feel better . . . why does it matter?"

I feel her sigh. "Because there will always be new Wards. There will always be people to take care of," she says.

"But if I can help just *one*—" She cuts me off.

"Stop being a saint. And anyways, you're busy taking care of *me*, ChumHead. And lucky for you, I'm a full-time job."

She puts her head on my shoulder and we walk the rest of the way to the Reserve in silence.

CHAPTER 13

MEADOW

The first time I went to the Rations Hall, my mother was still alive.

Peri was just a tiny being in her stomach then, growing bigger every day. We lived in an apartment on the edge of the city, and even though the murders hadn't started yet, the world was still far from safe.

"I don't want to go," I begged my mother. I wanted to stay home and feel Peri kick, and listen to my mother tell us both stories. Instead, she kissed my forehead and told me to follow my father outside. "Be safe," she warned me. "Listen to your father," she told Koi.

I still remember the sound of the three locks clicking

the second we left the apartment.

Koi's hand was clenched tightly over my own so I wouldn't get lost. His palm was drenched in sweat, wet, like he'd just come right out of the ocean, and he kept looking down at me, as if I'd simply disappear and never come back.

My father kept his eyes on the road the entire time, never checking on us, never slowing when we had trouble pushing through the crowds.

The second we walked inside the Rations Hall, I realized why my father wanted us to come.

Food.

There was food displayed behind one wall made of glass so we could see it. Koi let go of my hand. He rushed toward the wall and grabbed a bag of rations, so proud to have food for our family.

I cried out. I wanted to follow him, as I always did, but my father silenced me.

"You can both learn from this, Meadow," he said. I watched from behind my father's back as an Initiative soldier held a gun to Koi's head, finger poised to squeeze the trigger.

In exchange for Koi's life, we left with my father's eye swollen shut and not a single ration for the week. We were lucky the Initiative did not kill us all.

That night, my father chained Koi to the kitchen table and made him sleep standing up. "You must work for what you deserve," he told him. "Nothing the Initiative offers us is free."

There is a line of people standing in front of the Rations Hall, trailing all the way down the street and along the train tracks. A dead body lies near the doorway, flies swarming around the gaping eye sockets that have been picked clean by the gulls.

I'm not sure where to go in, where to start, so I just stand there for a while, counting the number of people.

105. 150. 210, before the line disappears around the corner.

"You the new recruit?"

I turn around. An Initiative woman is lying on her back on a generator box, popping gum. I have never had gum, but the way she's chewing it makes me want to try some.

I nod my head and swallow hard.

"Well, come on over," she says. "I don't bite. Name's Orion. Like the constellation, you know?" I hide my smile, thinking of the time Peri asked me if Orion was really fat, because his belt was so big.

I've never casually spoken to an Initiative officer, let

alone a woman. Her uniform is all black, with laced leather boots that reach her knees and a black pistol attached to her hip. But something about Orion is different. I notice a white-and-red band sewn into the fabric around her thigh. "You're a medic?" I ask.

"More of us are, these days," she says. "And we're about to be late."

I step across the train tracks and stand a ways from her, careful not to get too close. My blood is starting to boil. All the chaos, all the murders, and they do nothing but make us more afraid. They are the shepherds that turn a blind eye when the wolves come to play. "Meadow Woodson." Orion holds up a small handheld. My name, face, and Catalogue Number shine back at me from the screen. I am not smiling in the photograph. I remember when it was retaken, just days before my mother died. "Says here it's your first job. Things go well, you're stuck here for life, Blondie. Think you can handle it?" Her hair is chopped short, revealing a thick line of scars, like claw marks on her neck. Orion is tough. I can tell by the wiry muscles in her skull-tattooed arms, and the way she keeps swiveling her head, watching the citizens all around us.

But I bet I am tougher. "I can handle myself just fine,"

I say. I nod at the scars on her neck. "What happened to you?"

"Got jumped a few years ago. Wanna know why?" She rolls over onto her stomach, and the generator rocks a little as she hops down. "You'll find out soon enough." I hear the two short chirps that signal the start of the workday. "Follow me. Don't speak. Don't ask questions. You'll figure it out eventually." Orion waves her hand. "Move it people, move it!"

We shove through the crowd and go around to the back of the building, where there's less of a crush, but still too many people to really be safe. I stand guard while Orion scans her Catalogue Number. The door clicks open, and we slip into the Rations Hall.

As soon as we walk in I want to turn around and head back to the ocean, where the air is clean and crisp. Here, flies dip and dodge the swatting hands of the Initiative soldiers standing guard around the room. The air is sweltering hot, and with each step I get a dose of body odor and the scent of rotting meat. Rows of metal tables fill the center of the room. It looks as if they have not been cleaned in months.

"They told me I'd get used to the smell, eventually," Orion says. "They lied." She presses her forehead to a scanner embedded in another thick metal door. There are what look like fist marks in the metal.

I follow her into a massive room full of wood crates stacked to the ceiling. "Crates hold the rations," Orion says, slamming her fist on one of them. "It doesn't go bad, so don't worry about it not being able to take the heat."

So much food, just sitting here waiting. I can just imagine my father's face if he were to see this.

"Don't get any ideas," Orion says, raising a pierced eyebrow at me. She pats the gun on her thigh. But then, strangely, she smiles. "Nah. If you were that stupid, you'd have tried something already. This way." I follow her to a wall of thick glass. "Walls are bulletproof," Orion says. Before I know it, lightning fast, she has pulled out her gun and fired a bullet at the wall.

It sticks in the glass like a dart. My ears ring. "I just love that." Orion laughs, holsters her gun, and moves along like nothing happened. There is a counter underneath the glass, and every few feet, holes in the glass above the counter, just large enough for a plate of food or a bundle of rations.

"Those holes aren't bulletproof," I say, too loud. My ears are still ringing.

Orion shrugs her shoulders. "Neither are we. Makes it interesting, don't you think?"

Sweat drips down my spine, and I shudder. This is where the Initiative almost killed Koi so many years ago. I cast Orion a sideways glance.

"You look scared," she says. "Leave now if you want. I'm sure there are plenty of other little blonde girls who'd kill for this job."

I cross my arms and stare right into her brown eyes. "I'm not leaving unless you shoot me and carry my dead body out."

Orion laughs. "Good girl. Gear up." She tosses me a pair of thick gloves and directs me to stand behind a line on the floor. "The job's easy. Wait while they scan their numbers. Then check the screens, here. We're supposed to give them exactly what it says, and nothing more. You tough?"

I nod my head.

"Let's hope so. You got a weapon on you?"

I nod again.

"Anyone gets rough . . . use it. We lost a girl last week. Sick and twisted mess. You'd be surprised what people do for food."

"Probably not," I say. My lips purse together like the sides of a clothespin. Orion has probably never gone a day without food. I wonder what her life is like, what her apartment is like, inside the Initiative Compound.

Safe. Full of weapons and fruit and not a single threat when her head hits the pillow at night. A part of me hates her just for that.

"Here we go," Orion says. She pulls out her pistol and checks the clip. Five bullets, and one still stuck in the glass. I take a deep breath, turn to the doors, and watch as the Initiative soldiers let the citizens file in.

It only takes me a few minutes to get into the swing of things. When a number is scanned, I pull out a ration bag from a crate marked with the right serving size. Mostly it is sackcloths of dried meat, some so small they fit in the palm of my hand. Some citizens get a bundle of bread, depending on the Creds. I shove the rations through the slot above the counter, quick and steady, and move on to the next one. The work itself is easy, even with the heat and the smell.

But the citizens are rabid. They push and shove and claw at each other to get closer to the front of the line. I feel as if I am looking into the eyes of animals, like wolves that have not fed for weeks.

I grab a sack of dried meat. This one is so small, and it cost 25 Creds to get it. That is almost a week's worth of earnings for my father.

"What do you think I am, a Ward?" a man with a scarred face yells. "I paid for this food, I should get more!"

"There's nothing I can do about that."

The man grunts, then reaches through the slot, clawing for the other bags beside me. In an instant, my dagger is out of my waistband and I slam it down, right in between his middle and ring fingers. The handle vibrates with a menacing twang.

"Unless you want me to target an even bigger appendage, I suggest you take your food and move on," I say. I shove his rations bag at him, and he leaves me, his eyes focused only on his food now.

"Atta girl," Orion shouts. She's fast at what she does, so I speed up, too. I will not let a member of the Initiative outshine me. My father would be ashamed.

As the line continues to grow on the other side of the glass wall, I watch the women. Some of them are pregnant. My heart sinks. How many more people can we add to our society before we are all destroyed?

We have not a crumb of food to spare, or a square inch of space to make room.

Even if the murders continue, the hundreds of dead each month hardly scratch the surface of the problem. There are too many of us. Way too many. I've had nightmares of trying to swim in the ocean, but there are so many people I can't move, can't even rock side to side in the waves, and then I imagine that there aren't waves at all. It is a sea of people and I am stuck helpless in the middle of it.

Later, when the line is finally gone, I slump against the glass, staring at the hundreds of now-empty crates of food. There was so much this morning. Now there is nothing left.

Something lands in my lap. A slab of dried meat. I look up and Orion is sitting on one of the crates across from me, swinging her legs back and forth. "For your first day," she says. "Eat it or hide it before someone sees."

I close my hand over the meat, and suddenly all I want to do is race back home, where I can show Peri what I've earned, and see her smile. Orion is watching me with her strange dark eyes, and she won't look away. There is something off about her, something I cannot quite put my finger on.

I don't like it.

I put the meat in my pocket and give a nod of thanks.

I stand up, ready to leave, but Orion stops me. "Hold up, Blondie. Got your work badge?"

I grab it and toss it to her. Her reflexes are fast, like a cat's.

"This is temporary." She stands up. "Time for the real deal. You get a little adjustment to your Pin. Come with me."

We head to a small table in the back corner, with two rickety old wooden chairs. "Sit down," she says. "Hold out your arm."

There is a black box on the table. Orion opens it, and inside, there is a tiny black ball no larger than my pinky nail that I recognize as a Cred Orb. Koi does not have one, and he never will. The Initiative does not give us second chances. In the box there is also a can with a nozzle on top, and a syringe with blue goo that I think is pain medicine. My father told me about this, and as Orion reaches for it, I stop her.

"I don't want it," I say. She raises that same pierced eyebrow again. I don't need to explain myself. Pain is good. Every time I feel it, I get stronger. I learn how to push it down.

"I didn't want it either," Orion says. She watches me for too long, but I will not look away and show weakness. "You and me, we're not so different," she says. "Right arm on the table."

I could find a thousand and one reasons to argue with her, but instead I just sit in silence and hold out my arm.

The cut is not deep, but the pain is. I grit my teeth and take it in, and I do not close my eyes when she slides the strange black orb beneath my skin.

"This is where your Creds are tracked. You work, you get Creds. You scan your arm, you get rations. You step out of line . . . your Orb goes back to zero. Got it?"

I watch as Orion holds the can to my arm. Blood drips down my wrist. "These are liquid skin cells," Orion says. "Nasty smelling stuff. Like ham. You ever had ham?" I shake my head. I don't even know what that is. Orion sprays the stuff over the cut, and I watch as the tan liquid bubbles up on my arm. "Nanites can fix you up good. But this stuff will toughen the skin. You aren't getting this Orb out unless you slice yourself up real nice with a knife."

Seconds later, the bubbles fade, and I can see a fresh layer of skin under my own dried blood. The new skin is lighter than my own, and when I press a finger to the fresh patch, I don't feel any pain. "It's amazing," I say.

"And so are the Pins, you know." Orion stares at my wound for a second. When she notices me looking, she stands and puts everything back in the box. "Your Orb's programmed and ready to go. It's tough, won't break even if your arm snaps in half. Won't break even if you want it to. Now the Pin, that's a different story. Take that sucker out and you can say good-bye to your health. I knew the person who made them, you know. . . ." She trails off, and for a second, I think she's lost in her memories. They seem like sad ones, by the look on her face.

Someone pounds on the glass. We both jump, and an Initiative soldier motions for her to join him.

"Your next shift is tomorrow at dawn. I think I like you, so don't be late, Blondie." She leaves without another word.

CHAPTER 14

ZEPHYR

"The pre-Initiative Shallows were once known as the Everglades," Talan reads from a propaganda pamphlet we found after cleaning out the overflowing gutters in the streets a few days ago.

She could've been shot for stealing the trash. It's breaking Commandment Four.

We're supposed to send any propaganda to the Graveyard, so they can dig through the skitz and find whatever they want that's useful. I think it's just because they're scared we'll riot. But Talan has never been one to turn from the threat of danger, and she's obsessed with pre-Fall stuff.

While she reads, I'm so bored I feel like spearing out my eyeballs and roasting them for lunch. I'm hungry enough that I could. I swirl my fingers in the small pool of water beside me. Tiny minnows scatter.

I remember the first day I came here. The Ward Mark on my neck was still bleeding. I had a tent in my arms and a torn shirt on my back. I lost both before the moon took the sun's place in the sky.

That's when I met Talan. She was alone, too, but she was stronger, in her stubborn way. I watched her drop a boy twice her size for calling me a name, and from then on we were friends. We spent the night side by side staring up at the stars, telling each other stories about our parents. Telling each other we'd do whatever it took to stay on the same side and keep each other safe.

We kept our promise, but a lot has changed. I was softer then. I was scared of everything. Now the only thing I fear in this world is myself.

"You aren't paying attention to me, Zephyr," Talan huffs. "You want to figure yourself out? Then we have to do this. Either *you* read it, or you put on your big girl panties and listen up."

Why bother trying anymore? There is no conspiracy behind the murders. The pamphlet is just someone's pathetic attempt to deal with the loss of a loved one. What Talan and I should be learning about is how to survive. This crap is useless. "I'm so bored," I groan, and she slams the pamphlet down and stomps away from me, the ground making slushy suction noises with each step she takes.

"You're hopeless. Absolutely hopeless!" she yells.

Skitz, now she's pissed. If I could go back to that night we first met, I'd make her swear not to become such a girl about things. "Come back, Talan, I'll listen, I'm just messing with you. . . . "

But my words are cut short when the wind flips the pamphlet over. It takes me a while to sound out some of the words, but I manage.

"An anonymous tip from a long-time member of Propaganda Research states that the Dark Time is protected by the governing Initiative. The act of murdering may not simply be caused by Madness, but could be fueled by a common long-term goal to use the bodies as rations . . . "

"Oh, come *on*! That's sick." I throw the pamphlet aside. "Talan!" I've heard every crazy conspiracy theory before, but none of them hold any answers for me.

Like clockwork, I murder.

I can't stop. And I never will. Not unless someone finds a way to stop me.

Talan was right. I'm hopeless. There's nothing good about me, not really. No matter how hard I try to make myself better, I can never take back the things I've done.

My knife is homemade, sharp enough to cut through the bark of a tree. I clasp the handle. It feels warm and right. It would be easy to do it. To sink the blade into my chest, the way I've done to so many others.

I feel a jolt of pain.

Horrible, horrible pain, and in my head, there's a voice. *Stop.*

The knife falls from my fingertips. I must be going insane.

I try it again, put the blade to my skin, and there's the same pain, the same voice commanding me to stop.

For a second, I think I recognize her.

But no. That's not possible. Either I'm as crazy as the conspiracy theorists, or it's just my conscience. I should have Talan tie me to a tree each night, or give up all of my rations so I slowly starve.

But I'd still be here. I'd still be a threat to everyone, every waking moment of my life. I turn my knife toward my wrist. Slow and painful. That is the way I deserve to die.

The voice yells at me, and the jolt of pain comes, but I

push it all away, tell myself I have to be strong.

I cut myself like butter. Twelve times. Twelve even lines, one for each life I've stolen. I even try to dig for my Pin, take it out so the nanites can't heal me. But the dizziness comes, and I feel the world floating away.

"Freedom." I smile as I lie back under the warm sun.

Sometimes in the winter months, a thick fog rolls through the Shallows in the early morning.

It sticks to the sides of the buildings and blankets everything with a strange sort of coolness.

Right now I'm just like that fog, clinging to something that I know won't keep me for good. But it's worth a try. Somewhere through the darkness, I think I hear Talan's voice. "Stay with me!" she's screaming, but it isn't really a scream, I don't think. It's like she's calling to me from across the sea. "Don't you leave me, Zephyr James!"

Sometimes I think I can feel hands touching my skin, and I wonder if those are my victims, pulling me under. It's sort of like an ocean, but this ocean is cold, and the farther I sink beneath its waters, the harder it is to breathe.

"Why is he bleeding? What happened?" I don't know whose voice that is. Thomas, maybe?

There's a pounding on my chest, and for a second, it's

easier to breathe again. There is a scream, or maybe it's the high-pitched squeal of the gates opening, but I'm too tired to listen. I hear footsteps, running.

I think, for a second, that I might be floating.

I open my eyes and see the sky.

It is raining.

Fitting, I realize, for the day that I will die.

CHAPTER 15

MEADOW

I decide to take the shortcut home, past the Hospital. It is not as safe this way, but I cannot bring myself to go past the Catalogue Dome.

If they had found my mother in time, they would have been able to take her to the Hospital. They could have fixed her. I am sure of it. But of course it was too late. I never saw her body.

My father hugged me when he brought home her leather boots. There was still a bloodstain on one of the boots, and no matter how hard I tried to scrub it out, it never would fade away.

The sun is beginning to slip from the sky. There is a

rumble, and suddenly it starts to rain. It rains nearly every day in the Shallows. I can see the Hospital now, a small cement square tucked in between two towers.

I could make changes that matter, find a way to save lives, stop the deaths. My useless daydreams are interrupted by a group of kids, not much older than I am. They huddle in a circle, staring down at the blood-soaked ground. Most of them are Wards, with black X's on the backs of their necks. Their clothes are torn worse than mine, and they smell strange, even in the rain.

I should keep walking until my toes hit the sand and the water calls me home. But curiosity always wins with me. I stop.

I gasp.

Because it is him.

The same boy, lying in a bloody heap on the street. He is pale, his arm wrapped in a blanket that is pooling crimson all over the concrete. I shove my way to the front of the group. I kneel at his side. "What happened to him?" I say, as if the question doesn't belong to me.

"Who the hell are you?" someone asks.

"Get a doctor!" I scream, and then I pull off my belt and start to wrap it tight around the boy's arm, just above the wounds to staunch the flow of blood, the way my father taught me. "What happened to him?" I ask again.

"He tried to off himself, the ChumHead," a dark-haired girl says. "Selfish little skitz, leaving me to be the one to find him." Her eyes are bloodshot from crying, but she does not seem surprised.

Suicide is weakness. My father taught me this. Suicide is giving in to a world that we should be fighting against with all of our might.

I sit here, applying pressure, watching the boy, hating him for doing this to himself. His eyes are closed, like he could be sleeping, and his face is so pale. I should leave now, but I can't stop looking at him. He is beautiful. Shaggy brown hair sweeps across his face, and I am shocked at how bad I want to touch it.

Someone who looks like this shouldn't be so weak.

Someone who looks like this shouldn't die this way.

An Initiative doctor steps from the building, his white coat flying behind him. "What is this?" he yells at us. "Get off of my sidewalk, you filthy pigs!"

The crowd parts and the doctor gets a look at the boy.

I have seen bloody. I have seen gruesome. I've even seen a man's insides hanging from his open gut. But the twelve gashes carved into the boy's wrist are the worst thing I have ever seen. The boy did this to himself.

"Can you save him?" I look up at the doctor, my fingers skimming the boy's pale forehead. He is clammy, like wax.

"This is a waste of my time!" The doctor pulls a scanner from his coat and reads the boy's Catalogue Number.

"Zephyr James. Essential Citizen. Seventeen. Blood type AB negative." The doctor's face falls. There is no longer boredom in his eyes—there is pure terror.

"Essential?" asks the dark-haired girl. She is leaning over me, staring at the boy like she is furious she is about to lose him, like this boy is everything to her. "He's not Essential," she says. "He's just a Ward."

Essential. Essential means important. No Ward has ever been important.

No Ward could make an Initiative doctor so afraid.

I don't know why I even care.

But I do.

The doctor stares past us, as if he is trying to piece together the puzzle. But the boy suddenly moans, and the doctor rushes back into the hospital.

He appears again, two nurses flanking his sides. "He still has his Pin, at least. Get him inside!" he shouts. "And the rest of you, get off my sidewalk!"

I feel the boy's body growing cold. He seems so helpless,

so horribly alone. I cannot bring myself to leave him. What makes him Essential? What makes him different from the rest of us standing around him? I know my blood is type O. My mother had all of us tested. "Scan me!" I shout.

The doctor stops, turns slowly. "What?"

I stand up and cross the sidewalk in two strides. My hands are coated with the boy's blood. "I said scan me. My number." He doesn't move, so I reach out and yank the scanner from his hand, hold it to my forehead, and press the button.

"Meadow Woodson. Sixteen. Citizen. Blood type O. Rations Department."

"Take my blood." I thrust the scanner back into the doctor's hands.

"That's against protocol," he says.

"Screw protocol, take my blood! I'm not going to let him die!"

"The boy is in good hands, Miss Woodson."

My head drops. My heart sinks. I will pay for arguing, but something tells me I should not let the boy out of my sight.

A Ward is a Ward, and nothing more. This can't be possible.

"I'll give you every Cred I have," I whisper. "Just give him the damn blood."

He doesn't even take the time to consider it, and part of me wants to smile because I have outsmarted him. He doesn't know I've only worked once. Surely I haven't earned much. "We have a deal," he smirks.

Peri will lose a day of rations. My father will be furious. Koi won't speak to me for a week. My hands are shaking as I walk, and maybe it is from the shock of doing something for someone else. I like to think this is what my mother would have done.

Suddenly the boy is hoisted onto a hospital bed, and a nurse is gripping my arm, pulling me along behind him as we twist and turn through a maze of white hallways.

When we reach a room, and a needle slides into my vein, a part of me flows through the tube toward the boy.

Ward. Essential. Impossible.

I have to know what it means. I close my eyes and lay back on the cool metal table as a nurse silently stitches up the boy's mangled wrist. He moans as the doctor injects something into his arm and sprays liquid skin over his wounds. They are so deep the doctor has to spray them twice. Sometimes, the nanites do not work fast enough.

———

When I finally slip out the doors of the hospital, the world is coated in black. I consider running down the middle of the main street, along the train tracks.

But speed isn't always safe. So instead I walk silent and steady, keeping my breathing soft and slow. It is important to pay attention. To not miss a sound.

Some say the murders happen all at once, in a single, bloody moment. Tonight I see nothing strange, other than a handful of people still out taking their chances. The smart ones are in hiding, candles blown out, windows boarded up if they are lucky enough to have them.

I pass the Library, which reminds me of my father. I walk faster. I know he will be furious by now.

I hear no screams for help. Whenever I check over my shoulder, I am not being followed.

For the first time since coming to the city, I feel afraid.

The Shallows has turned into a ghost town.

When I turn a corner I can see smoke rising from the street. A cluster of people sit around a crackling fire. I smell something cooking. That is the kiss of death. "Stupid," I mutter under my breath. I make a big detour around the fire. In the distance, someone laughs.

I am almost to the beach when I hear it. The sound is soft, just a thump, and it comes from the alleyway to my left, from the way I need to go to get to the beach the fastest.

I hold my dagger in front of me. I walk on my toes, the way my father taught me to, and stick to the walls.

It is dark, but the moon casts enough light so that I can see where I am going. The alley looks empty from here. I run my hand along the brick. The solidity of it makes me feel safer.

Until I feel something warm and wet.

Lots of buildings have leaks. Old plumbing, breaking down over the years. But this is like touching wet paste.

I hold my hand up in the moonlight.

Crimson, thick and bright, coats my fingertips.

Blood.

I stumble away from the wall. A dark substance, almost black in the night, drips down the side of the brick.

I look up, slowly, following the trail.

When I see the body, I almost scream, but I catch myself. It is a woman. The long strands of hair hang down over the side of an old fire escape. I see her arm, dangling.

Suddenly I hear a scream, just behind me on the main road. It is high-pitched and awful, a sound that makes my hair stand on end. There is a splattering sound, like water hitting pavement, and the scream turns into a gurgle.

I do not go to help him. I know he's already dead. I hear footsteps, and a man steps into the alley.

He sees me. There is a cut on his face. Our eyes meet, and he says one word.

"Run."

I turn around and run, as fast as my feet can carry me, away from the City.

The Dark Time has come.

Tonight luck is on my side, because the dinghy is here, and the Pirates are nowhere to be seen.

I paddle out to sea as fast as I can, not caring that my boots are soaked with saltwater, or that my chest is heaving for air. I cannot paddle fast enough.

Stupid, stupid, stupid.

I never should have stayed so late, never should have veered from my path to try and save some strange boy who means nothing to me, nothing to my family.

It is about Peri. Peri and Koi and my father, our survival, and nothing more.

I am terrified that my father will have started up the boat and left me behind, to teach me a lesson.

But there it is in the distance, rocking gently.

Home.

The bow of the dinghy knocks up against the side of the houseboat, and I feel like I can finally breathe. But something's wrong. Normally, the wire perimeter would be in place, and Peri would be waiting.

Instead, there is nothing but the wind and the waves.

"Hello?" I call out. I knock my fist against the sides of the boat. "It's me!"

The rope ladder appears then, unfolding itself like a snake. I start to tie the dinghy and climb up, but someone is coming down.

It isn't my father.

It is Koi.

"Move over," he says, as he climbs down the ladder. I scoot back and wait for him. He settles down across from me. His face, so much like my father's, is angry.

"Nice of you to finally join us," he says.

"I got held up," I say, looking at my knees. "I made it back, didn't I?"

"Peri thought you were dead."

The words hit me right in the chest, like a hard punch. There is nothing I can say to defend myself, because my brother is right.

Koi leans forward and grabs the oar from my hands. I

notice that the wood is stained with blood. "What is this, Meadow? Blood?"

"It's not what you think," I say. "Someone was murdered."

"Of course they were! It's the Dark Time!" Koi throws the oar down between us. He glares at me like he hates me, like he wants nothing more than for me to fall into the ocean and sink to the bottom. I have never seen him this way before.

"Your work ends before sunset. You should have been home."

"I got held up!" I say, but he pounds his fist on the side of the dinghy.

"You're lying to me, Meadow. Dad wanted to come after you. What would you do if he lost his life because of your foolishness?"

"He . . . he was going to come look for me?"

"He loves you, Meadow," Koi says.

"He doesn't love me. He doesn't love anything but his training."

"That's how he shows love. Don't you get it? He lost Mom. He can't lose you, too."

The little boat rocks. Our heads sway close together for a second. Silver and bright. Koi says nothing. He just sits there across from me and waits for an explanation. I do not want to tell him what I did. It is none of his business.

But then I think of Peri, and I think of my father, and how hard we all work to stay together. Alive.

"There was a Ward," I start, choosing my words carefully. "He was bleeding out. I had to save him."

"He?"

"You don't understand, Koi. He was just lying there on the street. He tried to kill himself, and—"

"Then you should have let him die." Koi cuts me off. "Why should some stranger mean anything to you? What should *anything* else in this world matter, other than your family?"

"What is your problem?" I say.

He is acting just like my father.

I swallow hard. I try to explain. "The doctor scanned him, and it said he was Essential."

Koi just looks at me. His eyes are so dark. His eyes are not *his* tonight.

"Don't you get it?" I ask him. "A Ward is a forgotten person, not someone Essential, so the doctors brought him in, and I gave my blood to help save him, and " I stop talking when Koi grabs me by the shoulders and slams my head up against the side of the houseboat.

"What did you say?"

I try to squirm out of his grasp, but Koi has always been stronger than me. "I had to," I gasp.

"You had to do *nothing*," Koi spits. He presses my face hard against the houseboat. The metal is slimy and cold. "You could have been killed, Meadow. And then what would we have done? You would have killed Peri. Starved her to death."

There are tears in my eyes. I blink them away, because crying is a sign of weakness. "I had to know what it meant." I sound like a child. I *am* a child, who made a foolish mistake because I got curious. "Let me go."

"Not until you swear you'll grow up and do what you have to do. Nothing more."

He is right. He is. "Okay," I say.

He finally lets me go. My head is throbbing. The wind has picked up and the dinghy is rocking. I feel sick.

Koi leans forward and lowers his voice. He looks right into my eyes. He looks exactly like my father. Cold and hard and angry. "If you make this mistake again, Meadow, I will find that boy and kill him myself. Do you understand?"

I nod. He isn't lying. Koi never does.

We sit there, glaring at each other. And then Koi's

shoulders slump. He grabs my shoulders, and he pulls me into a hug, squeezing me so tight I can't breathe.

"I can't lose you," he says. "I can't be the only one holding us all together."

I have not hugged anyone besides Peri in years, so when I put my arms around him, it feels stiff. Awkward. "I'm fine," I say. "I can take care of myself."

"I know," he whispers. "That's what scares me the most." He pulls away. "You're becoming too much like her."

"What?"

But he shakes his head.

"Koi. Tell me. Who am I becoming too much like?"

"It doesn't matter," he says. I think . . . I think his hands are shaking, but he clasps them together and sets them in his lap. "Go find Peri so she knows you aren't dead."

I climb up the ladder slowly, and when I reach the boat and haul myself on deck, she is waiting for me with tears in her eyes.

"You made me cry," she says, sniffing. "Koi says you're an ass for making me do that."

"I'm so sorry," I say. I fall to my knees in front of her and wipe the tears away. "It's okay to cry, Peri."

"You never do."

"I do." I tuck a stray curl behind her ear. "But I do it when you're not looking."

"If you promise not to make me cry ever again, I won't be mad at you anymore," she says.

I nod. And then, just like that, I am forgiven.

I spend the rest of the night lying on the deck with my brother and sister, staring up at the stars. We tell Peri stories about our mother, and Koi teaches her about the constellations.

When Peri falls asleep, Koi brings out his fishing hooks, and a bottle of black ink he still has leftover from his tenth birthday. It is precious to him. He has not unscrewed the lid in years. "I want to give you something," he says. He takes my right arm and holds up the largest hook. The one with the sharpest, thickest point. I start to pull away, but his eyes find mine. "We're different, Meadow. I can survive in this world. But you can thrive in it. I don't want to know what you do out there. But you have to swear you'll always do it, so you can survive. Not for me or you or our father. But for *her*." He looks down at Peri. She is sound asleep. She is not having nightmares tonight.

"Ready?" Koi asks me. I nod my head and grit my teeth.

I hold back my scream while he carves the word *fearless* into my forearm. "Now you have a tattoo that isn't from the Initiative," he says. I watch as he puts ink on the wound, and wraps my arm with cloth. "You have to do what it takes to make it home," he whispers. "You can *never* end up like her."

Nothing matters but these people, on this boat.

Nothing matters but staying alive.

I will be fearless.

CHAPTER 16

ZEPHYR

When I wake up, I'm floating on clouds.

I keep my eyes closed, feeling around with my fingertips. Stars, are these . . . actual *pillows*?

I open my eyes. I'm lying in a hospital bed, in the middle of a stark white room that makes me feel small. My head spins. I look down at my wrist, and the memories come flooding back.

There was a knife. And twelve cuts. Twelve lines of blood, dripping from my wrist, and Talan, carrying me through the city streets as I died.

My wrist is marked with a light patch of skin that looks warped, like old scars. I touch it, and it feels fine.

How did I heal so fast? How am I still even alive?

"Welcome back," a voice says. One that's familiar. I look up so fast my eyes go out of focus. Standing in the doorway of the hospital room with her arms crossed over her chest is Talan.

"Hey," I say. My voice is a raw croak. I need water, and my head is spinning. "What happened? Where am I?"

Talan comes to my bed and pulls up a chair. "I hate you," she whispers. Her bottom lip trembles for a moment. And then she starts to cry.

The sound is strange, so out of place. She cries for what feels like forever. I let her lay her head on my chest and sob like a child, soaking my hospital gown with her tears. I don't know what to do about it, don't have practice with crying girls, so I just put my hand on her shoulder and tell her everything is going to be fine.

"You were dying," Talan gasps. "I didn't know what to do, so I brought you here, and . . ." The sobs just keep coming.

"It's fine now," I say. "Calm down, Talan. You're crying like a baby."

When she looks up at me, her blue eyes are rimmed with red. She looks like the girl I met so many years ago.

"I'm really sorry, okay?"

She smiles weakly, and catches her breath. "You're a ChumHead, you know that? Pretty much half of me *hates* you right now, Zephyr James."

"Just half? Well, skitz. I'll take it." That gets me laughing, and before I know it, I can't stop.

After a while, a nurse comes in. She's just a regular citizen assigned to the job, but she's good at it. "Welcome back," she says. She checks my vital signs, and Talan stands on the edge of the room, watching me like my mom used to do when I fell and skinned my knee. Like I'm some delicate kid, breakable.

Maybe she's right. But I feel better right now. Maybe I wasn't supposed to die. Maybe I'm actually meant for something more.

"Well, everything looks good." The nurse holds up my wrist, the one that should look mangled and bruised, and nods her head. "Skin is doing just fine. It'll be discolored for the rest of your life, but who cares, right?" She's looking at me like I'm supposed to laugh.

"Uh, yeah," I say. "Sure. Can I leave now?"

The nurse purses her lips. I've offended her. "You can leave. I'll have the doctor come and sign you out."

As soon as we're alone again, Talan comes back to my

side. "You ready to explain yourself, or do I have to start crying again?"

I smile weakly. "There's nothing to explain. You've always said I'm an idiot, and now I've finally proven it. I was stupid. End of story."

She winds a strand of dark hair around her finger. "I've thought about doing it before, too, you know," she says. That shouldn't surprise me. Talan's life is just as bad as mine. It's probably worse, because of Arden. But when she talks about suicide, I flinch. I've worked for so many years to keep her alive, to keep her eating and talking and getting out of bed each day. "I'm serious, Zephyr. I've thought about just drowning myself in the ocean. No one would try to stop me."

"I would."

She shrugs her shoulders. "Not if you were already dead."

I don't know what to say. I look down at my wrist with its new skin.

"If you died, Zephyr, I'd give up. I gave up the day Arden died, but it's *you* that's kept me alive. It's you that keeps me from dragging a knife across my own skin." She smiles, something Talan doesn't do all that much. "So let's make a new promise. You want to kill yourself again, and you might as well do me first. Got it?"

It takes me a minute for her words to sink in.

I thought the world would be better without me. But I forgot about Talan.

She needs me.

I reach out my hand and shake hers. "Deal," I say. "Now tell me how you managed to get a Leech doctor to save my life."

"Oh, then strap in," Talan says. "This story is *good*."

CHAPTER 17

MEADOW

There are not many belongings that I can call my own, other than my dagger and my boots. But there is one thing, so special to me that I know it's the right gift for Peri.

"I want you to keep this safe for me," I say, unfastening the bracelet around my wrist. My mother's seashell charm dances on an old chain that's tarnished from the salt air, but still beautiful all the same. "It was our mother's." I smile as her eyes go wide. I have to wrap the chain twice around her wrist, but it looks beautiful on her. "When you miss me, just press it to your heart. I'm always right there."

She smiles and touches the charm. "It's pretty," she says. "Just like you."

By the time I force myself to leave I am almost certainly late for work. I paddle fast to the shore, and the entire time, I feel Peri's gray eyes watching me go.

Bodies still lie crumpled in the streets. Some show evidence of a struggle, some simply lie on the concrete, apparently asleep. Seagulls swoop down, picking at the carnage. The corpses have been picked at by citizens, too, and some of them are naked, clothing stolen.

Orion is standing outside the Rations Hall when I get there, gun in hand. "One minute more and you'd have been late, Blondie!" she calls to me as I shove my way across the street. "Better be on your game today!"

"I am always on my game," I say, and shove past her to scan my Catalogue Number. Today she has me scan my Orb as well, so they can track my work hours and Creds.

"After you." Orion waves me in with her gun, the barrel staring me right in the face, but I am not afraid. I shuffle inside.

She catches me by the arm. "Interesting cut," she says, looking at Koi's gift to me. By now the nanites have caused it to scab over. "What's the story?"

I pull my arm away and press it to my side. "It's none of your business."

She grunts and lets it slide.

The day goes by quickly. I'm growing accustomed to working with the Rations bags, as if I've done it my entire life. I get trouble from a woman who manages to claw me, until the Initiative soldiers hold a gun to her head and force her to return her rations. I take them back because if I do not, it will be my life instead of hers.

Later, it gets worse.

A man with a gun comes in. When he lifts it and fires at the glass barrier, I already know it won't work. The Initiative is on him at once.

He is shot not once, not twice, but three times.

A waste of three bullets, a waste of one life.

I focus on my work.

That is, until the Wards file in.

I look up and see their faces. Filthy. Sunken cheeks.

The line moves forward enough for the Initiative officers to close the doors behind the first group. The sunlight disappears. I look up.

There, standing at the back of the line, is the boy.

Zephyr.

CHAPTER 18

ZEPHYR

Stars, it was her.

Her, the moonlit girl, who saved me.

"I don't even know if it was really her, Zephyr," Talan says. We're standing in line for rations. It's nearly 100 degrees already, and it isn't even noon yet.

"Silver-blonde hair, down to her waist?" I say, pointing at Talan's hips. "Gray eyes?"

"Well, yeah," she says, "But how am I supposed to believe some girl you've seen in your dreams is even real? Lots of girls have hair like that. It's from living under the sun, not haunting people's dreams. You sure you're feeling all right?

"I'm as healthy as a Leech, Talan. Promise."

The line moves forward, slowly. My stomach feels all soupy and mixed up inside. Before the doctor signed me out of the hospital, he pumped me with some sort of blue liquid that he said was chock-full of nutrients. "She's real," I say to Talan. "And if you say she saved me, then maybe there's a chance she's been dreaming of me, too."

Talan laughs under her breath, and winks at a boy with black hair as he passes by. "Life isn't a fairy tale."

"Well, it should be," I say.

She snorts. "Maybe you can draw a picture of her and start asking people if they've seen her. There's plenty of crazy people in the Shallows. Someone's bound to have an answer."

"You're kind of a ChumHead, you know that?"

Talan laughs, but then her expression grows serious. "There's something else, Zeph. When the doctor scanned you, there was something weird."

"What do you mean?"

She chews on her bottom lip. "Essential. That mean anything to you?"

"Never heard of it before," I say.

She frowns. "No, neither have I." She looks like she's going to say something else, but as we get closer to the front of the line, we hear shouts coming from inside the Rations Hall. A man's voice, claiming he's not getting his day's worth. There are three shots, and everyone goes silent for a second. I know without having to see it that the man's a goner.

The line moves quicker now. Talan is being scrappy as always, trying to barter for a pair of boots she wants from the girl in front of us. When we finally enter the Hall, the Leech guarding the doors locks them behind us. It's stupid, really. No one's going to try and push his way in when a Leech has a rifle pointed in his face.

"Another day in paradise," I say. I expect Talan to laugh. She usually thinks I'm pretty funny, but today she gasps.

"What? What is it?"

"Oh, stars," she says.

"See? I *told* you that word would catch on!"

Her fingernails dig into my arm, and she points across the room. "Just shut up and look."

My breath sort of stops, right there in my lungs.

Standing behind the glass, staring down at the blood soaked floor with anger warping her face, is the person I swear I've waited my entire life to see.

CHAPTER 19
MEADOW

I try to hide behind my hair, but the Rations Hall is warmer today, and Orion makes me pull it back, out of my face.

"Sanitation rules, Blondie," she snorts. "Besides, it looks good on you."

I keep my chin down, only looking up when I slide the next person their rations, but I'm slow.

"I feel sick!" I call to Orion.

"No one's felt sick in years, liar," she yells back. "That's a good one!" She laughs.

The boy is only five people away now. He looks better, his skin back to a color of the living. His arm has been patched up.

I am relieved. I am terrified. I am not sure what I am feeling.

"You're distracted," Orion says. "Pick up the pace before I shoot you in the foot."

I try to focus on my work, but he's getting closer. What would Koi say? What would my father say if he knew I was messing up?

Focus.

That girl is standing in line next to him, the one who watched him like he belonged to her. She has curves, and stands tall. I am strong and thin and small. I look down at my toes. "I said *hello*," someone says, and when I look up, it is the girl. She is watching me. "Are you deaf or something?"

"Scan your number," I say to her. The girl rolls her eyes, scans her number, and I check the screen.

Talan Banner. Ward. Seventeen. Ration Allowance: Level 1.

The Wards get a small bundle of dried meat, and a loaf of bread that barely fits in the palm of my hand—it is full of nutrients, I'm sure.

I slide her rations through the slot but she doesn't take them. "Don't even *think* about trying to take him from me, Skinny," she says. "Trust me, you're not his type."

Then the bundle is ripped from my hands and she winks, blows me a kiss, and moves away.

I laugh, because I do not really know what else to do. All I can do is stare back at him like I am a statue, and force myself to breathe in and out.

Zephyr.

"Hello," Zephyr says. His voice is not too deep. I both love and hate the way his voice sounds, all at once. "I wanted to thank you for saving me."

"I don't know what you're talking about. Scan your number."

He presses his forehead against the scanner, watching me the whole time. His eyes are the purest green.

"You don't have to be afraid," he says.

"I'm not afraid." Why won't he stop talking? I glance at Orion—she's talking with a guard, ordering him to handle a group of Wards who have started up a fistfight in the back of the line.

"You saved my life. I want to know why, and I want to thank you, in some way."

"You don't need to thank me," I say, keeping my eyes down. "It isn't smart to be seen speaking to me. Trust me."

"I already do. I'd be dead if you hadn't helped me."

I try to pretend I don't hear him. I try to pretend this isn't happening. I cannot see this boy. I can't look into his eyes, or think I owe him anything else, or have him think he owes me.

I gather his rations and place them in a bundle. My hands are shaking. I drop the bread on the floor, careless. "I'm sorry, Zephyr," I hear myself say.

Stupid, stupid, stupid.

"Blondie!" Orion yells. She waves a finger, signaling for me to pick up the pace. I scoop up the bread and stuff it into his rations bag. "Meadow! The day's not getting any longer!"

When I slide the rations to Zephyr, his fingers graze mine.

I start to pull away, but not before he squeezes my hand, just once. "Meadow, huh?" he whispers. "Well, at least I know your name."

The image of his face, with his oddly imperfect smile, and his emerald eyes, haunts me the rest of the day.

CHAPTER 20

ZEPHYR

Meadow.

I should've known she'd have a sweet name like that.

It's got nothing to do with how she acts. Shallows-sour, like she's pissed off at life. She's kind of a ChumHead.

"She'll come around," Talan says to me. She is gnawing on her rations like a wild dog. "I gave her good reason to want you."

"What are you talking about? What did you say to her?"

Talan shrugs, and kicks an old can across the street. It disappears in an instant, caught up in the current of shuffling feet. "I made her think you weren't free. Every girl wants what she can't have." She pats me on the cheek, a little too hard, and slips into the crowd, off to do what Talan does when I'm not around.

I should be looking for work today, or making sure the littlest Wards are safe back in the Reserve. But instead, I spend the rest of the day in the alleyway behind the Rations Hall, sitting with my back against an overflowing Dumpster, thinking of what I'll say to Meadow when she comes out.

Hi, I'm the loser who tried to kill himself.

Excuse me, miss. Have we met before?

Nothing is right. The look on her face when she saw me, like she was furious, keeps coming back to me. She saved me. She gave her own blood, risked her own safety to stand up to a Leech doctor for *me*. A Ward. Why?

I look up at the sky between the buildings on either side of me. It's hotter than normal, and even though I'm in the shade, I'm still drenched in sweat. The train rattles by, whistle blaring, and I imagine citizens diving out of the way. It must be nearly four o'clock. I have hours to wait.

Finally a Leech soldier comes out the back door of the Rations Hall, rifle slung over his shoulder. Three others follow. "Rations ran out early today, sir," one of them says into his cupped hand. Most Leech soldiers have mics embedded in their palms, and radio chips in their right ears. The soldiers laugh and walk past the alley.

I stand up and try to smooth out my shirt. The Leech Doctor gave me a new one, something that doesn't happen often, if ever, and a shower, too, and for the first time in my life, I might actually look presentable. Sweat drips into my eyes.

Skitz. Maybe half-presentable, then.

The door of the Rations Hall swings open, and the woman with the shaved head comes out. She eyes me for a second. "You'd be smart not to cause trouble with that one, boy," she says, shaking her head. When I say nothing back, she shoulders past me, muttering, "Suit yourself," under her breath, and disappears.

My heart starts acting all wrong in my chest. I feel like I'm gearing up for a fight, like adrenaline is pulsing through my veins.

The door swings open, and Meadow steps out, silver hair hanging just to her hips. Stars, she's perfect.

I swallow my nerves, step forward, and as she turns to shut the door behind her, reach out and place my hand on her shoulder.

"Hey," I start to say. It's the worst mistake I've ever

made, because before I realize what's happening, the world's upside down, and I'm lying on my back, staring up at the sky without a bubble of air left in my lungs.

I should be mad. I should be angry and embarrassed.

Instead, all I can think is I might love this girl.

CHAPTER 21

MEADOW

Zephyr is just lying there, staring up at me with a goofy smile on his face.

I must have given him a concussion.

"You shouldn't have snuck up on me like that," I say, even though I don't know if he can hear me. I pace back and forth, not sure if I should help him, or keep going on my way like my father and Koi would want.

Zephyr groans, and for a second I am worried he might be seriously hurt. But then I hear the strangest sound in the world.

He starts laughing.

I lean back against the wall and cross my arms.

I'll let him ask his questions. He must want to know who I am, and why I would offer any piece of myself to him.

After a while, he stops laughing, and pulls himself to his feet. He is taller than I thought he would be. Taller, maybe, than my father. Lean muscles ripple down his arms. "What do you want?" I ask him.

"I told you before," Zephyr says, holding his palms out. His hands are much larger than mine. Stronger, I bet, too. "I wanted to thank you for saving me."

"Okay," I say, shaking my head. I push off from the wall and start walking. "We're even now. Don't follow me."

"Meadow. Wait."

He does not yell it. He just says it, soft. I sigh, and turn back around. "Just give me a chance," Zephyr says.

No one has ever looked at me this way before, like I am something worth seeing.

"I promise I'm not boring," Zephyr says. He reaches up to scratch his chin, and I can see the pale patch on his arm where his jagged cuts used to be, where he almost took out his Pin. *Essential. Ward.* What does it mean?

I can let this slide, for once in my life. We can give each other the answers we need, and I can move on. Koi will never even know the difference.

"I'll let you explain," I say, "and after that, you never bother me again. Understood?"

"I'll try my hardest." Zephyr nods. His hair is as dark as chocolate. I want to run my fingers through it. I want to get away from him.

I do not know what I want.

"Thank you," he says. "Come with me."

He does not wait for a reply. He walks past me and into the crowded streets of the Shallows.

CHAPTER 22

ZEPHYR

When I look back, I think she's given me the slip, disappeared without a good-bye. But then I see a flash of silver, and I know she's still there.

The Leeches have plenty of buildings scattered across the Shallows. Plenty of buildings and plenty of cameras, giant watching eyes, to make sure the citizens don't step out of line.

There's one place that has the most eyes of all. The Cortez Pier, where I used to live with my parents. The citizens in this neighborhood worship the Leeches like they're gods come to earth. Even though the place is completely twisted, it's where I want to go now, for some reason.

I stop by the tracks and wait. Meadow is beside me, holding a dagger in her palm, the blade shining under the hot sun.

"It isn't dark yet," I say. "Do you really need that?"

She twirls it once, spins it over the back of her hand, and catches it in her palm. I guess the dark look in her eyes is answer enough.

I don't know how we make it onto the train. People are eager to get as far away from the Shallows as they can. But how far can we really go? The Perimeter is a giant coiled snake, squeezing tighter and tighter as our numbers grow.

I climb on first, shoving a man out of the way to make space for Meadow. When I reach down to help her up, she doesn't take my hand.

"After you," I say, laughing. She doesn't even smile. She's like Talan, but worse. The train accelerates, growling loudly beneath us.

"Where are we going?" Meadow finally asks. The wind blows her hair away from her face, and I get a good look at her eyes. Gray and angry. Curious.

"It's a surprise," I say. I watch as her dagger dances across the backs of her hands again. I wonder what else she can do.

We roar past the Reserve. I wonder if Talan is back

yet. I silently thank her for whatever she said to Meadow. "That's home," I say, pointing at the blur of green and brown. "Well, as close as a Ward can get to one."

She watches in silence as a flock of white birds rises from the swampy Reserve.

"What do you think?" I nudge her gently, and her body goes rigid.

"I think soon, there won't be anywhere that anyone can call home," she says.

Her arms and legs are littered with scars of different shapes and sizes, like shells. I wonder how many times she's almost been killed. I wonder if she'd kill me if she knew what I've done.

Probably.

"Your body," I say. "Your body is . . ."

"None of your business."

Skitz, she's beautiful. Terrifying.

"Where are you taking me?" She asks again. "Because I'm getting ready to jump."

"Where I can explain myself to you," I say. "When you see it . . . maybe you'll understand why I tried to—"

"Why should that even matter to me? I don't know you, and I don't want to."

"Come on. I'm not *that* bad."

We sit in silence. In the distance, beyond the marshes, I can see the towering black gates of the Perimeter. There's all kinds of stories about the citizens who've tried to sneak through, stupid enough to think they could just *leave*.

The rumor is that when the Pulse paralyzes you, you end up belly-up in the ocean. It's the ultimate Leech warning: No one screws with us.

A while later the train rolls to a stop at the only remaining station inside the Perimeter. We leap down from our car and I lead Meadow through the sea of people. Too many people. Way too many.

"Welcome to the City of Cortez" the old holograph on the station house reads. It hangs from the building, dangling in the wind, flickering every so often. No one has bothered to fix it.

I turn to look at Meadow. She raises her eyebrows and looks at me. "Where are we going?"

"Somewhere different," I say. I give her my best smile, then plunge into the crowd, hoping that she follows.

CHAPTER 23

MEADOW

People here are smiling. Some of them, at least. More than they do in the Shallows. A few children actually race back and forth in front of us, playing games. I feel like we have gone back in time, back before the murders began. Before my mother died.

We stop when we reach Zephyr's surprise. It is a massive boardwalk, stretching from the beach out into the ocean. I have heard of them. It seems impossible that the Initiative would still let one stand.

But of course. There at the end of the boardwalk, larger than life itself, is a giant silver globe, held up by a massive golden hand. Carved in the thumb is an open eye.

I see you. Nothing you do will be missed.

And suddenly the entire place seems sick to me. These are the people who support them, and love them. These . . . these are the Believers. The traitors. The ones who believe the Initiative is good. Holy, even.

"This is where I used to live," Zephyr says to me. "This is where I come from."

I look around at the houses and buildings just off the boardwalk, the Initiative soldiers patrolling the streets, rifles in hand. I look at the people laughing and talking and thinking that they are safe.

"This is where you came from?"

"My parents were Leech lovers." Zephyr nods, his shame on his face. "Me, I think Commandment One is the biggest sin there is. Come on."

We shoulder past a guard, the dark look in his eyes telling me that maybe, he might hate the Initiative just as much as we do. We slip through the large metal gates at the boardwalk's entrance.

"Today is the festival," Zephyr says. "They're celebrating the day the Leeches took control. That's when . . . you know, the Perimeter went up. And then the murders started."

"Why?" I think maybe they have all been brainwashed.

We stand in line to get our numbers scanned, and by the time we make it through to the boardwalk, I am shaking with rage. People are clapping. Celebrating. Singing.

They are *happy*.

"I want to kill them all," I say under my breath. Zephyr places his hand on my shoulder. He squeezes it, just once. "Be careful what you say here," he whispers.

There is one thing still working on the boardwalk. A giant metal mushroom, tall as a building, with peeling red paint on its rounded top. Hanging from the mushroom are at least a hundred swings on fat chains.

The mushroom lights up, and strange, tinny-sounding music plays, and as people file on and strap themselves into the swings, it begins to spin.

"Come on." Zephyr grabs my wrist. I flinch, but when I look at him, he is smiling at me. "Have a little fun, at least. The world isn't *all* death and destruction."

He is wrong. But I let him lead me to the swings. The spinning mushroom slows down. Citizens unlatch themselves and climb down, and soon, our line is moving. "We're up," Zephyr says.

I follow him through the maze of swings. When we reach ours, I feel Zephyr's strong hands on my waist. He lets them linger there, for a moment, before boosting me in.

Zephyr jumps beside me. Our legs touch. The space is tight and I could not move away even if I wanted to.

The mushroom lights up. We start to move. We go round and round, in a wide circle, feet dangling. It is like floating in a dream. Our swing is on the outside, so we soar over the sea every few seconds. I imagine the chains snapping, and our swing flying away and never landing.

We could fly over the Perimeter. We could go away and never come back.

The swing swoops low, and my stomach drops. I scream, giggling like Peri does when I tickle her, and suddenly I feel terrible.

I should not be here with this boy.

I turn to Zephyr, who I realize has been watching me. He does not smile when my eyes meet his. Instead he just stares, soft and questioning.

It makes me feel warm. It makes me feel wrong. I clear my throat. "I need answers," I say.

He nods, as the swing carries us away.

CHAPTER 24

ZEPHYR

She doesn't ask how I became a Ward.

She doesn't ask why I tried to kill myself.

She asks me about my parents.

"They died when I was eight," I say. "During the Dark Time." I don't go into the story. I don't go into the fact that I saw them murdered with my own eyes.

We glide over the crowd. People look up. Kids smile and wave.

"I'm sorry," Meadow says. "Who were they?"

"They were just people. Nobody important. Same as me."

Meadow frowns. "That's where you're wrong. I saw

the doctor scan you. It said something I've never heard before. It said you were Essential."

Her eyes go all wide when she says it, like it's supposed to mean something to me. Talan said it, too. But I still don't have any idea what it means.

The mushroom's music keeps playing, tinny and out of tune.

"Maybe it's just code for something else." *ChumHead. Murderer. Someone who has no hope of being wanted by gorgeous silver-haired girls.*

Meadow shakes her head. Her curls fall in front of her face, and if I weren't afraid she would snap my finger in two, I'd probably reach out and push her hair behind her ear. Talan says that makes girls melt. "No one is Essential, Zephyr. *No one* is Essential."

"Then it has to be a mistake."

"You should have died," she says. "You were practically dead. When the Doctor saw you, he knew you were a Ward. He wanted to let you die. But then he scanned you. You should have seen his face." She stops to take a breath. "He was terrified."

Suddenly the swings feel like they're moving way too fast. The music is too loud. "That can't be true," I say.

"Have you done anything, said anything . . . discovered

something . . . ?" Meadow asks.

I shake my head. But of course, I know.

I could tell her. I could spill all my secrets right now.

"Zephyr?" Meadow is looking at me. Like I mean something. And it kills me. It really does.

I know it's just because she's curious, and needs answers to justify saving me. Maybe she got in trouble. She thought it was worth it. Maybe she thought I was someone good.

This girl would probably take her dagger and thrust it through my heart if she knew the truth.

She never has to know.

I shake my head. I put on a good show. "I'm just a Ward," I say to her as the swings start to slow. "I'm an orphan who got tired of living in Cortez, and that's the only interesting thing I've ever done."

Her gray eyes hold mine like she's looking for the lie.

But if there's anything I know I'm good at, it's hiding the truth.

CHAPTER 25

MEADOW

At the end of the pier, citizens bow before the giant statue, pressing their palms to it, whispering. I watch a woman with a swollen belly waddle up. Her face is fat, like a puffer fish, and when she presses her belly to the statue, as if dedicating her baby to it, to them, I want to scream.

Zephyr takes my hand and I let him. It is a lifeline, a distraction. He tows me away to the end of the almost deserted pier.

I shake free and run, and when I leap off the edge, into the warm water, into *silence,* I am at peace. When I surface, I see him standing there on the pier, looking down at me.

"Come on!" I call.

I float on my back and laugh.

Zephyr leaps. When he surfaces, his hair is sticking to his forehead, and his eyes are even greener than before.

"I hate the ocean," he says.

"I think it's the only beautiful thing we have left," I say. "My father taught me how to swim. He tied my arms behind my back and made me stay afloat using only my legs." I run my hands across the surface of the water. It sparkles like fire in the setting sun.

Zephyr frowns. "Your own dad did that to you?"

"All he cares about is teaching me how to survive. Nothing more."

Zephyr dives. When he resurfaces and looks back at me, he is chewing his lip. It makes him look younger, like a child. I wonder how he protects himself on the streets. Something tells me he's street-smart, but I bet he would lose in hand-to-hand combat if it came down to it.

"Maybe that's just his way of showing he cares," he says. "I wish I still had my dad."

"It's better that you're alone. It's better that you don't have anyone to look after but yourself."

"I'm not alone. I have Talan."

Talan. The girl with the dark hair. "Do you love her?"

I ask, because I can't help myself. I feel all jittery, waiting for his answer, and I don't know why.

But Zephyr laughs. "Talan is like an older sister. Or a younger one, whichever way you look at it. I'm not with her in that way. I'm not with anyone." His eyes hold mine. We drift closer together.

"I have a sister," I blurt out, because it is the only thing I can think of to say without making a mess of things.

"Tell me about her," Zephyr says, still watching me with that look, like his eyes are seeing right into my soul.

So I do, because talking makes me feel better. I tell him about Peri. I tell him about my mother dying, and the houseboat we live on to stay safe. As darkness falls and the pier empties above us, I tell him about the blood that runs through the streets, and how some of it is from my own dagger, my own hands.

Zephyr reaches out, slow and gentle. He pulls me close, and studies my *fearless* tattoo. The nanites have nearly eaten away the scabs, and the ink has begun to show through. It looks strangely alive in the dying light. His fingers skim over the letters, and as they do, chill bumps scatter across my skin. "You're perfect," he whispers, "no matter what you've done."

I feel, for a second, brand-new. But I do not want to

forget. I want to be focused, always alert. I look up at the sky. The sun is an orange ball of fire, dripping into the ocean like hot wax. I slowly pull away. "We should go back now. Get on the train and head home. It's late."

"You're beautiful," Zephyr says. He moves closer. The waves rock us back and forth, and my heart hammers in my chest. His voice is velvet. His voice is saying all of the things I never thought I would hear anyone say.

I'm not sure I want this. As he reaches for me, I swim away, head toward the shore, moving underneath the boardwalk, until I am in its shadow. The waves lap against the wooden pilings. They are covered in barnacles and seaweed. I do not deserve his kindness. My family would say that he does not deserve mine.

I tread water as Zephyr swims toward me. I smile, but he does not.

"There's something I have to tell you, Meadow," he says. "Something about me you should know. I'm not—"

A rogue wave hits me, fast and strong. It pushes me into him. I grab his shoulders, and before I realize what is happening, his arms are around my waist. I can feel his heart hammering in time with my own.

"We should go," I whisper.

It is late, and soon it will not be safe.

We should go because I am falling, *fast*, and I am terrified of what that means.

"We'll go," Zephyr whispers. "But I want to try something first."

He is so close I can almost taste him.

CHAPTER 26
ZEPHYR

Her lips are about to touch mine. So close. Finally. My head feels fuzzy, and I tell myself it's just nerves, or the sea, rocking us back and forth.

I look into her eyes. I see the light blue sunburst that surrounds the gray pupil. I can't look away.

Suddenly everything goes dark, and I'm no longer in the ocean, no longer even a part of this world.

I'm standing in a mirrored room. I look left. I look right. I see myself, reflected a hundred times, dressed in black, fists clenched, eyes burning like fire.

A voice calls out to me from somewhere. I whirl around, but I'm the only person in the room. "Zephyr," the voice says again. Her voice is shimmery and bright, and it chills me to my very core.

"Welcome to the Murder Complex, Patient Zero. Initiate Termination."

I'm swimming with my arms wrapped around *Meadow Woodson. Sixteen. Target. Initiate Termination.*

All I want to do is kill Meadow Woodson. Sink a knife into her heart and end her feeble, undeserving life.

Meadow Woodson. Sixteen. Target. Initiate Termination.

I do the only thing I can do.

I obey.

CHAPTER 27

MEADOW

Maybe I am asleep, and it is just another nightmare. I will wake up and be back on the houseboat beside Peri, having made it home on time, having kept my promise to her.

But when the air leaves my lungs, I know that this is real. That Zephyr's hands, no longer soft and gentle, are actually wringing my neck.

I flail in his arms. I open my mouth like a fish out of water. I try to scream, but no sound comes out. He is killing me, lifting me over his head, out of the sea, as if I am weightless, nothing at all.

My vision begins to tunnel.

My father had Koi strangle me once. I am prepared for this.

My father.

Count to three. Relax. Now survive.

I stretch for my dagger. I do not think about the Zephyr of moments ago. I thrust it straight down, into his shoulder. There is a gush of blood, and when I twist the blade, his right arm goes slack.

I crash back into the waves, kick off a piling, and swim for the shore.

He is not Zephyr anymore. He is a monster.

CHAPTER 28

ZEPHYR

I am fulfilling my destiny. This is what I was made for.

The voice urges me on. Louder and louder and louder, until that's all I can hear.

"*Kill.*

Destroy.

No escaping.

No turning back.

This is your duty.

Purge the Earth.

This is the Murder Complex."

I lunge at the target. Flux, it's fast. A worthy opponent.

"Please, Zephyr! Please!"

I hate it when they beg.

Begging is the most annoying sound in the world.

CHAPTER 29

MEADOW

Zephyr lunges at me, teeth bared, a furious roar tearing from his lips.

"Stop!" I scream. It's like he can't even hear me. "Zephyr, please!"

He grabs my left arm and I throw my right fist into his jaw. I hear the thump of the hit, but his strength is incredible, and suddenly I am flying through the air, and I slam into an old wood piling, and my back is on fire with pain. I stagger to my feet, groaning, struggling to find my bearings in the sandy shadows of the boardwalk. Where is my dagger? How is he even *doing* this? "Are you insane?"

He's sprinting for me, arms pumping, blood dripping

from his shoulder. He leaps, and my head slams into the wet sand. He rolls off of me, grabs my ankles, and starts to drag me across the beach. Sand fills my mouth, my nose. I can't breathe.

Close your eyes. Feel your enemy's weaknesses. I twist away an ankle and sink my foot into his groin.

The freedom lasts long enough for me to spot my dagger at the water's edge.

I scramble across the sand, but Zephyr is way too fast. He grabs a fistful of hair and pulls me to my feet.

I stumble for a moment, then whirl around, and in one motion, pull his shirt over his head and slam his face down into my knee. There is a flush of warm blood, and he groans as he staggers back.

My feet skid across the sand. I grab my dagger, and then I am sprinting away. I can hear Zephyr behind me, like he is not hurt at all. Like he is a machine.

I jump up on the boardwalk and turn left. The town looks safe enough, but I am running blind. I bang on the door of a house. It is reinforced with a metal cage.

"Let me in!" I scream. "Someone help me!"

No one comes, no one ever comes. I huddle down in the shadow of an old car. A man with a child raises a homemade knife in my direction. "Scram, girl," he hisses.

"Get out of here or I'll gut you like a fish."

I turn and run. The sky is covered in clouds. Zephyr slams into me, clawing for my dagger.

His nails rip at the skin on my cheeks and I scream, writhing beneath him. But he is strong. Determined. Deadly. I lock my legs around his neck, slam him down sideways into the concrete; sink my fist into his face. "Zephyr, please!" I yell, as I leap up and stagger away from him, my whole body trembling. "What are you doing? It's me, Meadow!"

That only makes it worse. He lunges for me. I twist to the side and leap at him. My fingers close over his throat. I slam my head into his. The world starts to spin. Zephyr falls, crushing me. The air rushes from my lungs and soon I am gasping.

In the distance, I can hear the train rumbling, barreling toward us.

We both freeze, and it's as if he already knows my next move. He sits up, pulling me with him. I choke down a breath before he throws me back down, grinding me into the pavement.

I squeeze his chest with my thighs, until he can't breathe either. Then I stab him. When he growls and rolls away, I scramble up and run, heading for the tracks.

Mind over body. Mind over body. The sound of my father's voice makes me strong and focused. I will not die like my mother. I will not leave my family to face this world without me.

But then I look back at Zephyr, at the horrible expression on his face, like he hates me, wants me dead, wants to see my blood splatter the concrete as my head explodes. And he's still coming. Again.

The train keeps coming. I can see the trail of smoke rising from its back. I push myself harder. Zephyr is right at my heels. I stretch my arms wide. I take a deep breath.

And jump.

I slam into the carriage. I cling to a metal rung as my feet dangle above the ground.

"Do not resist!" Zephyr screams. The train takes a curve, and my body swings to the left. I see Zephyr, clinging to the next train car.

He pulls a knife from his waistband and lets it fly, the blade spinning at the perfect angle to sink itself handle-deep into my neck. I drop quickly to a lower rung and the knife barely misses me. The train keeps moving, racing down the tracks faster than I remember. The ground blurs.

I start to climb, one hand over the other, heading for the roof of the train. But Zephyr knows where I am going. I reach the top seconds before he does, and start running.

The wind slaps me in the face. I crouch low and keep moving, and when my car ends, and a dark gap stares up at me between it and the next one, I close my eyes and leap. My knees slam into the metal roof of the next car and I scramble to my feet again.

I don't know how many times I leap from one train car to the next, roll to my feet, and start running again.

The train rumbles over a bridge. I can see the waves far below. The wind is angry, blowing my hair back from my face, stinging my bloody knees.

I turn to see Zephyr leap onto my car. He rolls over once in a fluid motion, and then rises to his feet.

He is fire. Furious.

I have seconds to jump.

I turn around and launch my dagger. The blade spins wildly but with a menacing ring that brings a smile to my lips. He does not scream as it sinks into his thigh. I turn and jump, fly away from the train. It soars past above me, carting Zephyr off to the other side of the bridge. He is too late, and I am free.

We can only survive. We do not need anyone else. The world lives off hate.

And that is exactly what I feel for Zephyr James.

CHAPTER 30

ZEPHYR

"*Kill.*

Destroy.

No escaping.

No turning back.

This is what we must do to survive.

Purge the Earth.

This is the Murder Complex."

The voice is too loud. Like the sound of the train that still rumbles beneath my feet, and I don't know how I got here, don't know what I'm doing. I scream for help. Where is Meadow? I want to launch myself from the train. That would be better. Anything is better.

I want to die.

My body is not my own. My mind is not my own.

I'm being controlled, like a machine. *Remember your training. Remember that what you are doing is for the greater good.*

Training? What training? I've never been trained in anything other than ignoring Talan.

Who is Talan? I think I see a girl's face in my mind, but she slips away before I can grab her.

I am perfectly balanced on the top of the train, even in the wind. I'm good at this. Really good.

Find your target, and end it. That is the job, and you must do it well.

That's what I'm going to do.

When I close my fingers around her disgusting throat, I won't leave until the warmth rushes from her body. Until she's cold. Gone. Only then will my mission be complete. Only then will I have done my duty.

CHAPTER 31

MEADOW

This will be the first time I have hijacked a boat.

I will hold a blade to a man's throat and see the fear in his eyes. Maybe make him jump overboard, then speed off and leave him to drown.

My father has trained me and this world has made a monster of me.

So when the yacht floats past me, a black shadow as silent as the night, I do not even think. I reach for the dinghy that floats behind it.

I need to rest. I need to catch my breath. I need to heal.

I imagine Zephyr stretching bloodied hands from the deep. Grabbing me. Pulling me under the surface of the waves so that I can no longer breathe, so that soon, I am with my mother.

I swing myself into the dinghy. I peel off my shirt and start to rip at the seams, until I have a few strips to fasten around my bleeding knees. I take a deep breath and remind myself that soon I will return to Peri. I will never be so stupid again. I will never trust anyone but myself or my family.

I lie back and catch my breath. I fight the tears, because crying will mean that Zephyr has won. Crying will mean that I actually *care*. I should have buried my dagger in his heart.

Gone. My dagger is gone.

I sleep.

Slowly, I haul myself along the line that connects the dinghy to the boat. My strength comes from inside, from a place I keep locked away until I need it most, just like my father taught me.

I haul myself onboard the yacht. It is quiet and still dark out. The waves lap gently against the hull.

Fire spreads through my muscles as I rise to a crouch and look around the yacht. It is two stories, stark white and smells of bleach, as if it has been freshly scrubbed.

This boat is nothing like mine. No one should be allowed to own something this nice.

And that's when I see it. The large eye painted on the side of the first-story cabin.

I must be on the far side of the Shallows.

I hear voices coming from the second story, the clinking of glass. Laughter. Everything is so peaceful. I feel as if I have been dumped into another world.

I should not be here. I should turn around and dive back into the waves. But despite myself, I'm curious. And I need a place to hide.

Slow and silent, I tiptoe up the stairs. My heart is beating so fast I can feel it pound in my ears. I swallow the lump in my throat and slide up against a porthole.

The Commander of the Initiative sits just a few feet away, with his back to me.

I try not to gasp. I know it is him. I would recognize him anywhere.

So many nights I have dreamt about taking a sharpened arrow and letting it fly through his eye socket. Then I would claw out his brains with my fingernails and feed the rest of him to the fish.

I watch him relaxing in a plush leather armchair, a glass of some bubbling liquid clutched in his pale fingers.

Initiative officers surround him, and they are laughing. Celebrating. But celebrating what?

I take a step closer, to get a better look. I think they are watching a movie. I have never seen one before. My mother said they were beautiful, that they took you to other worlds. But now, as I watch people run around on the screen, slinking through the darkness to fight each other with knives and metal poles, I think this is not a world I would want to go to. Because I already live in it.

The officers cheer. I look from them to the screen, then back again. Just in time to see a bloody man with brown hair stagger across the screen. His face is pale. His arm is mangled and dripping blood like a faucet.

It is Zephyr.

I almost scream, almost stumble back. Because the Commander and his men are not watching a movie.

They are watching something *real* on a live feed.

Suddenly the screen goes black.

"What happened?" The Commander motions to one of his men. "Fix it. Now!"

The screen stays black.

They radio something in. I do not hear the answer, but I hear the soldier address the Commander.

"Headquarters is having the same issue. It seems like all the cameras are down, sir."

I stumble away. I have heard enough.

I am vaguely aware of the tears that blur my vision as I creep down the stairs. I huddle underneath them, behind massive wooden crates. I fall on my side and hold my knees to my chest. I do not want to think about the reasons for the killing, for the pain, the loss, the destruction.

But I know what I saw. I think about my mother, about the way her face would twist and she would run her fingers through her hair, anxious, as we listened to the Initiative's announcements on the radio. As soon as they spoke of the murders, she'd switch the volume off. She'd scoop up her radio and take it down to her office, leaving my mind screaming with questions I never had the courage to ask her.

Is this what they were doing when she was murdered? Watching it play out from the safety of this very yacht? Doing nothing to help her. Laughing and partying and wagering. Placing their bets on how fast she would go, on whether or not she would scream or cry.

I hold my hand over my mouth so I don't vomit.

I peer out between the crates, toward land. I wonder vaguely where Zephyr is, if he is still out there, hunting me. Or if the world took pity on me and let him die. He looked pretty bad.

The yacht is closing in on land now. I can just see the Initiative's marina up ahead, with its cluster of massive, seafaring beasts.

"Go, Meadow," I whisper.

It is the creaking of the door overhead that gets me moving, the footsteps on the stairs. They will find me, and know what I saw. Kill me. Slit my throat and dump my body overboard.

I wonder if Peri will cry like I cried when I discovered my mother was dead.

I bite down on the inside of my cheek, forcing the blood to run over my tongue. The taste spikes fear back into my soul. There are crates here. There are places to hide. I squeeze myself toward the back of the space, find a crate with rusting nails.

The voices overhead are loud enough that I think I am not heard.

I pry the heavy lid off and slip inside.

My knees are squished up against my nose and my neck feels like it is about to snap in half. There is hardly any room to breathe. And *oh*, it is so hot in here. Steaming hot. Sharp objects poke and prod me. I sniff, and realize I reek.

But it is not me. My hair is still wet, and I smell like saltwater. The scent surrounding me is so strong it is making my head spin. I let my hands slide from my cramped calves.

A sticky substance clings to my fingers.

I realize what I am sitting in.

Blood.

CHAPTER 32

ZEPHYR

When I was a boy, I got lost. I remember seeing my mom's face smiling down at me. I turned away for one second. When I looked back she was gone.

I cried like a girl. I got shoved and rocked by the crowd. I felt like I was drowning in a sea of people, and no matter where I turned, I only sunk deeper. That's when the Leech found me.

All I can remember is her voice. The voice was soothing, like a breeze on a cool spring night.

"I'm lost," I choked out through my tears.

She got down on one knee. I think she might have smiled, and wiped a tear from my cheek. "All you had to do was ask for help," she cooed.

I told her my mom taught me never to speak to strangers.

The memory isn't fully tangible, so it's sort of like trying to hold water in my hands. I can remember the way her Catalogue Number wrinkled up, though. I never forget a number.

"I am not a stranger, Zephyr." She smiled. I hadn't told her my name. "The Initiative knows you. Perhaps better than you will ever know yourself." She took me by the hand and towed me along with her. I followed in silence.

I don't remember what happened next. My past is all muddled.

I knew without a doubt that she could be trusted.

CHAPTER 33

MEADOW

I have to get out. I can't breathe. I am trapped. If I leave I will die. If I stay I will die. I reach up and slide the lid of the crate sideways, just enough so I can breathe. Then I lift my head, just the slightest bit, and get a look outside. A pair of feet is stomping toward me across the deck.

"This one, here," a man's voice says as I duck back down, and I am certain that they've caught me. I hear what I assume to be his knuckles rapping on the lid of my crate. This is it. In seconds I will be dead.

The man starts to lift the lid, and for a moment I am staring at the face of an Initiative worker. But he doesn't notice me. He turns away just before I stand up, just before I leap forward and twist his neck until it snaps.

"Don't open it, you asshole!" Another voice calls out. "It's full of Pins. That one goes to the warehouse." The lid slides back over me, and I am plunged into darkness. "Nail it shut. I swear this hardware is useless."

A hammer pounds two nails into the wood over my head.

Two nails, locking me in place, alone in a bloody crate.

But I am not alone. I am sitting on old Pins.

The only place this crate will end up is in an Initiative building.

I hear the whining of something loud overhead. I test the lid of the crate, but the nails hold. It will not budge. My heart sinks. There will be no running.

I hear groaning, and then I am moving, with the sticky Pins pressing against my shorts and my legs. I close my eyes and try to think of the ocean, of Peri, of my mother.

Despite everything my father taught me, I am going to end up just like my mother.

CHAPTER 34

ZEPHYR

I see Meadow's face. Her soft skin shredded because of me. Her silver hair matted, covered in blood, and it's my fault.

I don't want to hurt her. I never do.

But I fluxing *have* to. I have to do exactly what the woman says. I trust her. She saved me once. She could do it again.

As I run, I pass others who are the same as me. I wonder if they can hear the screaming in their heads, too. We look into one another's eyes for a fleeting second as we pass on the streets, and are reminded of our mission.

I see Meadow's face again. Skitz, it fills me with a rage

so deep that the only thing I can do is destroy everyone in my path.

The woman, Lark, tells me to stop. "Abort mission, Patient Zero. Abort."

She is angry. She's trying to pull out of my mind but I hang on with everything I have. It's all I have left.

Meadow made me look like an idiot. She's ruined my mission. The Murder Complex tells me that her existence still threatens the Initiative.

I decide that if I can't find her, then others will pay in her place.

A man steps in front of me. "Are you okay, son? You're bleeding everywhere."

I don't answer. I leap for his chest. I still have Meadow's dagger, so I use it. Then I slam into him. I hear his head hit against the pavement with a satisfying crack, and I smile.

Lark is furious. It hurts me to disappoint her, to deviate from my mission and take things into my own hands.

"Abort mission. Abort!"

But this time, I don't want to listen to her.

My mom said I was strong enough.

And I am.

I snap a young woman's neck and sprint for the next hopeless person within my reach.

CHAPTER 35

MEADOW

My father used to fill me with a fury so strong that once I swore to him that I would run away and never return.

Instead I buried myself at the bottom of his massive wooden tackle box. I figured I would stay there until he got scared. But then it got too hot. My head started to spin.

When I tried to lift the lid, it was locked. I remember the cold sweat, the pressing feeling of claustrophobia closing in around my body, suffocating me, like someone had shoved me into the Pit, and I fell to the very bottom of it, miles and miles beneath the city streets.

All I had to do was scream and bang on the lid, and then

it was lifted open in a burst of light, and my father was standing there, frowning down at me. He wiped my tears with the bottom of his T-shirt and gave me a moment to cling to him, apologizing. Then he set me gently aside and opened up the lid of the crate again. "Now climb back in and learn to cope with it, Meadow."

So I did. As he helped me settle back in, he smiled. "You *are* strong enough."

I wish my father were here now, to pry the lid from the crate and pull me out. Hold me to him and tell me never to be so stupid again. But he taught me how to do it right. He taught me to be strong. So now, as I sit here, thinking of him, I know that I must be.

Nine hours.

That is how long I've been sitting here.

They dumped the crate somewhere and moved on. But I can hear cranes beeping, doors slamming, maybe trucks, and I know it is not safe to try and escape. Not yet.

It is scorching hot. It feels like I am sitting in a dark oven, like everything is going to bubble and pop and boil around me, and I will die here, soaked in blood. My tongue feels like cotton. My throat sticks to itself.

Suddenly I am being lifted again. I reach down and grab a Pin.

It is rectangular and solid, as if it is made of titanium. I wonder if the nanites are still inside it, or if they died with their human host. What did Orion tell me about the Pins? *Impossible to destroy.*

I jam the Pin between the slats of the wooden crate. I lever it, side to side, twisting, turning. My palm is raw, so the Pin starts to cut into me. But I don't stop until a sliver of light pours in through the opening.

I suck in the fresh air, then scoot closer and press my eye to the gap. I am on the bed of a truck.

There are vines, twisting and snaking their way up fat trees. Everything is wild and overgrown. And there is water everywhere, brown and muddied with old gnarled branches bobbing up and down in it.

It is the place people talk about when they think no one is listening. My father once told me that if I ever found myself here, my life would be forever changed. He warned me that I would never, ever be able to forget what I saw. And as the truck lifts me along the overgrown path, I know that this is exactly where I am.

I can just see a brown building, well concealed in the foliage. As the truck moves closer, the side of the building opens wide, like a yawning mouth.

CHAPTER 36
ZEPHYR

I'm standing in the mirrored room again.

"You failed your mission, Patient Zero," the voice overhead says. Soft. But so angry it makes the skin on my arms crawl.

I turn in circles. My hands are covered in blood.

My whole body is covered in it. I start to feel pain in my shoulder, my leg, my head.

"Where am I?" My voice echoes back to me.

"You failed your mission, Patient Zero," the voice says again.

"What mission?" I say. "Who are you?"

The pain in my head gets worse. It pulses and grows like

a living creature, and before I have a chance to scream, a woman appears in front of me.

"Do you not remember me?"

Lark.

"You," I say. "I know you."

I think she smiles at me, the same way she did when I was younger, but I can't really tell.

"You failed." She sighs, and shakes her head at the floor. "I always knew you would." She paces around me, silent as a ghost. "Still," she says, stopping in front of me, "you were the first. It will be sad to see you go."

She reaches forward and places her hand on my chest.

Pain. So much pain.

My body seizes up and the world goes black.

"Is he dead?"

"I don't know."

"So then poke him!"

"No, gross! *You* poke him, Molly."

I hear the scuffling of feet. A high-pitched voice squeaks just above my ear. "Fine. Give me the stick, ChumHead."

A stick is jammed into my side. I ignore it, hoping the brats will just go away. But there it goes again. Poke, poke, poke. I roll over and open my eyes. The world comes in and out of focus as I blink. I see two browned faces peering down at me. "Go . . . away."

The two Ward children scream, and the stick clatters to the ground as they sprint off into the trees. I almost laugh. It takes all of my strength just to sit upright. My head churns and I realize I'm soaked in sweat and blood.

Flux. What happened to me?

"Oh, great, you're awake." Talan sits on the ground next to me, a plastic bottle of brown water in her hands. She shoves it roughly at me. Her voice is so loud it makes my head throb. "Don't ask where I found it. Just drink up, party boy."

"What's going on?" I ask, my voice a raw croak.

I've felt this way before. Twelve other times.

Except today, there isn't a body at my feet. My head feels like a sponge and nothing makes sense.

I unscrew the bottle and let the warm water slide down my throat. It tastes like acid as it goes down, but the whole thing's gone in seconds and my throat still feels like it's lined with cotton.

Talan punches me in the shoulder. "Enough games, already, Zephyr. Fess up."

Stars, that hurts. "What the hell are you talking about?"

"Um, news flash, pal. You disappeared with that girl

yesterday. And have you seen yourself?" She stares at me like my chest has just sprouted a fresh pair of boobs. "I mean, Zeph, you look like you've just come back from a war. You tell me what I'm talking about. Hey!" she snaps and the sound is louder than a gunshot. I just want her to shut up already. "I'm *waiting*. Where did you go with that girl?"

I look down at my hands. Stained with crimson, covered in cuts that have already scabbed over.

Why can't the nanites fix my brain, too?

"Fine. You don't want to talk. I get it. I, uh, had a little private meeting with your doctor yesterday," Talan says, her cheeks turning red. "And he gave me *this.*" She holds up a can of the fake skin stuff the doctor used on my arm.

"Talan," I groan, "you can't just pawn yourself off like you're a worthless Leech. You're better than that."

"Oh, *please.*" She rolls her eyes at me. "I'm a big girl. I can do what I want. Now shut up and take off your shirt."

She pulls it over my head for me. Skitz, that burns.

"Yikes," I hear her say. She starts spraying the liquid skin on my shoulder. Crusted blood covers the shirt in my hands. I toss it aside, disgusted, and see my thigh. "Here," I say, and Talan slices my pants with a dagger so she can spray the wound.

The weapon is silver. Sharp. It reminds me of Meadow.

"Where did you get that?" I ask.

It looks like Meadow's dagger. It *is* Meadow's dagger.

"You had it in your hand when you were playing Corpse Boy." Talan sprays the liquid on my thigh, closing up a deep wound. The nanites will heal me, eventually. But this is faster. This keeps the pain at bay.

I reach up and feel my face. I wince. There are claw marks that have scabbed over on my cheeks and forehead.

This can't be happening to me. No. Not again.

I lean over and spew vomit all over my chest. It splatters Talan. She curses and scoots away. "Are you kidding me? Next time you show up like this, you can find someone else to take care of you. Disgusting."

I put my head in my hands and ignore her. The pieces start to come together. Meadow. My moonlit girl. We were together yesterday. It was perfect. Free.

All of the blood. Her dagger. The wild spinning in my head. The throbbing pain all over my body. The bottoms of my feet are burned. It sounds like a train is barreling toward me, a loud siren wailing in my ears. The last person with me was Meadow. So why isn't she here now?

I already know why.

I think I murdered my moonlit girl.

CHAPTER 37

MEADOW

My mother stares back at me.

It's a painting. Gentle brushstrokes have made her come alive. She has my silver hair, my slender frame and gray eyes. But the artist got it wrong.

The expression on her face makes her look dangerous. Chin up, lips pursed. An expression of power, of fierce control. She is looking down on me, on all the Initiative scientists and officers who bustle about the massive warehouse. The painting is framed in gold, with ornate twisting designs littering the sides.

My mother was no one, especially not to the Initiative. Why would they ever honor her, a lowly citizen murdered like so many others?

Surrounding her painting is a group of photographs. Some of the faces I recognize. The young woman I stole lilies from on the streets. A man who whistles out of tune as he scrubs the streets on Collection Day.

And Zephyr.

He is younger. Much, much, younger, but I know it is him. I would recognize his green eyes anywhere, the curve of his jaw, his lips, the way his brown hair flips out from his ears.

Beneath the portraits are three words, scripted in bold, bloodred.

The Murder Complex.

"You can't escape destiny, Meadow." My mother's voice comes back to me now as I stare at the red writing. I had rolled over and closed my eyes that night. I never saw her face again. She never returned to the boat. But I remember now what she said as she walked away, just after she clasped the charm bracelet around my wrist.

I watch Initiative workers bustle in and out of my line of vision. Some are in lab coats, others in military greens. These are people who would never come in contact with someone like me. They pace back and forth, scribbling notes onto NoteScreens and talking in hushed voices.

Computer screens embedded in the walls all display the same information. Numbers. They tick, tick, tick, in rapid fire, like machine guns.

275.

290.

310.

I watch the count rise.

"Last night was successful," someone says. "Look at these stats!"

The numbers just keep going up.

367.

Somehow I know, as I watch the workers taking notes on their NoteScreens and nodding with approval, the same way the Commander did when he watched the live feed on the yacht, that the screens are totaling the deaths last night.

Deaths should not be celebrated. Deaths should be mourned. And I realize, as I sit here, trapped in blood, that the murders are not random. There is a system.

My father was right. He warned me that if I came here, I would never stop digging until I got answers. That I would never give up until it all made sense.

I have to know why Zephyr's photograph is on that wall. I have to know what the Murder Complex is. And I will not stop until I discover why my mother's face is staring down at me from the inside of a secret Initiative building.

CHAPTER 38

ZEPHYR

My feet can't carry me fast enough through the Catalogue Dome. I have to find it, the spot where her number would go. If she's really gone . . . if I've actually *killed* her . . .

I see her silver hair matted in dark red, her lips hanging open in a silent scream. I imagine myself on Collection Day, finding her body on the blood-stained concrete. And Talan, ripping the Pin from her once-beautiful flesh. "Oh, this is just some seriously sick skitz, Zephyr."

So I run, lungs screaming, because I have to know it's not true. When I burst through the doors the first thing I notice is how many mourners there are. More than usual, especially since it's the Silent Hour.

I keep my head down when I pass by the Leech standing guard. He's got a pistol on his hip, and I know he won't hesitate to use it.

Today everything seems out of order. It's totally chaotic. The place reeks of flowers and the muffled sobs swirl around me. I want it *all* to end.

"You," a woman croaks from the floor. She lifts a trembling hand and points at me.

"You did this," she groans. "You took my Robert from me." The tears are streaming down her face. "I saw you!"

"No!" I yell. "No, I don't even know him, I swear!" Everyone is looking at us in shock. No one speaks during the Silent Hour. Ever.

But the woman stands and lunges at me, screaming. A boy my age stops her just before she reaches me. He holds her back as she spits and claws like some crazy person. He puts his hand over her mouth and tries to silence her.

The Leech who was standing guard at the bottom of the Dome is running up the spiral hallway. I can hear his footsteps, and any second, he'll kill this woman for making noise.

"Just go," the boy whispers. His face, too, is stained from tears. "Go and don't come back."

I nod and keep moving, looking over my shoulder as

the guard comes up the hallway.

The woman stands, totally lost in grief, and lunges at him. "You didn't even help! You just let everyone die!"

"Mother!" the boy shouts, and then realizes what he's done, too late.

The Leech shoots them both.

"Honor the Silent Hour," the Leech says, looking at the mourners.

Now it's as silent as a grave again.

I turn and walk down the fourth aisle of the Dome. I fall to my knees and start to crawl.

I tell myself if I get to Meadow's number, and it's there, and she's dead . . . then it wasn't me.

It can't be me.

72048.

72051.

I sag with relief against the wall. Her number isn't here. Meadow Woodson is alive.

My fingers find the healing claw marks on my face. They're deep, like someone did it fast because they ran out of options. I sink all the way to the floor when I remember.

"Please."

One word is all I hear, but it's her voice.

She's alive. But it's only because I failed to kill her.

CHAPTER 39

MEADOW

"Patient C7 has done well," someone says. The speaker is tall and speaks with a clipped accent. "Progress is exactly as we hoped for."

"And the sister?" The two men in lab coats pause, right next to the crate.

"Coming along nicely," the first man says, and I can hear the smile in his voice. "They are both responding well to their supplements."

"Commander?" A woman's voice echoes through the massive space. I try to get a look at her, but the angle is wrong. "We have a situation."

"What?" I watch the first man's feet whirl around. He's

wearing black military boots. They are made of soft, supple leather that shines the way the sea does at night. Worth thousands of Creds.

The woman approaches him now. I can see her black high heels. "Well, as you know, the cameras across the city have been shut down. It could be a minor electric issue, sir."

"And if it's not?" The Commander asks. "If it's *them* . . ."

"It can't be," she says. "We'll solve the issue, sir. Not to worry. But . . . that's not all."

The Commander's boot taps on the floor. He does not speak, so the woman takes a breath, and continues.

"It's Patient Zero, sir," she says. "It . . . well . . . he hasn't quite finished his daily target yet. Our records show that he didn't even go for the right one, sir. But he's taken down others. Ones that the lottery did not assign to him. I thought we'd fixed his flaw."

"How much time do we have left?" the Commander barks.

"One minute, sir," she squeaks.

"He has performed unusually well since . . ." I think I hear the scratching of chin stubble. "Who was the target? And who did he go after instead?"

"The target was a boy his age, but Zero never got close

to him. And, well, who he went after is . . . the other part of the problem, sir."

It's quiet except for the ticking of the tallies. "He went after someone who should never have been in the system. He went after Lark Woodson's daughter. Meadow."

The Commander's NoteScreen clatters to the ground. The screens fall silent. The ticking stops. And when I hear my name, so does my heart.

CHAPTER 40

ZEPHYR

The ocean used to be a pretty place. At least, that's what the older Wards tell us.

Now it's just a big pool of waste, and I avoid it.

The second my feet hit the sand, I start thinking about my dad.

He had these deep crow's feet around his eyes that crinkled every time he smiled. He always kissed my mom all soft and gentle, like she was fragile and might break.

I never felt like I belonged. They looked so different from me, both redheaded, and blue-eyed. Where did I come from? The memories are sharp as daggers. They make me burn with a white-hot guilt that I can't escape.

Skitz.

I try not to think about them. I really do.

But standing here now, watching the gulls swoop down into the waves, water splashing up as they dive, all I can think of is my parents.

How they looked as I watched them sink beneath the waves.

The sand is warm and soft. Overhead, the sky is just starting to darken. A storm is rolling in, and when I look to my left I can see the distant shoreline fading, enveloped in fog.

"Where are you, Meadow?" I say out loud, and as I do, I notice a pile of rocks near the water, the sea spraying up as it crashes into them. Without thinking, I approach.

There's a group of men sitting around a doused campfire, polishing weapons in the darkness.

Pirates. The Leeches' brownnosers, who will do anything for some extra Creds.

"Gentlemen," I say. I know it's going to be trouble.

But for some reason, tonight, I want it.

The Pirate leader sees me and stands. He's a tall guy, big and muscular, and he looks ridiculous with a three-inch knife in his hands. "You want to pass, you gotta give us something good. By the looks of you, boy, you're a Ward."

"We don't let your kind enter the ocean," another Pirate says. I can smell alcohol, something worth thousands of Creds. They probably caught some kid collecting pre-Fall stuff, Commandment Four, and kept it for payment. It's disgusting.

I step toward them, hands outstretched. "I'm coming up empty." I want to fight. I want to . . . I don't really know what I'd do, but it feels like my body does.

"No payment, no passage," the leader says. He's got rotting teeth. Maybe I should knock them out for him.

"Let me pass," I say.

They all laugh, and two more of them stand up. "You want to die, Ward?"

"I was going to ask you the same thing," I say.

Then before I realize what's happening, I'm moving as fast as the lightning overhead. I'm striking punches, dodging. I snap a neck in an instant.

By the time it's all done, there are three dead Pirates at my feet.

The last one runs down the beach like a terrified child, and I laugh at his back. "Yeah! Run away, Leech Lover!"

In the distance, I can make out the ghostly shapes of boats. I run for the ocean, dive in, and swim. The boats flicker in and out of view as the waves send me up and down.

Thunder claps above, and rain appears, so sudden it's like a massive bucket of water has just been dumped into the ocean. I can't feel my tears as they slide down my face.

I remember screams.

Oh, stars, and I remember my mom begging for mercy, and my dad, telling me he loved me, that everything would be okay if I'd just *stop*.

Stop.

Stop . . . hurting them.

As I swim, searching for Meadow's houseboat, all I can think of is their corpses stretching toward me from the sandy bottom of the ocean, wanting nothing more than to exact revenge on the son who took their lives.

Because now I remember it all.

My parents were my first two victims.

CHAPTER 41

MEADOW

My mother. Me.

They are talking about *us.*

My mind is racing. Lark Woodson was a nobody. An engineer who worked on the Initiative's boats during the day and spent her nights locked in the bottom of our own. A woman who was murdered on the street, like so many others.

But my father said she was someone. Someone dangerous. Someone whose face is nearly identical to mine, whose blood runs in my veins, and because of her, I will never be completely safe. Because of my mother, I will always be watched. I shove my fist into my mouth and bite down so I don't scream. So I don't start banging on the sides of the crate.

It's Patient Zero, sir. It . . . well . . . he hasn't quite reached his daily goal yet. Daily goal. What is his daily goal? And the Commander's voice. Urgent. Demanding. *Who was the target? And who did he go after instead?*

Lark Woodson's daughter. Me. But I am a nobody. Just like my mother. Why would I be someone to be concerned about?

I heard his gasp when the tallies froze, saw his NoteScreen clatter to the ground when my mother's name was mentioned. When *I* was mentioned.

I lean back to the hole now and press my eye to it. The NoteScreen still sits on the floor. On the screen, I see *The Murder Complex. Patient Zero.*

Six digits. There are other words and notations I don't have time to read before the Commander bends down and scoops it up.

"Shut him down," he says with a sigh. "He's stronger than us now."

"Sir?" the woman says, as if she did not hear his words right. "We could bring him back in for a routine check, I'm sure there's a way to fix him—"

"Just do it!" He screams. "Take him out!" His voice

echoes. He stomps away and the woman begins giving her shaky commands to the scientists.

"We'll have to do it manually," a man with glasses says. "The Creator won't cooperate with us for an automatic shutdown. Especially not with him."

"He won't come easy," says someone I can't see. "He's smarter than that. He may have figured it all out by now."

"*No one* has figured *anything* out!" the woman says. She's pacing. "Do whatever it takes. Bring Zero in, or kill him, whatever you want to do. He's not fixable, not without the right codes. But the girl . . . bring her in. *Alive.* I want to know why that girl's in our system. And *how*."

And suddenly I realize why my heart has started to race and the sweat has begun to slip down my spine. I don't know what I'd rather do: burst into tears or laugh. Because it all makes sense now.

Six digits. Patient Zero has the same Catalogue Number as Zephyr James.

Patient Zero *is* Zephyr James.

He went after me. I am the girl he should not have gone after, the girl somehow in their system, whatever that means. And now, they want to bring both of us in.

It all happens so fast. One minute I am sitting here, soaked in blood and my own haunting realizations. The next, the crate is being pried open, and it feels like my world has been set on fire. Light. So much light.

"What the . . ." A blonde woman looks down at me, head cocked to the side. I read complete confusion on her face. She is weak. Incapable of defending herself.

I leap from the crate and close my hands around her neck. It snaps.

Chaos is upon me.

CHAPTER 42

ZEPHYR

Even with the storm, it's too quiet.

I find a houseboat that looks like the one Meadow described, and climb aboard.

I walk with light footsteps across the deck, whispering her name, like some creepy ChumHead. The boat rocks, angry, as the waves begin to rise with the wind, and soon it's hard to keep my balance.

I stumble for the small cabin and cup my hands on the rain-spattered windows. Worn curtains cover the glass, but as the boat thrashes, the fabric sways, and I get a glimpse inside.

Lamps litter an old wooden table, flames flickering

eerily. Two chairs are knocked sideways on the floor. And there are three mattresses in the far corner, empty, except for their twisted blankets.

Skitz. Meadow isn't here. No one is.

A wave hits the boat, and the curtains sway closed. The boat drops back, and the curtains move again.

Two gray eyes stare at me from inside the cabin.

I stumble backward across the deck and nearly fall over the railing. But cold fingers close around my wrist. "Meadow," I gasp.

Except it isn't Meadow.

I get one glimpse of a young man, his entire body covered with scars, like he's been shoved into a dull wood chipper. I open my mouth to ask him where she is.

He swings an oar at my head.

The world goes black.

CHAPTER 43

MEADOW

Always take in every detail of your surroundings, Meadow. Any daughter of mine will always know what is going on around her, where her opponents are, and who to strike down first.

There are eleven Initiative workers. Five men, six women. It will not be easy.

The man to my left is 6'2". Roughly 275 pounds, all muscle. Way too big of a target. I sprint past him, drop to the floor as he stretches to grab me, and roll. I fly across the floor like I am covered in oil.

"Get her! Get her!" voices scream. I have to run. I have to get away. I am a target that Zephyr should never have gone after, but did. They want to find me and question me, and they will stop at nothing to get their hands on us both.

I run for the computers. I see faces of people I recognize, faces of people that have been murdered. Children, young women, young men.

"She's one girl, you fools! Stop her!"

A man lifts a rolling chair and launches it toward my head. I duck, then stand and swipe the man's feet out from under him. He collapses and I don't even try to avoid him as I race over his body.

Others chase me but I caught them off guard, so it's easy, like playing tag with a child who is neither as fast nor as smart as I am.

I see a black, boxlike car in the far corner of the building. Unoccupied. I run for it, dodging workers, breathing in and out, in and out, focused only on escape.

I wrench open the car door and leap into the front seat. The key's in the ignition so I turn it, hoping it runs like a boat. The engine roars to life.

"The alarms! Hit the alarms!" The Commander's voice rings out through the chaos, and a wailing is so sudden and loud it makes everyone freeze for a moment.

I hear a shot. The bullet lodges itself into the steering

wheel, less than an inch from my hand.

There's a gear shift, like my boat. I slam it into drive, then stomp my foot down on the pedal, and finally, the car lurches forward. I steer it toward the massive metal door that is my only hope of escape.

The car crashes into the door. The metal buckles. I press the gas harder, and it starts to crumple, lifting over the top of the car. The metal rips, timbers tearing away with it. I hear yelling, probably for reinforcements, but I have already jumped out of the car and am heading into the mangroves, leaving the Initiative and the Murder Complex and my mother's horrible portrait behind.

CHAPTER 44

ZEPHYR

"What have you done with my sister?"

The boy with the scarred face leans over me in the darkness. He holds a candle in one hand, and a knife to my throat.

"I don't know where she is," I say. I can feel the cold steel now, stinging me. "Flux, man! I'm telling the truth!"

"Liar! Tell me!" He spits in my face.

"I swear! I don't know, I swear!" My voice is pathetic. Terrified. The ChumHead punches me with the handle of the knife, and my head spins as blood starts to drip from my nose.

"Perhaps my father will be a little more . . . persuasive."

He walks out of the cabin, leaving me alone.

I try to wriggle out of my bindings, but they're so tight I can't feel my wrists or ankles anymore. I can feel the fear, though, and I can't think straight. All I wanted was to find Meadow.

The door swings open and a man ducks in from the rain. He holds a tackle box in his hands. He sets it on the table beside me. "I've been a fisherman for as long as I can remember," he says, so casual, like we've been friends our entire lives. He's tall and tan, his skin worn from years under the sun, his hair so bleached it's almost as white as Meadow's. Oh, skitz. It's her *dad*. The psychopath who trained her.

"You a fisherman, son?" He opens the tackle box and pulls out a coil of fishing line. His eyebrows rise as he looks at me, waiting for an answer.

"No . . . no, sir."

He chuckles. "That's good news," he says. "Because today, I'm gonna teach you a little lesson."

He pulls a steel hook from the box. The thing is *massive*. I gulp and focus on his face.

"Fish are smart creatures," he says as he threads the fishing line through the eye of the hook. "You've got to hook them in just the right place. . . ." He tests his knot. It holds. "Or else you'll lose your catch."

His eyes meet mine again. I stare back. I'm about to piss myself.

"Meadow's a smart girl," he says as he pulls a chair toward me and swings it around so he's sitting on it backward. "She's a lot like her mother. A survivor."

"Her mom's dead," I say. What is *wrong* with me?

He just shakes his head and laughs. "Did you kill her, boy? Did you kill my daughter?"

"I would never hurt her." He doesn't believe me. I wouldn't either.

"Of course you didn't," he says. "Because she's my girl. And do you know what *I* do when someone tries to hurt *me*?"

All I can do is sit there, staring at the hook. He stands and grabs my chin.

"I teach them a lesson." He grins. I thrash, as best as I can, but he only holds on tighter.

"You hurt my daughter," he says. "Well . . . that hurts me."

He sinks the hook into my cheek. I hear the pop as it breaks through the skin inside my mouth. I hear myself scream.

"You see, boy . . . I know how to keep a fish on my line.

You tell me where my daughter is, and I'll set you free."
He starts to tug on the line.

"I dun- ho!" I scream.

"That's a lie!" he yells back at me. "What did you do
to her? " He gives the line a real tug. I can feel my flesh
stretching, ripping, as he takes slow, deliberate steps
backward.

"Please!" Every movement is pure agony. I'm on fire.

"Got a fighter on the line, Koi!" The cabin door bursts
open and Meadow's brother runs back in. "Last chance,
boy."

"Ahh swear!" I try to tell him. His face twists with fury,
and suddenly he freezes.

"Dad?"

Outside, it's still raining. I can hear it hit the ocean. And
there's another noise. Like a whirring. Meadow's father
crosses to the big, plate glass window and moves the curtain aside. I can see a blinking red light in the distance. A
Leech boat, on this side of the Shallows? Meadow's dad
drops the curtain and curses under his breath.

"What did you do?" He whirls around. "Did you lead
them here?"

"W-huh?" I mumble.

"Did you lead them here?" He gets in my face, and I

shake my head, not understanding what he's asking. "Koi, get your sister, we're leaving!"

"But what about Meadow?" Koi says. "We can't just—"

"I said get your sister and let's go! Now!" Meadow's father grabs an old brown sack lying discarded by the mattresses. I hear the clanking of metal as he rushes past me, and I'm almost positive the thing's full of weapons.

"Where to?" Koi asks.

A little girl steps through the door. Skitz, Meadow wasn't exaggerating. She's a miniature version of Meadow, with silver of hair that hangs to her waist. It's Peri. Who she loves more than anything in the world. She stares at me, at the bloody mess. She looks back at her dad.

"Daddy?"

"Oh my . . . no . . ." I can't hear him anymore. All I can hear is shouting. Something bumps up against the side of the boat. Meadow's dad turns and punches out the window with his fist. The glass shatters all over the floor.

He grabs Koi by the shoulder, pulls him toward him. Kisses him on the forehead and pushes him out into the waves.

Meadow's father turns and takes one last look at me, at the hook hanging slack from my cheek. "Go to hell, boy," he says. He wraps his arms around his daughter, and disappears with her through the blowing curtains. The door of the cabin bursts open, kicked right off of its hinges.

It isn't Leeches.

It's something even worse, because I recognize the guy who steps inside. He has a big Initiative eye tattoo on his neck. "Well, well, well . . . what do we have here?" He cracks his knuckles, and I know I'm about to die.

This is the guy I just left on the beach, after I killed three of his men.

And there's five more Pirates standing behind him, every single one of them just as pissed off as the first.

CHAPTER 45

MEADOW

I run until my feet bleed. I run until I cannot run anymore, and even then, I keep going, through the crowded streets of the Shallows, shoving people aside. I race past the Rations Hall. Orion is standing out front. I was supposed to be at work today.

"There you are, Blondie!" she cries out. "Come here!" She lifts a hand in greeting, but I keep going. I hear her calling my name, screaming for me to stop. But I will not. I lose her in the crowd, and keep running until I reach the ocean.

When I stare out at the water, relief washes over me.

myself one moment to catch my breath. When I get to the boat, I will ask my father to explain it to me. I will finally get my answers. I dive into the waves and start the swim.

CHAPTER 46

ZEPHYR

The Pirates take turns beating me.

They laugh each time they stick a punch in my gut, or slam my skull with an elbow, or fist. I start seeing stars. I think I actually do piss myself, and the Pirates can't stop laughing.

"We came here for the girl, but it looks like we got an extra treat instead," the leader says. I'm seeing three of him.

"You think you can just get away with killing my men?" He spits in my face.

"Goh ew hell," I say.

Once I actually *do* pass out, but they dump saltwater

on my face, and it burns so bad I wake up screaming. I'm going insane. I think I see Meadow, her face frozen in horror as she looks at me through the shattered window.

Meadow is *here.* She's here right now, and if these guys see her, they'll do worse things to her than they're doing to me.

But it's good, because Meadow slinks behind the men, sticking to the shadows. I watch her head for the door at the opposite end of the cabin. She slides it open. I hear her gasp, and she leans down to grab something small and silver. She holds it up, and the moonlight makes it shimmer. A seashell charm. For a second, she wavers. She bends over like she's been hit in the gut. But then she straightens up, faces me, and smiles.

Then she disappears.

CHAPTER 47

MEADOW

My family is gone.

There are Pirates on my boat.

The Pirates are beating up Zephyr.

How did he get here? I know the Pirates are here because the Initiative sent them to find *me*. Maybe they sent Zephyr here, too, so that he could finish me off.

My father will understand that if Pirates are here, it means the Initiative sent them. He will keep Koi and Peri in hiding. They'll be someplace I don't know about, some place I can't find. The Shallows is miles wide, full of thousands and thousands of people.

I might never find them. I might never see them again.

I want to scream, but instead I focus on the only thing I have left.

I slink past the men, sticking to the shadows. I head for the door to belowdecks. Just as I slide it open, a glint of silver stops me.

Peri's bracelet.

I pick it up, fingers trembling. It feels like I have been hit in the gut. But there's no time to waste. I creep down to the belly of our houseboat.

This is where my mother always disappeared, locking the door behind her. This may be my last chance to come aboard this boat, and I will not leave until I discover what lies behind the door.

I take it at a run, letting my body slam shoulder first into the old wood. The Pirates are shouting overhead, Zephyr is screaming. I pray they can't hear me. The wood splinters. I see something silver behind it.

Confusion drowns me. I tear furiously at the wood, and in minutes, I have peeled it all away.

A steel door stands before me.

Everything that is left of my mother is behind this door. I have to know her secrets. I have to know what she knew.

I hear Zephyr scream in agony, and I tell myself I do not care. He deserves it. I turn and slam my fists against the door, and after a moment, I realize that there is an insignia etched into the metal.

It reminds me of my mother's seashell charm. The very same one I have worn on my wrist since the night she left me, until I gave it to Peri. With shaking hands, I lift the bracelet so that it dangles just before my eyes, and there it is. The same pattern.

I press the charm up against the door. It fits. It locks into place, and suddenly there is a hissing noise, like compressed air being released. The door slides open.

The room is small—it's a closet, really. The walls are covered with photographs. Charts. Newspaper clippings. Equations and symbols that make no sense to me. There is a NoteScreen embedded in a tiny desk.

When I touch the shiny black screen, it flickers to life.

I tap it again.

A photograph of the Commander, standing side by side, arm in arm with a woman and a team of scientists in white lab coats, appears on the screen. The woman holds a pair of scissors. She is poised to cut a red ribbon. The group is standing in front of the Initiative building I just escaped from. The woman is my mother.

I hear footsteps.

I look around quickly. There is an emergency kit in the

corner of the galley. Inside are matches, and rope, and what looks like a container of fuel.

I unscrew the lid and dump it on the floor, splash it on the walls of the galley and closet.

I am getting ready to strike the match when something catches my eye. An envelope, tacked to the wall with all the other stuff.

Meadow it reads on the front. In my mother's handwriting. Did she know I would find this here? Did she know I would discover a way into her locked room? I grab it and put it into the emergency kit.

The Pirate is stomping down the stairs, calling out my name, like he knows I am here. I can't go into the engine room. I'll be trapped. I sling the emergency kit over my shoulder and sprint into the hall.

Our eyes meet, and the Pirate smiles. I skid to a stop.

"Got her, boys! Down here!"

His eyes trail up and down my body. I rush at him. I let him grab me from behind as I try to pass, just like my father trained me to do. I let my body go slack. I swing my legs behind his knees, then put all my weight into the trip. He goes down easy, and lands in the wet fuel on the wooden floor.

He is heavy, and I caught him off guard, so I am able

to scramble away and get to my feet before he does. I hold the matches out in front of me so he can see them.

"What are you gonna do, girl?" The Pirate throws his head back and laughs. "Are you gonna burn me?"

"Where is my family?" I ask.

The Pirate smirks. "They're probably being skinned like rats. I betcha the little girl's long gone by now."

"You're going to die," I tell him. "You're going to burn for what you are and who you serve, and no one in the world will ever miss you."

I strike the match. The fire ignites instantly, and I drop the match to the ground. There is a whooshing sound, and in a flash, the Pirate, the floorboards, and the walls are all engulfed in flames.

I stand frozen for a second, watching my world as it is consumed by fire, listening to the Pirate's screams as he burns.

Overhead, the deck starts to crack and buckle. The other Pirates are shouting. I hear their speedboat as it starts up. "Meadow!"

I whirl around and Zephyr is there, a broken piece of chair still tied to his wrist. He must have busted his way out of it, and now he is running down the steps toward me, his bloody mouth open in a scream, hands outspread for me. "Watch out!"

I look up just as the wood overhead collapses.

The last thing I hear is my mother's voice, whispering my name.

And then everything fades away.

CHAPTER 48
ZEPHYR

Meadow almost looks peaceful. I smile, because I'd like to see someone try and sneak up on her, thinking they'd found an easy target. As soon as she felt hands on her body, Meadow would give a new meaning to the words *dead wrong*.

"You're something else," I say. It's a huge mistake, because the second she hears my voice, her eyes fly open. She leaps from the sand and pins me. The air leaves my lungs before her fingers find my throat.

"You killed them!" She spits in my face. Her voice is ragged. So full of pain and confusion. I don't fight back. I lay there with her body on top of mine and let her choke me. She stops when she sees I'm not fighting.

"Fight back!" she screams. "Hit me!"

I close my eyes. By now the hole in my cheek has closed up. The injuries inflicted by the Pirates are just ugly bruises.

"You're pathetic." Meadow spits and rolls off of me and staggers to the ocean, stumbling over her own feet.

She collapses at the water's edge and sits with her back to me. It's still raining but not hard enough to put out the fire. In the distance, her houseboat fights to stay afloat as the flames eat away at it. But in minutes it sinks.

When the rain stops, she stands up and walks past me. She disappears into the trees. I hear leaves rustling, and see glimpses of her climbing.

I settle down against the trunk of a nearby tree and listen to her whimper for the rest of the night.

In the morning, we will have to hide.

CHAPTER 49

MEADOW

I have watched the sun rise from the sea so many times that it no longer makes me smile.

The sky turns seashell pink. Then mandarin orange. Then a red so deep it reminds me of blood. It reminds me that everything I have ever known is lost.

Zephyr is still sleeping when I climb silently down from my tree. I consider slitting his throat. Snapping his neck. Getting it over with.

But I need to know where my family is. I have to know what he has done. So instead, as I pass him, I spit on his face, and smile to myself as I walk away. The beach is crowded as it always is, and I have to weave my way around sleeping bodies to reach the water.

The ocean is warm when I slip into the waves. The salt stings, but I don't flinch. I'm almost healed by now. I let my hands dangle in front of me and stand motionless. A huntress.

When I feel the slippery touch of a fish gliding past me, I slam my hands together and dig my nails into its scales the way my father taught me to. I turn and throw it on shore and watch as it flops around on the sand.

Zephyr is beneath the palms. He does not look up when I approach and drop the fish in front of him.

"Dagger," I say, and he tosses it up at me without a glance. It is my father's dagger. Having it back again makes me feel strong. I sink down across from him and begin to rip out the fish's guts. "You tried to kill me."

"I know," he says as he piles sand over his feet, patting it down smoothly.

"So why did you save me from the fire? Why not let me die, finish off what you started?"

"I didn't want to kill you, Meadow."

"Why did you do it?" The feelings I had for him, just yesterday so strong, will never come back. "Why did you try to kill me?"

"Flux, Meadow. It wasn't *me*." He growls, and turns his

back to me. Like a child. "It's never me. I can't explain it."

I don't know why I am still sitting here. Why I haven't thrust my dagger straight through his heart. Maybe it is the pain in his voice. The way he just sits here. Broken, like me.

"Tell me where my family is," I say. "Did you kill them?"

"No," he says. "I went to the boat to find you." He winces as he speaks, and reaches up to touch the scab on his cheek. "Your dad is proud of his fishing hooks."

I nod. "And you expect me to believe you because . . . ?"

"Last night I had a gaping hole in my cheek. I was tied to a chair. Pirates were beating the living flux out of me, Meadow. Doesn't exactly look like I had the upper hand in that situation, does it?"

I glare at him. I am not thinking straight. My father and Koi would never let someone get the upper hand. I am surprised Zephyr wasn't cut into a million little pieces and thrown to the sharks.

"You blew up your own boat," he says. "Why?"

"Some secrets need to burn," I say. "Where is my family?" I look down at my wrist, at the charm. I can't bear to think about Peri.

"They abandoned ship when the Pirates came." Zephyr shrugs. "Left me to die."

"You deserved to die," I say. "And you still do."

"I know. I wish you had just let me die the first time you met me."

We sit in silence for what feels like forever.

"What do you know about the Murder Complex?" I ask finally.

Zephyr's body stiffens. He turns, slowly, to look at me. "What did you say?"

"The Murder Complex." I shove a piece of raw fish into my mouth and shiver a little as it slides down my throat.

"I . . . I don't know." He picks up a shell and throws it into the trees behind us. "I hear it sometimes. Those words. In my dreams. I hear it after I kill, like an echo. When I wake up covered in blood. It's always there. But I don't know why."

"I found a secret Initiative building, in the everglades," I say. "Ever been there?"

"I don't think so." Zephyr shrugs. There are dark circles under his eyes. He must not have slept last night.

"They were watching the murders on televisions or computers or something. And there were photographs. My mother was in one," I say, drawing a swirl in the sand with my fingertip, "and so were you."

"*Me?*"

Zephyr's eyes are massive. He shakes his head. "No. It must have been a mistake."

"I'm not blind," I snap. "I know what I saw. And I know that they said you weren't supposed to try and kill *me*, but you did try . . . and because of that, they're going to bring you in. Both of us, actually."

"Who is?"

"The Initiative," I say. "You can stop lying. I know you're in on some disgusting plan they have. Patient Zero."

Zephyr gasps. "Patient Zero," he whispers. He looks down at his hands like he's seeing them for the first time. "I think . . . I think they turn me into a monster."

"No. You're a monster because you're a monster," I say. "And I'm not buying the fact that you don't know what any of this means." I stand up and start pacing. That's when I notice a duffle bag at the edge of the trees. Zephyr must have taken it from the boat. I pull it toward me across the sand.

"I dream about you, you know," Zephyr says, his back to me. "I dreamt about my parents, too. Before I killed them. And the old woman. The little girl. It's like . . . like I know who's next to die. And no matter what I do, I can't stop it. I always kill them. Until you."

His words roll off me like the crest of a wave. "Meadow?"

he says, but I do not answer. "If what you're saying is true, they'll be sending someone else after us. They might even come themselves. We can't just sit here and wait to be taken."

"Just go away."

He stands up and walks into the trees.

I start to wonder just how long I will last.

I reach into the duffle bag and grab the envelope from my mother. I peel it open.

A key. She left me a key.

"450 White Ave." is inscribed on the key. I trace the numbers, as if somehow they will whisper to me the secrets that they hold. I reach back into the envelope, eyes closed, my blood pulsing in my skull.

When my hand closes over another hard object, I take a moment to breathe. To promise myself that I will stay strong. I open my fist. It's a silver Initiative badge. The symbol of the Eye stares back at me.

I drop it and scoot away from it on the sand.

There is a name inscribed into the metal.

COMMANDER LARK WOODSON, INITIATIVE SPC

CHAPTER 50

ZEPHYR

Meadow crashes through the trees when the Leeches finally come. They've all got these strange shiny black NoteScreens in their hands.

Like they're searching for us on the screens.

Tracking us.

"It's for both of us," Meadow whispers to me. She pulls me down into the undergrowth and we lie flat side by side. Her face has gone pale. Her Catalogue Number looks darker than ever. "The Initiative wants to find you and shut you down, whatever that means. They want me, too, for what I saw in that building."

"Guess it's our lucky day, huh?"

We wait while they question people on the beach. A woman points at Meadow's fish bones. Probably selling us out in hopes of getting a big payday. It doesn't work out for her. They spread out and walk into the trees.

They walk right past us, so close one of them almost steps on my hand. Some trackers.

We wait until we're sure they're gone. Then Meadow stands up, brushes herself off, and glares at me. "I'm leaving. Don't follow me."

But I do. I won't let her go that easy. I don't even care how pathetic that makes me. Stars, Talan would laugh at me right now.

"Whatever you think, you're wrong," I call after her. "I'm not a Leech, and I don't know what the Murder Complex is." She just walks faster, so I jog to keep up with her.

"As soon as you let your guard down, I'm going to kill you," Meadow says. Her eyes are cold. "And don't yell. We're not clear yet."

She swipes a palm frond out of her way. It whips me across the face. "All right." I shrug my shoulders. "That's fine."

We make our way through the undergrowth, stopping now and then to listen. "Your family's safe, you know," I say to her back. Her hair sways back and forth just above her waist. "They got away in time."

"Hmm," is all she says. But I'm not stupid. I know all she cares about is them. I know she's hoping.

Soon the skeletal buildings of the city loom in the distance. I smell hot human waste, the stench of the Graveyard. I notice the key in Meadow's hand. "Where are you going?"

"It doesn't matter," she snaps. But then she sighs, and shows me the key. "Know where this place is?"

I read the label on it and smile. "White Avenue is this way," I say, grabbing her wrist. She whirls and slams me up against a tree trunk, her dagger pressed to my throat.

"Touch me, you die," she says.

"Hey. Relax. I can take you there. I'm not going to hurt you, Meadow."

"Why should I trust you?"

I run my hands through my hair. "Because we're in this together. We both want answers. You need me to figure this out."

"I don't need *anyone*," she says. "Especially you. Patient Zero."

"Well, I need you. I need to figure this out. I need to

figure *me* out. Please." I take a deep breath. "I'm begging you."

Her eyes hold mine. I swear she can hear my heart thrumming in my chest. "You're lucky my father taught me how to tell when someone is lying," she growls. "Well, this is all great." She laughs, a cold hard sound. "The sad thing is, I have to keep you safe now, because if I don't, they'll kill you, and I'll never get any answers." She tosses the dagger up, then catches it on top of her knuckles. Lets it teeter for a second, then whirls it around again. "Plus, if the Initiative kills you . . . I won't get to. Make one wrong move and this blade goes through your heart."

"You should threaten me more often. I like it."

She looks like she's about to slam her fist into my face.

"Okay," I say. "No jokes. Got it."

Skitz.

"This way," I say. "Keep your head down. Move with the crowd. And stay close to me, if you can handle that."

We keep our heads down while we walk, just like everyone else. We step over dead bodies and try not to gag at the stench. The street's still wet from the rain. Cicadas bounce off our shins. I pull a hat off a dead man's head and slip it on top of my own. Meadow grabs a scarf and wraps up her hair. We both walk faster.

"Flux. The Pirates are here," I say. They hardly ever leave the beach. This isn't good.

There's a group of Pirates huddled up against a building, all of them covered in tattoos. One of them has on a pair of the strange black goggles the Leeches use sometimes, the kind that can search for and *find* a single Catalogue Number in the middle of a crowd. He falls into step behind Meadow and me.

"We should have covered our numbers better," Meadow whispers. "Walk faster!"

"How many people did you kill in that building?" I ask, but she ignores me.

We're being hunted, and I think we've been found. I can see at least ten of the ChumHeads. They keep using their signals, and whistling in code.

"Left," I say, and I nudge Meadow's hip. "Trust me," I say into her ear, and I take her sweaty palm in mine. Then we start to run.

Left, right. I can hear them clambering after us, anxious to catch us and get their Creds.

We're fluxed.

I see White Avenue up ahead, the old holographic street sign bent almost in half, its screen flickering sadly. I run faster, hauling Meadow along with me. The address is on the edge of the Pit.

It isn't what I expected. It's way worse.

The place Meadow wants to go to is the old lot full of storage units, all dented and covered in bird skitz, most of them probably abandoned or ransacked.

And that's because half of the units have fallen right into the Pit. I've walked past it thousands of times, hauling dead bodies with Talan. No one goes in the storage units anymore, because the ground is so unstable.

"We can't go in there," Meadow says. She skids to a stop and rips her hand out of mine. "What if the ground falls in?"

"It's better than being Leech bait," I say. "Come on."

There's an old chain-link fence that surrounds the place. We duck through a hole in it and lose ourselves in the maze of units, and the whole time I'm begging the stars not to let the ground crumble and suck us in.

"The units, they're in the units!" I hear someone shout, and then we're sprinting down the rows, searching for 450.

"Oh, come *on*!" Half of 450 is dangling over the edge of the Pit. A Leech steps out in front of us, eyes bulging wide with a predatory hunger when he recognizes us. He's about to shout, but he never gets a chance.

Meadow's dagger whistles through the air and lands handle-deep in the guy's throat. He drops, blood gushing from his wound, and then lays there. Lifeless.

"Stars," I say. "Your aim is amazing."

"Move him," she says, as she plucks out the dagger and heads for the padlock on the unit's door. I hear the clanging of chains as she turns the key, but the door doesn't budge. "Damn it!" she says. We try to pull the padlock up, make it move. But then I spot something on the metal, low to the ground. A strange insignia, like three tiny lightning strikes.

"What *is* that?" I say, and Meadow gasps.

She stoops down, presses her bracelet to the insignia, and the metal door slides open on its own, revealing a small gap for us to crawl under.

I guess her bracelet was a second key.

"Pull him inside," Meadow commands, and I do, rolling us both into the darkness. I hear Meadow take a deep breath, and then she rolls in after me.

CHAPTER 51

MEADOW

I do not know what I expected to find when I turned on the light bulb hanging from the ceiling.

Maybe I expected to find a NoteScreen with my mother's face on it, explaining everything.

The words are painted everywhere. *The Murder Complex.*

They are on the floor. On the metal walls. The ceiling. In different shades of red. Crimson. Scarlet. Maroon. Everywhere, like blood. Besides the words there is splattered paint, as if someone stood in the middle of the unit and threw buckets of it all over the walls. Screaming.

Why would she want me to find this place? My mother,

who I used to love, is an entirely different person than I thought she was.

I rise to my feet. The whole unit creaks, and I feel the ground sway.

"Be careful," Zephyr says. "Slow movements."

He pushes the dead Pirate to the far right, and squats beside him. "Weight distribution. I don't know about you, but I don't feel like crashing down to hell in that sinkhole."

"If I have the chance, I'll push you," I tell him.

The wall to my left is covered with sheets of paper. They are all numbered, and the word MURDERER is painted in a deep red across the top of the wall, in massive dripping letters that take up several feet. I take a moment to gather myself.

Number one. It is dated, like a page in a diary. Twenty years ago. Before Koi was even born. The handwriting is rushed, but I can tell it is hers. I touch it with my fingertips.

October 2nd. The Initiative Research Team has finally come together. The government has given us money to fund our experiments. Today, our patient responded well to our commands, twitching his fingers when triggered. We have hopes to bring him out of his coma soon.

My mother was not a doctor. She could fix up my scrapes and cuts, sure, but bringing a man back from a coma? I read once in one of my mother's books that a coma was an endless sleep, that people could get stuck inside for years. Decades, even. The thought of my mother curing a coma patient is so ridiculous I almost want to laugh. I scoot to the right, to the tenth page tacked on the wall.

October 17th. I've discovered a way to heal paralysis. Trials are all ending with 90% positive results. But it isn't enough. Not for me. I want to do more for the greater good.

My mother did this? No. It's not possible. I stumble to the other wall, and my foot catches on a stack of newspapers. And there is a photograph of me.

No. It is not my face but . . . but my mother's. When she was younger, with soft eyes and hair that is identical to my own. I lean over the image, my blood-crusted curls scraping against the paper. She is smiling, the way I remember her.

"Young Woman Cures the Plague – New Hope for All" the headline says.

"Lark Woodson, the 20-year-old daughter of Professors Adam and Jane Friedman at the University of Southern Florida, has discovered a cure for the human weakness to

disease. *The cure will render the Plague completely ineffective, thus saving humanity from its untimely end. Woodson was recently placed as head of a research team called the Initiative. Their mission? Rewiring human DNA in order to improve the Cure and distribute it widely. Just weeks into the trial stages, Woodson solved the puzzle that has baffled scientists for years . . . "*

There is a hole in the page, and half of the story is missing. But I understand enough.

"It's so overwhelming," Woodson said, *from her Florida home. "I have discovered a way to arm the human immune system, so that it is impossible to contract the Plague. From this day forward, the only way a person can die is from unnatural causes. Disease is a thing of the past. The world finally has a future. We will go on."* There is another picture of my mother standing in front of the Perimeter. A huge smile is on her face, and in her outstretched palm, she is holding something small and rectangular.

A Pin.

The room is too warm, and closing in around me with these dripping red walls. The newspaper flutters to the floor, but I can still see my mother's face, staring up at me from the page.

"This is impossible," Zephyr says. He takes a step

forward, and the entire unit sways. "Get back before you kill us both!"

But he doesn't seem to care. "Your mom invented the Pins? And the Pulse? *She* is the one who cured us of the Plague?"

I turn back to the wall. My mother's rushed handwriting stares back at me.

"Read it to me," Zephyr says. "Please."

"December 24," I say. The year is missing. *"The Initiative has exposed the population to the Cure through Water Distribution.*

I skim further down.

"Everything is falling apart. The Cure is keeping us all alive, but it killed many of the larger land animals. We are running low on resources. Citizens are dying of starvation. I am blessed to be a part of the Initiative. We have purchased a million acres in Florida with the funds we have received from our efforts. We can now start experimenting on a Cure Controller. I have been granted the position of Commander in Chief of the Scientific Population Control team. John will be pleased with the rations we will receive because of this. . . ."

My father. How much did he know?

I move to another article. *The Perimeter has finally been*

240

sealed. The rest of the country is in shambles, but here, we have the chance to start again.

And another . . .

Tonight, we commence the first trial round of The Murder Complex. In exchange for lifelong rations, our patient will undergo our procedure. We will send her out into the Shallows, and we'll be watching as we make her decisions for her. Sometimes I second-guess myself . . .

I scoot away from the wall and sit down in the middle of the floor. I swallow and try to think rationally, the way my father would if he were here next to me right now. The way he trained me. He would breathe. And adapt to the truth of the situation.

He would face the facts, and the facts are right here in front of me. Written in my mother's handwriting.

CHAPTER 52

ZEPHYR

I want to tear the photograph from the wall and rip the thing to shreds.

It's two bloody children fighting to the death. They're both bald, heads shaved slick as glass. They have additional Catalogue Numbers tattooed on the tops of their heads.

A7. A8. Their faces are dead. Devoid of all emotion. Like machines. It's bullskitz.

Scientists stand behind a wall of glass, taking notes. It's like they're all betting on who will win a dog fight, like the kids aren't human beings. But the lists are worse. There's all these names and numbers covering one wall from top to bottom. Thousands of them.

Patient X. Allen Troy. Patient U78. Sicily Peters.

We scan the names, and even though I already know what I'm about to discover, I try to make it not true. "Look at my scalp," I whisper to Meadow. "There's nothing there . . . right?"

She moves toward me in the flickering light, careful not to move too fast. The unit groans again, and she freezes. I slide the rest of the way to her. She touches my hair, gently brushing it aside. I hold my breath.

"There's nothing here, Zephyr," Meadow says. But she keeps searching. Suddenly her breath catches in her throat, and her fingertips fall from my scalp. "What's that word you use again?"

"Which one?" I ask.

"The worst one," she says. "It's there, Zephyr. I'm sorry."

We both turn back to the list, and see Patient Zero. Zephyr James.

"Flux," I say.

"Yeah," she breathes. "Flux."

CHAPTER 53

MEADOW

"What does it mean?" Zephyr asks me. His hands linger on the wall where his name is printed, as if the answers will come to him the longer he stands here.

I shove his hands away. "Stop looking at it. And get away from me, for the last time."

There are other things in the unit. Stacks of old wooden crates.

I have to move, do *something* besides stand here with my mind reeling.

"Open the crates," I say to Zephyr. "But be slow. Be careful."

He moves to the first one and starts prying it open.

It's full of knives, nice ones that cost thousands of Creds. My heart rises into my throat. How would she have gotten her hands on so many of these? But of course. She had everything she wanted.

The second crate is full of blueprints. I take one and smooth it out on the floor.

Initiative Building A – Scientific Research

It is a plan of the cooling systems. My mother was the Commander. So why would she need to know the utility entrances to the Initiative buildings? Better yet, why would she have a hidden storage unit full of blueprints and knives?

"Stars, Meadow, I know that building," Zephyr whispers, when I hold up the blueprint.

"Have you been there?"

"No. Never," he says, shaking his head. His eyes are glazed over, confusion making him look younger, like a child. "But . . . I've had dreams about it. And I'm starting to think maybe my dreams aren't exactly dreams at all."

I hear feet pounding by outside. The unit starts to teeter up and down. I hold my breath.

I can hear chains clattering to the ground. They're prying open the padlocks. We don't have long before they open up the right one.

"Take these," I whisper, and shove a handful of blue-prints into Zephyr's arms. He finds a dusty backpack against the wall and starts filling it with them. No questions asked. He just does what I ask him to do, as if obeying me will be enough of an apology.

I open the next crate, keeping one hand on my dagger, one eye on Zephyr's back. This crate is long and rectangular like a casket, and for a second, I am afraid I'll find a body. But when I open it up, a huge grin spreads across my face.

"Oh," I gasp, and Zephyr appears at my shoulder. I ignore him. It's my mother's crossbow. I poise my finger over the trigger and remember the way she used to shoot down seagulls from the deck of the boat. Koi and I would race through the water like hunting dogs. Whoever got to the bird first was the one who got to shoot the next arrow.

It was always me. And I never missed.

Why didn't she feed us? Why didn't she move us to the Compound with the others, where we would always be safe, and never hungry, and always far from the murders? Why didn't she tell us who she really was?

The crossbow already has four arrows attached, the feathers on the ends red and black. Beautiful. Lethal. So familiar. They seem to buzz with life.

246

The ground moves again. More papers flutter to the floor.

"What are you doing? We can't stay here!" Zephyr says, but I hold up a hand to silence him.

I slide over and reach into the box of knives. Zephyr tucks several into the backpack. I find two leather thigh sheaths and strap them to my legs. I slide two knives into them and stand, slinging the bow over my shoulder. Feeling confused about my mother. Feeling angry. But feeling strong.

That is when we hear the clicking. They have found us.

"This one," a voice says, and my heart nearly stops beating. Someone laughs. "We could shove this one into the Pit."

"Oh, man. Imagine their screams."

The first voice barks, "They're wanted *alive*. Hey. You! Open this thing up!"

Zephyr tries to step in front of me, but I shove him to the side and position an arrow onto the bow. I hold it steady in front of me, finger on the trigger, and let the memory of my father's voice settle me. *Breathe. Steady arms. Focus.*

"They don't have the bracelet. They can't open it," I whisper.

The door explodes. I fall backward onto Zephyr.

"Come on out, kiddies, before you fall!"

We have no choice. I have four arrows, and there are ten of them. Seven Initiative soldiers, three Pirates. I drop the bow.

"Atta girl. Now be a good little citizen and come on out."

The unit tilts. Zephyr pushes me through the blasted-out door just as the entire thing goes careening into the Pit.

CHAPTER 54
ZEPHYR

The Leeches tie our wrists together so we can't get away.

Not that we'd be stupid enough to try. They've got guns jammed into our backs as they haul us down the streets.

"You know we aren't worth much," I say to the two Pirates holding me by the arms. The Leeches walk up front, moving citizens aside. "I'm just a Ward. You really think the Leeches will give you Creds for turning in a worthless kid like *me*?"

"And the girl's even worse than I am," I add. "You don't want her. She's crazy."

"Shut up and move," one of them grunts.

Meadow glares at me like she'd rather kill me than her captors, even though I didn't mean what I said about her. I'm *trying* to get us out of this.

We walk along the train tracks, and I know that now we're just waiting for the metal machine to show up. As soon as it does, we'll end up inside of it, soaring right to the Leech Headquarters.

I can't let that happen.

Most of the crowd is going in one direction, but there's someone moving toward us, pushing and shoving. It's a man in a mask.

It's just a ripped-up shirt tied over his face, with holes for his eyes and mouth, but it catches me off guard.

"Go to hell, Leeches!" the man screams.

He holds up a sign, hand-painted on a thin sheet of scrap metal.

It's a painting of the Leech symbol, an open eyeball.

But there's a dagger stuck right in the middle of the eye, and blood dripping from the corner of it. It's incredible.

"Kill the Initiative!" he yells. "They don't stop anyone from killing us!"

People stop walking and watch him in disbelief. Everyone knows the last protestor was sent straight to the chopping block.

But today, it's different, because I'm here. I'm already caught.

"Kill the Leeches!" I scream. "They deserve to die!"

"Go and get him, I can't get a clear shot," the Leech soldier tells the Pirates. "We'll handle these two." All three of them leave, chasing after the protestor. He keeps screaming as he runs down the street, and people actually *part* to let him pass.

"Foolish," the Leech says. He's about to say something else, but just as he opens his mouth, something amazing happens.

His body kind of seizes up, like he's been stung by a wasp and can't handle the pain. For a second, his eyes go wide. Then he coughs, and blood trickles out of his mouth. He clutches his chest, gasps for air, and not a second later, he falls to the ground. An arrow sticks right out of his back.

"Holy *skitz*," I hear myself say.

The Leech is dead.

The crowd starts screaming as arrows rain down from the sky.

CHAPTER 55
MEADOW

My mother's arrows.

The feathers are black and red, the shaft silver and lethal.

One hits the soldier holding me in his left eye. He falls to the street.

The crowd is screaming. They push and shove and try to get away, but there are so many people. Another arrow lodges itself in a soldier's heart.

There is only one person I know who can shoot with such precision.

It is my father.

There are two soldiers left, one holding Zephyr, and

one holding me. If I wanted to, I could take my captor down, then scramble for the other. But instead, I will give my father the satisfaction of killing them both.

There is a whistling sound, and an arrow flies right past my ear, skimming my hair, but not harming me. It dives deep into the throat of Zephyr's captor, and the man is dead instantly.

I wait for the last arrow. The soldier holding me drops my arm. He tries to run, but the crowd around us is so dense he cannot get away. People are frozen in place, staring with surprise at the dead Initiative men.

Thirty seconds pass. The arrow does not come, and I realize my father wants to see *me* do the job. Of course.

In the distance, I can hear a siren wailing. Soon they will come with their pistols and rifles and gas, and there will be no chance of escape. Behind the soldier, I can see my father's blond hair as he climbs down an old fire escape. He is coming for me.

Zephyr and I rush the soldier together. We shove him to the ground, but instead of killing him, I retrieve my dagger from his belt loop and hold it to his throat, where it belongs.

Then I look up at the people around us, their starving

faces, the hope that is shining in some of their eyes.

"Do what you want with him!" I shout. "He's yours now."

We rush into the shadows of the nearest building, where my father is waiting.

CHAPTER 56

ZEPHYR

Meadow's father holds the crossbow to my throat.

"Why aren't you dead?" He asks. His face is covered in sweat and dirt. He looks scarier now than he did on the boat.

"*Dad,*" Meadow says. She puts her hand on the crossbow. "He's not what you think."

"A thank you would suffice, Meadow. I've been tracking you all day," he says to her. But he smiles and places his hand on her shoulder. "Good move back there. You've given them hope for the first time in years."

Meadow's cheeks flush red. Stars, this guy probably *never* compliments her.

"Where's Peri? Is Koi with her? Are they okay?"

Her dad smiles. "They're fine, we'll see them soon. You still have your mother's bracelet?"

It's not an expected question, not when we're all huddled in the shadow of a building, just waiting for the Leeches to come haul us away. But Meadow lifts up her wrist anyway, and shows her dad the seashell charm.

His face relaxes. "It's a reverse transmitter. Your mother made it herself, so that when you had it on, the Initiative couldn't track your Pin. *And* anyone else's within a five-foot radius."

Meadow gasps, and stares at the bracelet with awe.

"Hold on," I say, shaking my head. "Those ChumHeads *track* us? Through our *Pins*?"

Meadow's father laughs, and shakes his head. "They can do a hell of a lot more than that."

A gunshot rings out. "Follow me. Stay close to Meadow," her father says. "And run fast."

We duck into an alley and run. Somehow we reach the salt marshes. I'm about to scan my Catalogue Number at the gate, hide us away inside the safety of the Reserve, but Meadow's father grabs my arm.

"When you scan in, it alerts them. Use your brain."

I can hear the train rumbling. It comes and goes

through the center of the Shallows like clockwork.

We race for the tracks. The engine comes into view. Its hulking mass of rusted metal is covered in old, dried blood.

"Try not to die!" Meadow smiles, and her eyes are on fire.

I jump and cling to the first thing I can find. My legs are dangling over the edge. Skitz, I'm going to fall, or be swallowed up by the tracks and split into a million pieces.

But Meadow's father grabs me by the wrist and hauls me up. In seconds, I'm lying facedown inside the car, feeling my heart slam against the hard floor.

"Iss our train! Get the hell out-a here," a man hisses from the corner. I smell alcohol and sweat. And oh. There's a young girl beside him with tears in her eyes.

Her dress is all ripped up, her hair is in tangles, and there's red marks all over her arms and legs. She clutches her chest, and looks at us like she wants to scream for help, but no words come out of her mouth.

Meadow takes the crossbow from her dad. She aims at the ChumHead's drunken face. "Jump out of the train, you sick bastard," she says.

"I do what I wan-do." The man laughs.

"Jump out of the train, before I shoot this arrow

through the back of your throat," Meadow says, stepping closer to him.

"I can kill you slowly. You can drown in your own blood. Or I can use a dagger and cut your eyes out. Your choice."

"You're crazy," the man says, but he stands up, stumbles forward, and stands, toes dangling over the edge of the car, ready to leap from the train.

He doesn't have to. Meadow shoots him in the back of the neck. He disappears as the train sweeps around a corner. The girl gives us a wide smile.

"Are you a good swimmer?" Meadow asks her.

She nods her head, brown eyes wide. "My mommy taught me."

"When this train passes over the bridge, I want you to jump into the water. Swim to shore, climb a tree, and stay there until morning. Understand?" The girl nods, and as the train rattles over the bridge, she leaps without hesitating.

CHAPTER 57

MEADOW

The train stops.

"I was afraid of this," my father says. "They're shutting down all transit until they find you two. Meadow, I don't know what you did. But I've heard them talking, and they'll do whatever it takes to get you. They might even capture your brother and sister if it will draw you in. We're going somewhere safe. Let's move."

We leap out of the train and run, following my father.

He leads us right to the edge of the Graveyard.

It looms overhead like a giant beast, the smokestacks making it look like the Graveyard is alive. A monster breathing in and out, waiting to swallow us whole.

I skid to a stop, and Zephyr does the same beside me. My father turns when he realizes we are no longer following.

"It's the only place, Meadow. For now, until I can make contact with the others."

I do not ask who the others are. I swallow my fear and follow my father into the only other place in the city that I swore I would never go.

There are two trash mountains on either side of us. The steam makes it feel like a thousand degrees. My clothing sticks to my body, and it's hard to breathe. As we walk, I can hear clicking noises, from cockroaches and crickets, crawling amongst the garbage.

"Are Peri and Koi in here?" I ask.

"They're with an old friend," he says. "They're safe."

He leads us to the left, under another steam tower. Through the steam and fog, I can see far too many others, huddled against the trash. There is a woman with an old harmonica, playing a song. I see a man and a woman tearing at each other's clothes, kissing. A little boy standing knee-deep in garbage hisses at us and backs away. He has a rat in his hands.

I skirt around him, closer to Zephyr.

"Where's all the Gravers?" he whispers to me.

"They come out at night, I think," I say. "I don't like this place even in the daytime. I can't believe Peri is here somewhere."

My father leads us deep into the Graveyard. I don't think I could find my way out of here without him. There are huts made of old wood and metal scraps fused together, nestled against the piles. As far as I can see are mountains of garbage, pathways twisting and turning. We finally stop before a hut with an old car hood for a door. My father knocks three times.

I hear rustling from the other side, and the door swings open on rusted, makeshift hinges.

I nearly fall backward, but Zephyr catches me.

Because the man standing in the doorway before us is one of the men I saw in my mother's old photographs.

He is a member of the Initiative.

CHAPTER 58

ZEPHYR

The man in the doorway looks insane.

He's got white hair that hangs in dreadlocks to his shoulders. His right eye's covered by an old eye patch, and I can see a jagged scar sticking out from under it.

The second Meadow sees him, she pulls out her dagger and holds it up to his throat.

"Meadow!" I yell. "Stop it!"

"He works for the Initiative!" she hisses. "I saw him in my mother's photo!"

The old man gasps. Then he *slaps* the blade of the dagger away, and Meadow looks so shocked and confused that I actually laugh.

"Put that knife down, child!" he says. "I'm *retired,* and if you're near as smart as your momma was, you'd know that. Now get inside before they spot you."

Meadow's father laughs and ducks in through the doorway, but she doesn't follow.

I put my hand on her shoulder. "Sometimes, you have to trust people. It's fine. You've got your dagger, and you've got me. Crazy automatic weapon here, Meadow."

She almost smiles, and follows me inside.

The hut is empty. Nothing but a bare space, with a dusty tarp covering the floor. The old man sweeps it away, revealing a trap door.

We all climb down into the darkness.

The trap door opens up into a tunnel, a big metal cylinder that looks like it used to be a part of a giant machine. The old man lights up a lantern. It shines with blue light, something that's got to be pre-Fall.

We follow him through the tunnel, crawling deeper under the garbage. There are boards and poles holding the ceiling up in places where the cylinder is corroding. I'm afraid if I even sneeze the whole thing's going to come crashing down.

"Found this beauty a while back," the old man says, tapping the cylinder. "She needed fixing up in places.

Helps that I was an architect, way back when. And an engineer. Bah, it doesn't matter."

The tunnel finally opens up into a small room. The walls are covered in steel and a mess of wires. "Anti-transmitter, just like your little bracelet there, missy," he tells Meadow. "Keeps my old coworkers from finding me here."

There's all kinds of crazy stuff in the room. A pre-Fall wooden desk, filled with copper and bronze trinkets that buzz and whir. I think I see a piss bucket in the corner, and stockpiled bags of rations.

There's also a small pile of blankets in the corner, and two sleeping figures on it.

Meadow gasps.

"Koi!" she screams. "Peri!" She runs forward and pretty much body-slams them, and I watch her siblings wake up. It's like some reunion, with all of them smiling and laughing.

I don't have that. I'll never have that.

Then Meadow turns and points at me, and whispers something to her brother.

Oh, skitz.

When his eyes meet mine, I swear to the stars he's going to kill me.

"I'll deal with you later," he says. He clenches his fists in his lap.

Meadow and her family sit together on the floor. I sit next to the old man, who introduces himself as Kansas.

"I know what you are," he says to me. He watches me with his one good eye, like I might explode at any second. "I know all about you."

"That makes one of us," I tell him. "Meadow doesn't trust you. I want you to know that I don't either."

"I don't trust myself no more. Not after the things I've done. Now it's time to eat up. I worked forty years to stockpile this stuff."

We dig into the rations bags and have the first good meal we've had in forever.

CHAPTER 59

MEADOW

After we eat, I excuse myself. The walls are too close. I need a second to breathe. When I get outside, it's late afternoon. I weave my way through the piles of trash, and as I do, I can't help but wonder why my father kept all of this from me. A secret Graveyard hideout, ex-Initiative workers on our side. The truth about my mother.

"You know it's not safe out here," a voice says behind me.

I turn around and my father is there. I had not heard him sneak up on me. If he were an enemy, I might already be dead.

"Sit with me," he says. I can tell from his stillness that

his thoughts are just as heavy as my own.

"How long?" I break the silence between us. "How long was my mother one of them?"

He sighs, a sound that is heavy and ragged. Full of pain. "You should hold on to the memories that you do have of her, Meadow."

"I need the truth."

He turns his back to me, and as he does, something inside of me breaks. I thought I would feel a piece of my world slide back into place. Instead, he's pulling me into a darkness that threatens to swallow me whole.

"Haven't the two of you done *enough*?" I say. "I've been chased all over the city. I had to destroy our *home*, and I've had to kill too many. I'm still being chased. I want the answers. I *deserve* the answers."

"You deserve what you earn," he says, and as he speaks, his hand closes over my shoulder.

I know this feeling. I know what he is about to do, and I welcome it.

I turn to face him. But before I can move, he holds up his other hand. A strip of black cloth hangs from his fingers. "Nothing will be given to you. You will take it."

I sit quietly as he ties the cloth over my eyes.

"Listen to the sounds around you." His voice comes at

me from the right. I turn and lunge, but I can feel the whip of wind as he dodges my hit. He takes my legs out from under me, and I crash to the ground. I get a mouth full of dirt and grime.

"Not good enough, Meadow. Focus."

I grit my teeth and stand, listening for my father's voice, for his breath. To the left. I kick out and this time I connect, but he moves quickly. I whirl around and his fingers close over my throat.

"You're dead," he says, releasing me. "Again."

I fail twice. Three times. Blood drips from my forehead, soaking the blindfold.

"Make it *mean* something. You have to want it."

And I do. I think of Peri and Koi. I think of my mother and how she hid who she really was from us. Darkness is all I have ever felt inside. This should be no different.

"Don't look them in the eyes. Listen to their breathing instead, and follow their movements." My father's voice is to the right of me now. He's talking about people like Zephyr. But are they enemies, if what they are doing is beyond their control?

I listen, but he is silent as a predator.

There's a breeze. Metal clinks, paper rustles, cockroaches hiss. Steam falls across my shoulders, making the

268

heat unbearable. I release my senses to my surroundings, and imagine him circling me, waiting for me to fail. I will not fail.

There is a slight change in the tone of the world when something blocks me from the wind. It is the absence of sound, as if my father absorbs the noise. I visualize sound waves rippling around him and take the chance. I dive for him, fueled by my anger, my pain, my fear. We slam into the ground and I shove the tip of my dagger up against his throat. For a moment, I want to cut him. I want to put scars on his body and make him hurt the way he has hurt me. But it would only make him prouder, so I slip my dagger back into its sheath. "Give me the damn answers."

I roll away and lay back on the dirt. I tear off the blindfold.

"She was godlike, your mother. Changing the laws of the universe. Her parents worked their entire lives in science. When they died because of the Plague, your mother dedicated herself to avenging them. She found a cure."

"The Pins and the Pulse," I say, and he nods.

"They set up stations all over the country. Soon, everyone was healed."

I close my eyes and will myself to listen and not judge.

"But death has its place in the world," my father

continues. "You cannot eradicate it without consequences."

My father rolls over onto his side and looks at me.

"Do you remember when you used to collect seashells?"

I nod. My mother would take me to the beach every day when I was a child. We'd scour the sand and find treasures. She would tell me stories about where each one came from. A mermaid. Two friends standing on separate shores, sending tokens of their love out across the sea. But soon I had so many. There was not enough room in my jar to keep them all. And suddenly I understand what my father means.

Without death, there is only life. I remember how my mother and I had leaned over the side of the boat and watched as my precious treasures drifted away into the sea.

"We'll start over, Meadow," she told me.

Is that what she decided to do with us?

"There was no way to take back what she had done. You give the world a *miracle*"—he says it like it is quite the opposite—"Well, there's no taking it back. So the Shallows came to be, and the walls went up to hold us all in. And the Murder Complex was born."

Nausea churns in my stomach, threatening to rise up my throat. I don't want to hear what he is going to say next. I don't want to know that everything I have learned is true.

"Originally it was just a testing site. She played god. She took back from the people what she had given, and then some. She used the Murder Complex to decide who would die, and when."

"I don't understand," I say. "Why not just reverse the Cure? Couldn't we just take out the Pins?"

My father laughs. "The Pins are just a cover-up, Meadow. There are no nanites in our Pins. They were released into our blood streams, through the water, a long time ago. They're still in us, Meadow, but we all have a Pin so that we can be tracked. The Shallows is a testing center. We are *all* a part of an experiment. Or at least it started that way. It was only supposed to last a few years. Now they keep us here. We are trapped and the world out there is much worse. The Pulse, believe it or not, keeps people *out*. Well, assuming there is anyone left out there."

"And the Murder Complex?" I ask. "Why keep it going?"

My father sighs. "The Cure is in everyone's blood, and once it's in, it stays, and it gets passed on. No one dies, Meadow."

"And the people like Zephyr? What about them?"

271

He turns away and stares back up at the stars. "They are *created*, Meadow. The Patients. Not by birth, but in the lab. Their bodies grow at a rapid rate, and once they are mature enough, the surgery is simple. There is an implant that is activated when the lottery chooses them for a mission. They are given happy memories. Sad memories. Whatever will make them believe they were born and raised in the world, with everyone else.

"They are made Wards. At night, they are watched inside their Reserve. It was your mother's idea. What citizen would suspect the orphaned Wards? In reality, they are far from worthless. It's all a cover-up. They're like machines."

Zephyr. Poor Zephyr.

"Things changed when the lottery chose *you*, Meadow."

"What?"

"The Murder Complex chose you. To die. You weren't supposed to be in the system. But there you were, like someone had programmed you into it. Maybe as revenge."

"Did she stop it? I mean . . . she took me out of the system, right?"

The wind blows my hair back from my eyes, and I can see my father is watching me. "She loved you, Meadow."

"I asked you if she took me out."

He pinches the bridge of his nose with two fingers. "She believed that the lottery was law. There is no changing it. No altering it."

"So she sacrificed me?"

"No. She took you out before anyone could murder you." He sighs, placing his hand on my shoulder. "We never did figure out who put you back in after that. They could still be out there. And someday, Meadow, your time might come. Your mother is gone. She cannot protect you anymore. You will have to do whatever you need to do to survive. It is what you have trained your entire life for."

If what he says is true, then whoever it was has struck again. Zephyr wasn't supposed to go after me. But he did. He tried to murder me. I have been programmed into his brain. Maybe for years. "Why me?" I ask. "Why not Koi or Peri? Or you? And mom is dead. There's no point in getting back at her now. Why can't they just let us be?"

My father closes his eyes. He sighs. "Because you were always special to your mother," he says. "And murdering an entire generation is not something that most people can let go, Meadow. Putting you into the system was an act of vengeance against your mother. To take away the two things she loved most. Her system . . . and you."

"And mom?" I say as I take this all in. My voice is

strangely calm. "What really happened to her?"

"They didn't need her anymore. She wanted to quit, and take us all out of the Shallows, back into the real world, to take our chances. So they killed her before she could. I saw her, Meadow. She was . . . completely destroyed." He stands to leave me, but turns and stops.

"There is a Resistance. If anything happens to me, I want you to find them and join them. I want you to fight against what your mother started."

Then he is gone.

I will do whatever I can to stop what my mother started. That I know.

CHAPTER 60

ZEPHYR

Meadow comes back when the Night Siren starts to wail.

"Hey," she says. "Let's go talk. Away from . . ." She nods her head toward her brother.

"Fine with me," I say. "I don't like being alone."

We crawl down the dark tunnel. I stay totally silent until she asks, "What are you afraid of?"

"Honestly? I'm afraid of myself," I admit. Because it's true. I don't want to see the faces and the numbers tonight. I don't want to see the people I've killed because of her mother's psycho experiment.

Meadow takes my hand.

No one ever touches me.

"I'm glad we didn't kill each other," she says. Maybe I should laugh. She almost does.

"What's your story, Zephyr?"

"You already know my story. You know exactly what I am," I say.

"You're not a *what*, Zephyr. You're a *who* . . ." Her voice is careful, like she's searching for something that she's afraid she'll actually find. "Can you feel it? The Murder Complex?"

"It's hard to explain," I say. "It's like there's another person inside of me. This crazy person who just wants to hurt people. The other day, when I came to find you on your boat . . . I killed three Pirates. And it felt *good*."

"But you were triggered on them, right?" she asks. "And it only happens during the Dark Time?"

"No. I wasn't triggered. It's like it's changing me. Someday I might be as bad as the Leeches."

She frowns. "Do you have memories?" she asks. "From before all this?"

"Some," I say. And it's true. I have memories. I feed off of them to keep myself going.

"Tell me one," she says. There's something weird in her eyes I can't figure out. She leans forward like she needs to hear my stories.

No one's ever *needed* to hear anything I have to say. Not even Talan. "We used to sit on the boardwalk. Watch the sunset, me and my parents."

"Mmm . . ." she says, and when I look over her eyes are closed and she's leaning up against the wall of the tunnel, a smile on her lips, like she's feeding off of my memories. I wonder what's wrong with her own.

I keep talking, because I want her to keep smiling. "I had a big brother, too. He had a baby girl and every time I held her she'd giggle and squirm in my arms. It was the happiest sound I'd ever heard. She didn't know what the world was like yet."

My mouth keeps spilling the words and I don't try to stop. For the first time, someone wants to listen. "I have lots of memories. Happy ones. But a lot of them are fuzzy . . . when I . . . when my parents died, they said they couldn't find my brother . . . it's like he wasn't even real."

"I don't want to hear about that. Tell me more about you when you were little."

"We used to go to the park . . . the one that overlooks the ocean," I say. I want to wrap my arm around her shoulders. But the second I start to, she stiffens. I hold her hand instead. We climb out of the tunnel, into the entrance of the shack.

"My father would push me on the swings and it felt like I was flying . . . I have a favorite memory, though," I say. "It was the morning I woke up and found you standing in the Rations Hall." I reach toward her and pull her chin up. "Look at me," I say, but she shakes her head. "Hey. I won't hurt you, Meadow. I owe you my *life*, remember?"

She looks up slowly. "My father said that if you're triggered, you'll try to attack me when our eyes meet," she says.

"Then I'll keep them closed," I tell her.

I close my eyes and I feel her breath on my cheek.

"I want to believe you," she whispers. "It's like I've known you all my life."

I reach out and touch her cheek. Her skin is so soft. "I wish I could find the words to tell you how beautiful you are," I whisper.

"Your eyes are closed." She lets out a nervous laugh. "How can you say that if you aren't even looking at me?"

"You're ruining the moment."

"You're wrong," she says, breathing in. She starts leaning toward me, and I start leaning toward her.

I'm about to kiss her when a voice calls out from the darkness of the tunnel. "That's close enough, Zephyr."

I turn and see a figure coming our way. "Ah, skitz," I whisper. "Really?"

It's her brother.

"Koi," Meadow squeaks, backing away from me. She studies her fingernails like they're the most interesting thing in the world.

Is she *embarrassed?*

"Get away from my sister," Koi says. He reaches for her, then takes a half-step in front of her like she needs protecting.

"Koi, it's fine," Meadow says. "Nothing happened!"

"I've been waiting a long time to do this to one of *them.*" Koi's voice is hard. He keeps his arm in front of Meadow, holding her back from me. And then, before I realize what he's up to, he *punches* me, square in the face.

"Koi!" Meadow screams, and tries to pull him away, but he pushes her off and lunges at me, pinning me down with his body.

The punches come fast and hard.

One to the cheek. One to my brow. One that almost hits me in the temple, but I flinch and dodge the blow.

By the time Meadow manages to pull him off, my face is dripping blood, and the world's spinning in and out of focus.

"What the hell are you doing?" Meadow screams. Her voice is furious, hard like sharpened steel. "Zephyr! Get out of here."

"No! He *stays*," Koi says. "So I can kill him."

"Like hell you will," Meadow yells, and she steps in front of me. "We need him."

"For what?" Koi groans. "He killed her, Meadow. He killed Mom."

She stumbles backward. "What are you talking about, Koi?"

"The Patients! She created them, and it made her crazy! They killed her!"

"You *knew*?" Meadow gasps. "All this time you *knew*, and you never told me? How could you do this to me?"

She pulls him away, and the two of them speak in hushed voices. I catch bits and pieces of what they're saying about me. About the others like me.

I don't want to hear.

I stumble away from them, out into the Graveyard. There are tears in my eyes, blood in my mouth, questions in my mind. None of this makes any sense.

Somehow I make it to the steam tower. I stand there under it and let the heat and darkness drown out my thoughts. For a second, I consider finding something sharp. Ending my life for *good* this time, when Meadow can't stop me.

But then I remember my promise to Talan. And stars, now there's Meadow. I don't want to leave Meadow.

I hear footsteps. I hear her calling my name, but I don't respond.

I don't feel like being found.

But she finds me anyway, and her ChumHead of a brother's with her.

"What am I?" I ask, looking at him.

"You're a machine," he says. "Your brain is programmed. It makes you kill. When the Initiative wants you to murder, all they do is press *play*."

"We have to stop them." Meadow's eyes are on mine. Her body is wet with sweat, and her hair sticks to her skin. She turns to her brother, then back to me. "We have to stop the Initiative. We have to stop what our mother started."

"I want in," I say, because I'll do anything for this girl. I'll even follow her down to hell if I have to. And knowing her, that's probably where we're about to go. "Is there a way to reverse it? A way to . . . take it out of my brain?"

Koi stares at me. I half expect him to lunge at me. But then he looks at Meadow. She's watching me.

"You care about him?" he asks her.

"*Yes.* It's not his fault what he does. I understand that, and you should, too, Koi."

They are the best words I've ever heard.

"I wish you didn't," Koi says. His breathing slows. His shoulders droop, and his eyes go all soft, like their little sister's. He shakes his head and turns to me. "I don't know much about the Murder Complex. But if you want answers, you won't find them here."

"The Initiative," Meadow says. A piece of paper gets picked up by the wind and dances past her feet. "They're going to bring Zephyr in. Shut him down."

Koi nods. "You could turn yourself in." He shrugs. "I would be fine with it."

"Stop it," Meadow hisses.

I look down at my hands. They don't feel like my own.

"If I turn myself in . . . will they stop chasing you and your family?"

"You are *not* doing that, Zephyr. They'll kill you." Meadow crosses her arms over her chest. "We'll find another way to get answers. There must be someone who can help us . . . someone who knows more about this . . . "

"There is *someone*," says Koi. "But all I have is a name."

Meadow stares hard into his eyes. "Well? Who is it?"

"A woman," he says. "She worked with our mother. I don't even know if she's still alive, Meadow. It was years ago."

"Who is it, Koi?"

A scream comes from the darkness. A girl runs in our direction, pushing past us, tears running down her face.

"What's wrong?" I yell.

"Gravers!" she gasps, then stumbles away. "The Gravers are here!"

CHAPTER 61

MEADOW

They come like locusts.

Slowly, in packs of two or three, then all of them at once.

Where they hide in the day, no one knows. The Graveyard is a maze. There are plenty of places to slip away. At night, they swarm the pathways. They take everything from everyone, and leave broken people in their wake.

A Graver woman comes for me, wearing armor made of trash. Old flattened soda cans cover her chest. Forks and spoons are twined together, shielding her arms. She has black paint smudged all over her face, and when she approaches me, I am so horrified that I nearly back away.

"Give me the knife, little girl!" she screeches. "I'll tear the hair from your scalp piece by piece!"

Koi takes her down, and the three of us run.

"What's the point?" Zephyr asks. The night is pitch-black, and the steam is thick. "They *live* in a trash pile. Why do they need more stuff?"

"Because all the good stuff is with the living," Koi says. People push past us, running in all directions. We are like ants trapped inside of a crumbling mound. "Most people that come here to hide are weak. They hope it's safer than the city."

We skid around a corner. A Graver is trying to rip a tooth out of an elderly man's mouth. I swipe the Graver with my dagger, slicing his back. Koi shoves him into the trash mountain, and we keep running.

We've almost circled back to Kansas's house when one of the Gravers points at us, and shouts, "It's them! Bounty's five thousand Creds! *Get them!*"

He blows three loud bleats on a whistle.

Gravers come out of nowhere, hooting and hollering like they are hunting animals.

We take off. Zephyr is just ahead of me. He grabs my hand. My foot catches on an old coil of wire, and I tumble to the ground, hard. Zephyr turns to help me up, but a Graver grabs him by the shoulders and whirls him around. More come for me, but Koi is there. He pushes me into the shadows, then takes down two using only his fists, and snaps a third's neck with effortless grace. Their comrades scream. They want my brother now.

"This way, you Leech Lovers! Come and get me!" Koi starts throwing trash and rubble at the Gravers. "Take Zephyr and hide," he says, loud enough for me to hear. "Don't go to the shack."

"We'll fight them together!" I say. "There's too many."

"There's never *enough* for me, little sis!" He smiles. "Better run."

I turn to Zephyr. He's rolling in the dirt with a Graver, trying to get the upper hand. But then Zephyr's face contorts, and he looks furious. He shoves the man away with a twisting move only a trained fighter would know.

"Come on!" I scream, and as we run, I hear radios chirping in the distance.

"They're this way!" a Graver woman shouts. "This way!"

A spotlight bounces along in the darkness behind us.

The Initiative is here.

CHAPTER 62

ZEPHYR

Meadow and I make it to Kansas's shack a second too late.

The Leeches are already outside the door. They've got spotlights lighting it up. This isn't good.

Meadow pulls out her dagger and starts to run for them, but I grab her and hold her back. "Are you insane? It's a trap!"

"My . . . my sister!" Meadow gasps. A pack of Leeches come out of the shack.

There's Meadow's dad, holding Peri in his arms, and five Leeches with guns pointed right at their heads.

Gravers come down a passageway, hauling a body along with them. "We got the boy! We got him!"

My heart sinks. It's *Koi*. His hair is all covered in blood. He gave himself up so Meadow and I could run.

Meadow struggles in my arms and I clamp my hand over her mouth. Let her bite me, I don't give a skitz. Meadow's dad is screaming, whirling in circles, telling the Leeches to stay the hell away from his daughter and his son.

He looks in our direction, like he knows Meadow is there.

"The stars!" he screams. I think maybe he's gone crazy, but his face is angry. Not afraid. "Trust the stars! Find them where the darkness is safe!"

I pull Meadow deeper into the shadows, and she stomps on my foot. *Hard.*

"Meadow, do you want to die? Stop fighting me!"

The Leeches tie up Meadow's dad. His arms, his feet. They gag his mouth with a rag. Peri starts crying, and it's the worst sound I've ever heard. Koi is passed out on the ground in front of her, and I don't even know if he's alive or dead, and now Meadow's sobbing. I pull her to my chest.

I see Kansas come out of his shack. A Leech guy hands him a bag of rations, and a brand new rifle, shiny and new. "Nice doing business with you, friends," Kansas says.

Traitor. He's a *traitor*.

"Hey! Where's *our* pay?" a Graver asks, stepping out of the shadows.

The Leech leader turns his rifle on him. "You didn't deliver the girl or the boy. You told me you could deliver them within the hour."

"They were here! We saw the girl! Jackson almost got the boy! Swear!"

"But you didn't," the Leech snarls at him. "And Trackers can't find them. I owe you nothing, you fool."

The Leech lifts the gun and shoots the Graver in the head. Then he turns it on Kansas and does the same.

The Leeches grab the rations and gun from Kansas's dead body. They start hauling Meadow's family away. One of them picks up Peri and tosses her over his shoulder.

Meadow writhes against me. We've got her bracelet, so they can't track us. But they can still see her. No one, not even her, can take on a group of gun-toting Leeches alone.

So I do the only thing I can do to keep her safe.

I reach behind me and grab an old metal pipe sticking out of the trash. She starts to run, and I grit my teeth and slam the thing as hard as I can over her head.

She drops like a swatted fly.

"Sorry," I whisper, as I bend down and scoop her into my arms.

Then I haul her into the darkness to hide and wait.

When morning comes, I've got Meadow tied up tight against one of the steam vents.

"Let . . . me . . . go!" She thrashes against her bindings. She slams her head backward against the metal and I watch her eyes glaze over from the pain.

"I'm sorry," I say. My voice is hoarse. "Not until you calm down."

She looks so small and terrified right now. I lean forward to wipe the sweat from her brow and smooth her tangled hair from her forehead. But when I try to wipe the dried blood from her lip, she recoils and a warm glob of spit hits my face.

"Skitz, Meadow! Would you calm down?" I stumble backward, shattering an old burned-out light bulb. "What do you want me to do? It's your fault they're gone! Can't you see that? You had to go snooping around, and you got them into this mess!"

The second I say it, I know I've screwed up.

I watch her face twist with rage. Her gray eyes smolder back at me, and her bottom lip starts trembling.

Ah, stars. I know what's about to happen. "Nope. No way Meadow, don't even think about it."

"I. Hate. You," she says. And then she bursts into tears.

I turn around and leave her there to cry herself dry.

CHAPTER 63

MEADOW

"If you don't let me go, I'll kill you."

"You'll kill me regardless of what I do, Meadow. Drink."

Zephyr shoves an old bottle of water to my mouth. I have no choice but to tilt my head back and let the cool relief slide down my throat.

"You have to calm down," he says after he takes a sip for himself. I sit here, watching him, as the sun dances across the tops of the huge trash mountains. I stare at his jaw. I imagine what it would feel like to have it crack beneath the force of my fist. I imagine the satisfaction of knowing that he paid for keeping me from my family.

I think of what my father would say to me, what he

would *do*, were he in my place at this moment.

He would breathe until his heart became steady. Force himself to push his emotions aside and focus on what matters. So I do what I have always been trained to do. I channel my father's strength and reign myself in.

I am emotionless. I am strong.

The Initiative will pay.

CHAPTER 64

ZEPHYR

By the time late afternoon comes, Meadow's breathing has slowed down. She stares unblinking up at the sky. She looks like a ghost.

"I have to find the Resistance now," she says. Her voice is hers again, calm and steady. "It's what my father wanted."

I settle down in front of her, but she doesn't take her eyes from the sky. "If I cut you loose, you have to promise me that we'll fight for this together," I say.

Silence.

"Meadow." She tilts her chin up even further. Refusing to look at me.

"You're being a baby," I say. "What happened to the girl

who gave me her own blood?"

"She's right here," she says. "And if you don't cut me loose, the Initiative will kill my family. They might already be dead."

I swallow hard. She's right. But if something happens to her, I'll never forgive myself. "Then I'll let you go," I say, and lean forward to cut the bindings. "But . . . you owe me something first."

"And that is?" She's still staring up at the sky.

"A kiss," I say.

Her eyes never meet mine.

"Well?" I ask.

She nods and smiles, finally throwing me a stare that's as deadly as poison. "You can kiss my ass, Zephyr James."

I cut her bindings loose anyway.

In the distance, the Pulse flashes blue to purple and back again.

There are no nanites in our Pins.

We've already got them in our blood, and the Pins are trackers.

When the Night Siren wails, I know what needs to happen.

"Meadow," I whisper. We're leaning up against another

steam vent, back to back, keeping watch in both directions. Waiting for dark.

"This will make you happy," I say. "It's my turn to be tied up now."

She turns to look at me. I think she's going to make some crack, but instead, she just nods. I know she understands. If I hurt this girl somehow, or actually kill her . . .

We find some thick wire. I sit back against the vent and Meadow winds it round and round, as tight as she can get it.

"If I get free, I want you to stop me," I tell her. "I don't care what it takes. Do you understand?"

She nods her head. "I know."

"If I . . . if I say anything to you, Meadow, you have to know that it isn't me. Not really."

"It's my mother." Meadow nods. The bindings tighten around my chest, my arms, and my waist.

I shift my weight. "Tighter," I say, and suck in my breath while Meadow pulls the wiring hard against my body. When she's done, she sits down across from me and pokes at the ground with her dagger.

"Come here," I whisper. She settles next to me, leans her head against my shoulder. "Meadow, I . . ."

"Don't speak. Not now."

CHAPTER 65

MEADOW

In the morning I wake to the sound of a woman wailing.

I do not have to wonder why she is crying. There must be hundreds of dead bodies lying in pools of blood on the concrete, hundreds of Catalogue Numbers that will soon appear on screens in the Dome.

But I smile as I stand up and stretch. Because Zephyr is still tied up, sound asleep. He did not hurt anyone last night.

We decide today will be our last day in in the Graveyard. We will hide out until sunset. I scavenge through the garbage and make a bolo weapon with what I find. When a seagull lands and picks up a cricket, I throw the bolo.

It ensnares the bird, and Zephyr whistles as he starts up a fire.

"You're making me look bad, Woodson."

"It's okay. All women should know how to cook. You're doing great," I say, and his laugh is so musical and sweet it reminds me of Peri's.

At sunset, when the sky is bleeding red, we walk to the edge of the Graveyard and stand in its shadow.

Find them where the darkness is safe. The stars will show you the way.

My entire life, I have been taught that darkness is death. Darkness is horror, and blood, and now, darkness is when my mother sets her monsters loose.

Darkness is the furthest thing from safe.

"It must have something to do with the Resistance," Zephyr whispers. We have found an old pair of pre-Fall binoculars. One lens is broken, but the other still works, so we take turns watching the city. "What do you think they're going to do with us?" Zephyr asks.

"They said they want to shut you down manually," I say. "Maybe they'll reboot your system or something. I don't want to think about what they'll do to me."

"Don't worry," Zephyr says. He slips his arm around my waist. It feels strange to be held, but I let him.

"What if I lose my bracelet? It could fall off, or we could get separated, and then it will only work for me."

"You want to cut our Pins out," he says. I can feel him sigh. "You know we can't do that. Everyone says that you die if you try to take them out. Like . . . from a shockwave or something. It's the same thing that happens when you try to leave the Perimeter. Only worse."

"We have to risk it," I say. I run my thumb over the bump in my forearm. My entire life I thought it kept me safe from diseases, helped my wounds heal faster, helped my heart beat steady and true.

We are living in hell. The Pulse has always been the only piece of heaven we have ever had. Now even that is a lie. I want it out of me. "And we'll probably die as soon as we leave this place, anyway," I say.

"I wish I was more positive, like you," Zephyr jokes. But then he thinks for a moment, and his smile turns to a frown.

"We could die right now," he whispers. I feel his hand on my arm, closing over the spot where my Pin lies just under my skin. "We could die the second we cut these things out, and we'll never know what could have become of this."

"What do you mean . . . this?" I ask.

Zephyr shakes his head. He runs his fingers through his hair, and he groans. "I've been trying to get the courage to tell you how I feel about you ever since I met you, Meadow. But I can't put it into words. So don't kill me, because I'm just going to *show* you."

He leans forward, his eyes smoldering like coals, and takes my face gently in his hands.

Then he presses his lips to mine.

The moment is fast. A single second in time, and I try to tell myself that this is what *he* wants, that I am doing this for him and not myself. But my heart slams against my ribs and I am suddenly more alive than I have ever been.

I pull away, gasping for air. Our foreheads stay pressed together, his lips so close I almost taste them. "You got your kiss," I whisper, even though it was *my* kiss, too. "Now you owe me this."

In the darkness, we cut out each other's Pins. We hold back our screams, and we are fearless, just like Koi would want, just like my father taught me to be.

"Nothing happened," Zephyr says. He kisses me again, harder this time, and I kiss him back.

We wrap scraps of our clothing around the wounds, and we drop our Pins in the Graveyard where they belong.

We live, for the first time in our lives, without the Pulse tracking us.

Together.

CHAPTER 66

ZEPHYR

Stars. Meadow's father said it had to do with trusting the stars.

In the distance, I can hear the train rattling along, coming closer.

"Let's go!" I say. I take Meadow's hand and we run, sticking to the shadows. The Dark Time is almost here. We don't look at each other, now that we know how the trigger works.

The train's bright light is about a half-mile behind us when we run past the Pit.

Meadow drops my hand.

"Well, lookie here, lookie here," a voice says. A man steps out of the shadows, and this time, it's not a Graver or Pirate.

It's a Leech, and he's got his gun trained right on us.

The Leech whistles, and a bunch of them come out of the shadows. Skitz. They were hiding right here on the edge of the city, waiting for us. We didn't stand a chance.

"Stupid boy," another Leech barks. This one's got nothing but a tiny pocket pistol in his hand, and I almost laugh at him.

"Let's kill 'em," one of them says.

"The orders were to keep him alive. Both of them."

The barrel of another gun is pressed to my temple. "Where is the girl?"

"She's . . ."

I turn. She was right *here*.

Skitz, where did Meadow go?

"I uh . . ." I look around. I think I see a flash of silver, someone sprinting between two buildings.

"She's dead," I say. "I killed her myself."

I hear the click of a bullet sliding into a chamber.

"*Alive,*" one of the Leeches says. He stomps forward and rips the gun away from his comrade. "We bring him in alive!"

"Fine. Brock, bring those MagnaCuffs over here. Lock him up good."

A scrawny Leech walks forward. He looks like a new one, fresh on the job. He's got two thick silver cuffs in his hands. He slips them over my wrists, and they form real tight against my skin. When he presses a button on them, the cuffs light up, and they slam together from magnetic force.

"All right. Good enough. Brock, let her know we've got the boy."

"Sir," the Leech boy says. He's lifting the radio to his mouth when a gunshot explodes into the night.

The kid falls onto his knees. He's been shot in the chest. There's a whistle and a squelch as the soldier closest to me gets a knife through an eye socket.

I smile. It's not a knife. It's Meadow's dagger.

I can't see her, but she's here, somewhere in the shadows.

"Come out, little girl!" the Leech next to me shouts. He hauls me to my feet. "Move!"

"Nah. That's okay," I tell him, and then I watch as he falls. Another guy drops right after him, and a second later, another.

Another gunshot, but it misses the last Leech and hits *me* instead, right in the thigh.

"Flux!" I scream. Meadow comes out of the shadows, holding a rifle.

She stops, takes a deep breath, and shoots the last Leech just before he puts a bullet in her skull.

"Get up!" she yells at me. "Run! Go for the train!"

"You shot me!" I scream at her.

It hurts like hell.

Meadow hauls me to my feet and I start running, hobbling. It takes everything I've got in me, and when I leap into the moving car, I land face-first on the hard metal flooring.

"You shot me," I say, catching my breath. "I can't believe you shot me."

"You'll be fine." She isn't even winded. "Stop being a baby. Look, it's already healed up."

"You have the worst aim ever!" I groan, because *no,* it hasn't healed up all the way. It's still trickling blood, and it still hurts like hell.

"We can't stay here long," Meadow says. "They all radioed someone, and they'll probably shut the train down soon. Start looking for a sign. Stars. He said it had to do with stars and darkness."

The next thing happens so fast we're both caught totally off guard.

A woman leaps onto the train. All I see is her black uniform, her bald head, her pierced eyebrow, and I recognize her at as the Leech worker from the Rations Hall.

Meadow cries out. "Zephyr!"

We both lunge for the woman, but I reach her first. Hands still cuffed, I use my body weight to tackle her to the floor of the car. She struggles to fight, but I'm bigger. Meadow holds a dagger to her throat, but before she cuts her deep, the woman says one word.

"Resistance!"

"What did you say?" Meadow shouts. A drop of crimson bubbles up on the Leech's tattooed skin.

"Resistance!" she gasps again. "The stars!"

Meadow's dagger clatters to the metal floor.

"What are you thinking? Kill her!" I say. "She's lying!"

But Meadow shakes her head. "My father has that scar." She points at the mark on the woman's neck, just above her collarbone. There's three tiny stars in a row, cut so they mimic that Orion's belt constellation Talan and I used to love looking at. "It means something."

"Are you sure?" I say.

"I'm positive," Meadow says. Her voice is so sure, but I'm not. "She's with us. Please, Zephyr. I know it."

"Get the hell off of me," the Leech woman snarls, and before I can pull away, she launches me upward, flips me, and rolls on top of me. She locks her hands over my throat. "If I wanted to kill you, Patient Zero, you'd already be dead." Then she pulls out a key and unlocks my MagnaCuffs.

"The stars," Meadow says, nodding her head. "Of course." She turns to me and takes my hand, smiling for the first time in days. "Zephyr. This is *Orion*."

CHAPTER 67

MEADOW

All this time, and I never knew.

"That was a suicide mission. You know that, right?" Orion says. She stands across from me, arms locked over her chest. Watching me with those strange, dark eyes. "The way you took that guy out in the alley, and stole his rifle? You're a clever one. I'll give you that."

"How long have you been in the Resistance?" I ask her.

But Orion only shakes her head. "Answers come later, Blondie. I've been searching for you since you went on a killing rampage in the Everglades. I've got no patience left. Now hush, and get ready to jump again." She lifts her pierced eyebrow toward Zephyr, and he turns away, embarrassed.

The train leaves the city. We pass by the Ward Reserve. I hear the buzz of Orion's radio chip. *"Boss. Hey boss. Commander needs your report."*

"Not a *sound,*" she hisses to us, and lifts her palm to speak. "Caught the little bastards on the train. The girl was a tough one. Boy went out like a light." She winks at Zephyr, and the muscles in his jaw twitch.

"Hold your position, Soldier. We'll come to you."

Orion reaches into her ear, pulls out the tiny chip, and throws it out the open door of the train.

"This whole time you were on my side," I say. "This whole time, you could have warned me about the Murder Complex. You could have warned me about my mother."

Orion shakes her head. The light of the moon makes her skin glow a soft white. "Some things are better left unsaid, Blondie." She looks at the wrap on my arm and on Zephyr's. "Did you remove your Pins?"

I nod. "Just before you found us."

"Shouldn't have," Zephyr groans beside me, but Orion smiles.

"Well . . . welcome to the Damned life. Now you're running around this town like a ghost." She winks.

The train lurches left, making us sway on our feet. We are past the marshes now, heading toward the Perimeter. I look at the Pulse, blinking, but no longer tracking me, and I know Zephyr and I made the right choice.

"I stuck my Pin in a Ward's bag a few hours back." Orion smiles. Her teeth are shiny and white. She has lived the life of an Initiative soldier for a while, judging by her well-fed looks.

"The Reserve's gonna be lit up like a Christmas tree before too long. 'Course it means I'm done. Ah, it's all well." The train speeds up, making a turn along the side of the Perimeter wall. Soon we will hit the bridge and cross to Cortez. "You two good to jump?"

"Why wouldn't we be?" Zephyr says, putting his arm over my shoulder. I want to shrug him off, want to do this on my own as I always have. But his warmth calms me. I do not always have to be by myself. I can have a partner. And maybe, if Orion leads us to the Resistance, I can have an entire team.

Together, we all move to the edge of the train car.

"They always said you were a tough one, Z. Blondie shot you in the leg, eh?" Orion laughs and looks at Zephyr. "Wait till you meet the Others."

"Others?" He asks. "Like me? Where are they?" He

leans forward, eyes lit up with questions, but before he gets an answer, Orion laughs again, winks at him, and leaps from the train. She disappears into the darkness.

"Come on," I say, taking his sweaty hand.

"I don't trust her," Zephyr says, his green eyes slits, like a snake's. "Do you?"

"I don't have a choice," I say, because right now, Orion is the only lead we have to finding the Resistance, to finding Peri and Koi. Thinking of my siblings fills me with a rage that rocks me from the inside out.

"Fine. But if she kills us, Meadow, this one's on you. Not me."

"You should worry less. It doesn't look so good on you," I say.

I drop Zephyr's hand, take a deep breath, then leap out into the unknown.

CHAPTER 68

ZEPHYR

I've pushed a cart full of bodies to the Leech Headquarters every week, dripping sweat, holding back my vomit, for as long as I've been a Ward.

The routine's never really made me think twice about my safety. It's never made me feel afraid, because I've always imagined the Leeches thought I was dead, too. Totally worthless. A pathetic Ward.

Now that I know what I really am, what the Murder Complex is, everything's turned upside down.

"That's where they train the Patients," Orion whispers beside me in the darkness. We're crawling in the dirt like bugs. The sky rumbles and lightning cracks overhead.

Rain starts pelting us. Soon the dirt turns into mud, and the crawling gets painfully slow.

Orion continues. Skitz, she's as bad as Talan.

"It's also where they're holding Blondie's family, if I'm right. And of course, it's where they've got the Board."

"What's the Board?" Meadow asks. I see her look at the Leech Headquarters, and the anger in her eyes is scary as hell.

"It's what we call the Motherboard," Orion whispers. "The person who controls the Motherboard controls the Murder Complex. It's how they turn the damn thing on."

She leads us to the oldest part of the Shallows, through a maze of old palms and moss-covered trees, until we reach an old, pre-Fall road. Most of it's covered by overgrowth, but the pavement is still visible in places. Finally, Orion stops. Lightning strikes, and the world lights up for a second like someone's turned on a lantern above the trees.

"This is where we disappear." Orion grins, pointing at an old metal grate. There are ones like it all over the city streets. I've found dozens of dead bodies on them. I've always been concerned about what's on *top* of the grates. Never what's hiding under them. Orion lifts the grate and slides it away. I can see a ladder. Below that, just darkness.

"Get in," Orion says.

Meadow and I just sit there like ChumHeads, staring down into pitch-black.

Orion groans. "Hurry up."

Meadow slips her legs through the hole in the ground and disappears down the ladder.

"After you, Patient Zero," Orion says. I step in and grasp the ladder. I'm about to start down when I feel her hand on mine. I look up and her face is so close I can see her sweat.

"You make one wrong move down there, you let that freaky Murder Complex mind trick make you hurt any *one* of my team, and I promise you I'll slit your throat before you even know what's happened. You understand?"

I don't answer her. I climb down the ladder and hold my tongue the entire time.

CHAPTER 69

MEADOW

When I was little, Koi and I used to race to the ocean floor. We would hold our breaths and dive deep, open our eyes, and see an entirely new world. So beautiful and peaceful.

"It's always been there, Meadow," my father said, when I told him about it. "Some things are better when they stay hidden beneath the surface."

Going to the Resistance Headquarters is like discovering the ocean floor for the first time. The ladder leads us to tunnels so dark I cannot see my hand in front of my face. Orion takes the lead, talking quietly the entire time so we can follow her voice. Her murmurs echo off the walls, and there is a constant drip-dripping of water that soaks our heads.

We finally reach the end of the tunnel and enter a massive underground room. The space is lit by flickering torches, and I can see the shadowy figures sitting in huddles around the concrete floors.

"Honey, I'm home!" Orion says, whistling, and I hear laughter from all sides. In the corner, two boys are sparring. One is far larger than the other, but the smaller one is winning with effortless grace. Others stand around watching them, cheering them on. A rat scurries past my feet, and a little boy runs after it. He is even smaller than Peri.

"What is this place?" Zephyr asks.

"This is the Cave," Orion says, sweeping her arms in a circle. The place smells like waste, and the air is thick with a foglike heat that makes it hard to breathe, and water continues to drip down over my head and onto my clothes.

But something about the Cave makes it the most amazing, welcome place I have ever seen.

"It's not much, but it's home. We've been here a few years now. Work is slow. We're gathering our own troops. Our own army of *Patients,* if that's what you want to call them. Zombies, more like." She laughs.

Zephyr flinches.

"Come on," she says. "I'll give you the grand tour."

There are groups of people clustered around torches, speaking in hushed voices, holding out books, scribbling on salvaged scraps of paper. I see photographs of my mother plastered on one of the dry walls. Zephyr points out photographs of Initiative soldiers, buildings, the trains, the Reserve. In one corner, marked by glowing white candles that line the floor, there are names and dates scratched into the walls. Some have notes scratched beside them. *RIP.*

I love you.

You still owe me 5 Creds.

"Our memorial," Orion says, "for the ones we've lost. There's no Catalogue Dome down here. No toilets, either, but we're living in one I guess, so you can drop your pants and do your business wherever you like."

I hold back a short laugh, and wish Peri could meet Orion. She would giggle at every word this woman says. I feel like now I am meeting the *real* Orion for the very first time.

The whole Cave is one wide circular space, with more tunnels leading outward into darkness. And on the far right side, tied down with heavy metal chains, are three figures with bags over their heads.

"Who are they?" I ask Orion.

"Patients," Zephyr says. His arms are crossed. Fists clenched. "They're Patients, aren't they?"

Orion nods. "They chose to join us and fight the cause. But they're still Zoms when the Initiative wants them to be. We haven't figure that out. So far, at least."

"So you tie them up." Zephyr nods. There is sweat on his forehead, and he's soaked, and I want to reach out to him, but keep my hands at my sides instead.

"We protect them from themselves," Orion says. "It was their choice."

She introduces us to people, some who look as if they have not seen the light in months, pale as flounder. "Everyone has a different job," Orion says. "Some gather food. Some gather information. Some," she says, eyeing a massive dark-skinned man chewing on a bone, "go out and recruit Zoms who want to join us in the fight."

"And what is the fight, exactly?" Zephyr asks.

"You don't pick up on much, do you, Zero? We're going to shut down the Murder Complex. Someday, at least."

Finally she takes us to the center of the room, where a small stage made of wooden slats has been erected. There is a NoteScreen, like the ones the Initiative Evaluators carry, and on it, I see a slideshow of faces with Catalogue Numbers. "Patients," Orion says, nodding at the images. "We were lucky enough to hack into their system a few weeks back. The other day, we knocked out all their cameras, which is probably the only way you two got here alive. Problem is, we lost our tech girl. She disappeared suddenly—we're guessing she's dead. Now we can see when the Patients will attack, and lucky for you, Zero, it's not your special day. But the problem is, even though we know—"

"There's no way to stop them," a voice says behind me. I whirl around and there is a young man with hair as black as the night, and eyes blue as the summer sky. I have never seen anyone like him. "You're the Woodson girl," he says, studying me closely. "My father worked with yours."

"My father?" I ask, and Zephyr's hand skims my back. "My father worked . . . here? With all of you?" There are faces in the darkness, watching us, but I don't care.

"He sent us information," the young man says, shrugging. "Taught a few of our people how to fight, way back when. Word is you're his protégé. We've been waiting on you to join us for a long time."

He exchanges a glance with Orion. Then he turns to Zephyr. "So. You're the precious Patient Zero."

Zephyr's hand squeezes mine hard. "Zephyr," he says. "I prefer my real name."

"Nah. I'll stick with Zero. The name's Rhone," he says. "Welcome to the Resistance."

"Why are we here?" I ask, because I am confused. Because my father never told me about a Resistance, or Rhone, or Orion.

The more I uncover, the more I realize that my father never really shared anything with me at all.

Rhone grins at me. "You're here because your father promised us that when the time came, you'd help us do a little something. In return, we'll help you get him back."

Zephyr stiffens beside me. I can tell he does not like this. But I look at Rhone and nod my head. "Go on."

"It's simple, really. You're going to break into the Initiative Headquarters. You're going to find the people who control the Motherboard, and you're going to kill them."

Kill them. Finally, words that settle me. Words I understand.

"Now you're speaking my language," I say. Rhone laughs, and Orion pats me on the shoulder.

The only person who does not smile is Zephyr.

CHAPTER 70

ZEPHYR

I sit back against the wall and watch Meadow for the next few hours, while Rhone and Orion show her maps of the Leech Headquarters. They give her codes to doors, until she can recite them back by memory. They pair her up with their best fighters, men and women both. She beats almost all of them like it's no big deal. I watch with a group of others, off to the side, as Meadow's body gets all bruised and bloody. She's spectacular.

She's bought into this whole place, but it doesn't bother me that much. It's Orion and Rhone that really do.

The way they watch her, nodding, whispering and

scribbling notes, makes me feel a rage so deep that my body goes cold.

It's like she's an experiment, and they're so damn proud of their work that they can't take their eyes off of her. My anger pulses and festers, and suddenly, before I can get a grip on myself, everything goes cold, and dark.

I feel myself hit the floor as a memory or something takes over me, and when I try to fight it, the world fades away.

I'm not inside the Cave anymore.

I'm in that mirrored room again, staring at my own reflection. My face is younger and softer. But flux, my eyes are so cold they almost look black.

"You're progressing quite well, Patient Zero," someone says. When I turn around, it's Lark, smiling at me like she's proud. "Soon you will be able to go out into the world."

"I am afraid," I say, looking at my bare toes.

Lark's smile falls away. "What did you say?"

"I am afraid. I do not want to leave here." I'm wearing all white, but there's a splash of color on my clothing that gets my attention. When I look down, I see red on my hands. Red on my sleeves.

It's blood.

In the corner, there's a body that lies crumpled on the floor.

It's a woman way older than me. Her neck is stuck at an awkward angle, and her hair's splayed across her face. She's bleeding.

"I killed her," I say to Lark. "Why did I kill her?"

"You obeyed protocol," Lark says, but instead of smiling at me, she looks . . . tired. Or sad. It's impossible to tell. "Come here, Patient Zero." She makes me sit down in front of her and tell her how I feel.

"Did the woman deserve to die?" I point at the body. I stand up to move closer to it. "What did she do to deserve to die?"

"Stay where you are, Patient Zero."

"I don't want to." I know I should probably listen. But I feel like I'm strong enough that I don't have to, so I go over to the body, push her hair from her face so I can look at her eyes.

The pain is horrible.

A shockwave of electricity.

I whirl around. Lark is pushing that awful red button in her hand. It causes pain in my head. Pain behind my eyes.

I scream. I drop to the floor.

"You need to listen," Lark tells me. She puts the button back into her lab coat. "You need to obey."

"I'm afraid," I tell her. I'm shaking, but the pain is gone.

A woman's voice comes over a loud speaker, crackling in

my ears. It sounds like Lark. But darker.

"He shouldn't be speaking like this. We've been pushing 60 watts. He shouldn't have feelings, not when it's turned on this strong."

"And yet he does, sister," Lark says, looking at me. "It's fascinating." She takes me by the shoulders and pulls me close. "He's stronger than the others. He's special. Just think of what he'll be able to do someday. Think of what we'll be able to use him for. . . . "

The memory is sucked away. I see Meadow, kneeling over me, feel her shaking me. I try to call out to her, but my body feels so weak.

My eyes fall closed.

I sleep.

CHAPTER 71

MEADOW

Zephyr does not wake for hours.

I sit beside the cot Rhone brought for him, studying the articles about my mother that Orion gave me. A whole box of them.

My mother was 19 when she married my father.

She was 21 when she had Koi, and 26 when she had me, and even though I know all of these things, have always known them, I feel like she is a stranger. That this is the story of someone else's mother, not mine.

She was 17 when she discovered a cure for the common cold, right after her parents died from the Plague. *Teenaged Einstein,* the caption reads. She was 20 when she created the Cure, which held the nanites, and was released all over the country in the water.

She was 26, the same age she was when I was born, when she created the Murder Complex, but the information is not printed in ink. The details are scribbled in pen inside a notebook. I think by Orion. She talks about how the original citizens of the Shallows were tricked into getting their Pins. Extra nanites. A lie. People were so foolish to believe them.

But I guess they were desperate for rations, desperate for a place that they thought would be safe.

By the time I am finished looking through the papers, I feel sick.

Finally, Zephyr wakes up.

His eyes flutter open, and I am so relieved that I fall on top of him, press him into a hug that is tighter than I meant it to be. He gasps, but wraps his arms around me anyway.

"I thought you were dying, you ChumHead," I say into his ear. His hair is soaked with sweat and sticks to his forehead. I brush it back and bury my face in his shoulder. "I thought . . . you were gone."

"I feel like a million Creds," Zephyr says to me, joking, but I can tell something is wrong. "I promise, Meadow. Hey. Look at me."

He pushes me off, and we sit side by side on the cot. "I saw something. Or dreamed it. I think it was a memory."

"Of what?" I ask. His face is white, almost as pale as those who live down here.

"I was with your mom," he says, wide-eyed as a child. "I was younger, in this room inside of the Leech Headquarters, I think. And she was punishing me when I wouldn't listen."

"I'm sorry," I whisper. I cannot picture my mother hurting anyone, ever. Especially not Zephyr.

"But that's not the point." He shakes his head. "There was someone watching us. A woman. She said I was stronger than I should have been. Whatever it is, some system or something, was on . . . and I was disobeying your mother. I heard your mom call her *sister.*"

There is a whistle behind us, as a figure steps out of the shadows. It is a girl, younger than me by the look of her. She is thin and dark-skinned, her cheeks hollowed. Her hair hangs in dreadlocks just past her shoulders, and on her arms are black horizontal lines, tattoos that run from her wrists to her elbows. "So it's true," she says, looking at Zephyr. Her voice is sweet, like a melody. "You're really as great as they say you are."

"Um . . . excuse me?" Zephyr asks.

"Sometimes you get the best information from people when they think no one's around. I saw your little episode over there. You dropped like a dead fly. Let me guess. You had a flashback?" She approaches us, sits down cross-legged on the floor in front of the cot. There are black tattoos on her legs, too.

She sees me staring.

"Kill marks," she says. "I tatted them myself. I'm a Zom, too. And I was a good one, apparently, before the Resistance found me."

Zephyr breathes in fast. "We're the same?"

"The same, but different. I'm like *you*, is what you should be saying." She picks at her toenails and smiles up at Zephyr like he is on display. Almost like he is holy.

"You were in the first group they made. Around here we call you guys the Originals."

CHAPTER 72

ZEPHYR

The Originals.

I shouldn't be surprised anymore, not after everything I've discovered with Meadow. But I can't help myself. "You're lying," I say.

The girl, whose name is Sketch, just laughs. "I've only met one of you guys before. She was a girl. Sweet thing, but she died a long time ago. She had flashbacks, too."

"Do you have them?" Meadow asks. Then she looks at me, *stares* at me, like I'm some crazy Graver or something.

"Nope. Sorry," Sketch says. "Only the first Zoms do. It's a glitch in the system, maybe. Or could be I've been hit in the head one too many times. I barely remember what I ate for breakfast this morning. And in case you're wondering, it was a rat."

She reminds me of Talan.

Talan.

Skitz, I hope the Leeches don't do anything to Talan.

"How do you know he's one of the first?" Meadow asks Sketch.

"Cuz we've all studied the history," Sketch says. She spits on the ground, just misses my foot. A real lady. "I was a Third Gen. They fixed all the kinks by my time. But you, dude, you've got a screwed-up brain in there, don't you?"

I chew on my lip. I stare at her.

"Someday, I'll get my hands on that psychopath Creator," Sketch says, then looks at Meadow. "No offense."

Meadow shrugs, but says nothing.

"So they told you what we have to do, right?" Sketch asks me. Her eyes are this really weird shade of yellow, like a cat's. "We've gotta go in there and fight off the Protector. *The* Protector, dude. The one who guards the Motherboard."

Protector. Not Protectors. "And wait . . . you're going?"

"Of course I am. I'm going to shut that Board down,

even if I die trying." Sketch laughs. She stands up and brushes off her tattooed thighs. "It's a good thing your girlfriend is such a skilled fighter. Because word is you fight like a kid. We've only got a day to get you prepared. I don't think you realize what we're up against."

An hour later, I'm surrounded by a ring of Resistance members, looking like the biggest ChumHead in the history of the Shallows.

Everybody's shouting my name. And they're laughing at me, sometimes so hard they can't even breathe.

I hit the cave floor.

Again and again.

"Stop wasting your energy!" Meadow yells. "Swift motions, Zephyr. Choose your target and focus only on it."

I haul myself to my feet and ready my body for her attack. But this time, when she lunges, I'm more prepared. I drop to the ground and roll sideways, away from her. When she turns, I kick out my feet and make her crash down beside me. Everyone cheers, and Sketch screams something vulgar.

Out of the corner of my eye, I can see Orion and Rhone. They don't look impressed at all.

Meadow smiles. "Better." Dried blood speckles her

face, and it sort of makes me feel sick that I've been trying to beat the skitz out of her. But she looks like she hasn't been this happy in years. She's grinning like a crazy person. "Zephyr, *look* at your body. You're all muscle, and you're fast. Somewhere inside you know how to do this. Now do it again."

Again and again I attack, but her instincts are way too quick. She avoids every punch, sinks more than a few of her own in my gut, and soon, I'm on the ground, heaving for air like some dying fish.

One day. *One day,* to prepare myself. They should've given me months.

This is totally impossible. It's humiliating. I'm an Original, and I fight like a little girl. "This isn't working." I say. "There isn't enough time!"

Sketch pushes through the laughing spectators until she's at Meadow's side. They both stare down at me.

"Muscle memory, dude," Sketch says. "All the Zoms have it, but it's deep down in your brain. Pull it out. They did this to you. Now *use* it."

Sketch extends a hand and pulls me to my feet. It's worth a shot to listen to her, I guess. I close my eyes as she circles around me. I tell myself I've got to hang on to her every word, and focus.

"You know you're a murderer, Zephyr. So prove it. Try to kill me."

"Stop it." I clench my fists.

"You've done it before," Sketch says. "You can do it again. Try to hurt me. Try to kill me, Zephyr."

"I said stop." The hair on my arms starts to stand on end.

"Make yourself *feel* something. Get angry! Do it!" Her fist connects with my jaw, and I stagger backward. Flux, she's strong. I focus on how bad it hurts, letting the pain fuel me like fire.

When it starts to throb, I feel something different.

Fury.

I turn and run for her. Sketch's mouth spreads into a grin just before I slam her body into the floor. Everything around us fades away. My muscles take over, and everything clicks into place. I'm making all the right moves, taking all the right steps, blocking her kicks and throws like I've been training for this fight my whole life.

The crowd is cheering me on, trading Sketch's name for *mine*. It feels so good to hear it, and I fight like my life's on the line. Someone throws Sketch a knife, and the mood changes. I trade anger for hatred, move faster than I've ever moved before, as Sketch starts swiping at the air. The knife skims close, and the tip of it slices my arm open.

"Not so fast now, are you, Zero?"

Meadow watches me with her eyes on fire, her fists clenched.

I have to win. I've got to prove myself to this girl.

I reach for everything from the past, everything that's inside of me, and suddenly I feel myself changing. I see flashes of moments from long ago. The mirrored room, an opponent that's dressed in white, like me. I see a man, training me to make strong punches, take even breaths, and move on the balls of my feet. There's a woman, spraying my wounds, fixing me up only to send me right back out again. I feel pain when Lark pushes the red button every time I lose a fight, and I feel pleasure when she pushes the blue button every time I win. I hear my name, Patient Zero, over and over and over.

Suddenly I'm fighting with grace, like the battle is a dance. I see Meadow's face in the corner. Her mouth drops open, her gray eyes go wide. I strike Sketch's throat with my fist. She coughs, sputters for air, staggers backward. I slip my arm over her wrist, twist it, and laugh when her knife clatters to the ground.

"Get her, Zephyr, get her!" Meadow's screaming, and I have the knife in my hand.

I set a trip with my foot and push Sketch to the ground. She cries out, furious, but before she gets the chance to stand up I'm right on top of her, straddling her with the knife pressed to her throat.

Her yellow eyes are wild.

"Good," she says. "Very good."

There's something dark in me. It wants me to push the knife right through Sketch's throat. But Meadow starts cheering. I look at her face, and the knife falls out of my hand.

I stand up and disappear down one of the tunnels. Then I throw up everything in my stomach before I collapse against the cold, wet walls.

"You did great," Meadow says later that night, as she chains me up just a few paces away from the others like me. "You're ready."

Meadow sits across from me, wiping the blood from my mostly healed wounds. "They'll do whatever they can to stop us, you know," she says.

"I don't think I care anymore."

She found clean water somewhere. It feels good on my skin.

"I feel like I can protect you now," I say. "I feel like

when we go in there tomorrow, we're going to be okay. We'll make it okay, together."

It's a long time before she answers. When she does, she speaks so soft it's not even a whisper. "Did you ever think that . . . maybe it's not *you* they want? Or my family?"

"What do you mean?"

A fire nearby lights up the scars on her arms and legs. When she looks back up at me, my heart almost stops. There's something I've never seen before in her eyes.

Fear.

"They took them," Meadow says. Her voice cracks. "They took my family. But they didn't take me. And I think I know why."

I reach out to her, but she pulls away. "It's just because they couldn't *find* you, Meadow. I kept you safe."

"You shouldn't have!" She hisses. She is so angry that I look away. "They want me, Zephyr. Not you, not my family . . . me."

I wait a minute for her to calm down. "You don't know that," I say. How could she? All we've done so far is run blind. We don't really know anything at all.

"I see the way Rhone and Orion look at me. You don't think I've heard the whispers? Everyone knows something about me that I don't."

"Skitz, Meadow, you're Lark Woodson's *daughter*. That's kind of a big deal."

"Maybe so," Meadow says. "But my father told me something in the Graveyard. He told me that there's a person out there who keeps trying to put my name into the lottery system . . . to get me killed, I guess to get back at my mother."

I close my eyes and let her words settle. Nothing should surprise me anymore, but this does. "So my dreams about you . . . it's because I'm the one who was chosen to kill you . . . because of this person."

She nods.

"Well . . . then that settles it, Meadow. There's nothing wrong with you," I say. "You're perfect. It's this crazy person that's the screwed-up one."

Her eyes snap to mine. "Would you stop with all of that? This isn't a fairy tale. This is real life, and right now, Zephyr, something is wrong. I'm going in alone." She stands, checks her dagger, and gives me one last look. Her eyes are dead. "If I turn myself in, they'll let my family go."

"Are you insane?" I try to leap to my feet, but of course I can't move. "What, you think if you just . . . show up, they'll smile and hand you your sister, Meadow? No.

We've got a job to do. We have to shut the Motherboard down, and end *all* of this skitz for good."

I hold her gaze. I'm not going to let go of this girl.

Not ever.

"You think we can just walk in there, kill one person, and end the Murder Complex? It's ridiculous. There's still the Perimeter, Zephyr. It's going to keep everyone stuck in here forever. No one will die for a long time, even if we shut the Murder Complex down, and then the world will keep growing, and children will starve, and . . . oh, this is insane! We won't make it out of Headquarters alive. We've been lucky so far. We'll go in there tomorrow and we'll die. And my family will die. And you will, too. All of this will have been for *nothing*."

"You're *wrong*," I cut her off. "You are. But this isn't just about us. It's not just about your family. It's about all the Wards out there. It's about the Leeches, controlling us, holding us in the Shallows. Killing us all off, one by one. We might die. Your family might die. But . . . it's worth a try, isn't it?

She slumps down on the floor. Her eyes shine with tears. She swallows and looks at me. "It would be easier to give myself up."

"We're in this together, Meadow, you and me. Until

they rip us apart, and even then, I'll fight."

I watch her eyes flick from me to the exit tunnel and back.

"You're not a machine, like me," I whisper. "It's okay to be afraid. For once in your life, just be *human*."

Finally, her shoulders sag. She lets out a deep breath, and her tears fall fast and hard. I want to wrap my arms around her, but I can't, so I hold her hands in my own while she sobs into my shoulder.

After a while, she settles down with her head on my lap, looking up at me. Her face is full of a darkness so deep that it sucks all the light from her eyes. It's all anger and hate, and a million emotions twisted and tied up into one, but these aren't meant for me.

"Tomorrow," I whisper. "Just wait until tomorrow, and we can both get the revenge we deserve."

"Are you afraid?" she asks me. I have to look deep inside of myself for the truth. And I realize that for the first time, I'm not. If I die, I die. At least I'll know I died fighting for something *right*, and the girl I love will be beside me. "No," I whisper. "I'm ready."

"Good," Meadow says, as she closes her eyes to sleep. "Because tomorrow we kill them all."

CHAPTER 73

MEADOW

I wake to the sound of Orion's laugh.

Everything dances in the torchlight, strange shadows that, today, make everyone's faces look menacing.

"You ready for this?" Sketch asks me. She is drawing lines on her face with white paint. The patterns are beautiful, in a way, and for some reason, I think Koi would like this girl.

"War paint," she says. "People used to do this, I think. To get ready for battle."

Battle. Today we are going into battle.

Orion and Rhone call us all together. Zephyr has a gun at his hip, I have a crossbow slung over my shoulder, and my dagger, and Sketch has knives strapped to a vest, her legs, her arms. They run over the building codes with me again. We all look down at hand-drawn blueprints from Orion's journal. I have the entire layout memorized. "The holding cells and the Motherboard are in the same wing. You'll stick to the air ducts," Orion says. "Once you're done, the only way out is back the way you came. Stay quiet or you're dead, you got that?"

Sketch laughs. "We're dead the second we set foot in that place."

Beside me, Zephyr crosses and uncrosses his arms.

Rhone draws a line on the map, through the air ducts. "The building is bigger than it looks from the outside. We've got a route, and you'll stick to it. The Motherboard is here"—he circles a room at the back of the building—"and the Protector's going to be with it. Unfortunately, the air ducts don't lead right into that room. So . . . you'll have to find a way down, kick some Initiative ass, and get to it."

"Or die trying." Sketch grins, and a part of me thinks she *wants* to die in there, really craves it.

It is Zephyr that asks the question none of us focused on. "So . . . how do we get inside the building? Are we going in through the Perimeter exit, in the back?"

This time, it is Orion who answers. "It's too heavily fortified. We keep eyes on all the Zoms, all the time. The Initiative does, too. The only way in is *through*. And lucky for you, Z, we've brought in someone to help, someone I think you'll be happy to see."

I hear footsteps, and something being dragged across the floor. "She's a fighter, this one," one of the men holding her says, pulling the bag off her head. I see her bright, baby-blue eyes. My heart sinks to my toes.

"Talan." Zephyr gasps.

CHAPTER 74

ZEPHYR

"Oh thank *God*." Talan falls into my arms. I crush her to my chest.

I'm so relieved that she's *alive* that I don't notice for a while that she's actually crying. Talan, *crying*. Her right eye is all swollen and purple, so fat that she can barely open it.

"You smell like death," Talan says to me, sniffing my torn shirt, and her voice is still her voice, but I push her back and look her over, checking her arms, her hands, her neck, to make sure she's okay.

"Did they hurt you? Did they do this to you?"

"Stars, no," Talan says. She winks at me. "This is from

that sad sack of a Reserve boy who always tries to get into my pants. I gave him a good show this time, Zeph. You should have seen it."

"They had a bag over your head," I say, but she just shrugs.

"They also gave me fifty Creds to come here. Hell, they could've tied me up and thrown me out to sea for that much."

Reckless. So damn reckless.

I can't believe she agreed to go with these strange men, with a bag over her head, for a measly 50 Creds.

"We've been using Wards for a long time," Rhone says to all of us, scratching the dark stubble on his chin. "They take Creds to do jobs, they keep it secret, and the best part is, the Initiative doesn't give a rat's ass about the unprogrammed ones like Talan, here."

"Easy, boss," Sketch says, when I clench my fists and wrap my arm tighter around Talan. "Don't make a Zom angry."

For the rest of the day, we sit around the fire and go over the plan. It gets old fast, because Meadow keeps making everyone repeat the steps, and Talan won't stop talking, and Orion won't stop talking, and I kind of want to blow my ears off. And out of nowhere it hits me. I'm part of a family. It's a broken one, and it's not what I expected. But it's real.

We eat a full meal. Seagull, and dried rations and roots. Orion even brings out an old, dusty bottle of whiskey, which we all take a sip of. It burns like fire, and I wish I hadn't ever tasted it. Talan laughs, and Meadow holds my hand, and Sketch puts war paint on our faces.

It all ends when Orion tells us that the Night Siren has gone off. We make our way slowly out of the Cave, and a part of me is pretty sure that I'll never come back.

CHAPTER 75

MEADOW

I have smelled death for as long as I can remember.

It is all over the streets. Always, the scent in the air like a thick fog that causes you to turn and go the other direction once it hits you, to cover your mouth and wipe your watering eyes as the mourners wail in the streets.

But I have never smelled it as strongly as I do now, buried three bodies deep beside Zephyr and Sketch in the body collection cart.

Orion and Rhone zipped us up in plastic body bags. They took us to the edge of the Disposal Road and set us down in the street.

Once, two Initiative soldiers came by, but Orion

handled it with ease. "Keep walking, boys, these are your fallen comrades. Find those runaways and bring justice to the cause!"

Talan came after a while, pushing a cart. Orion and Rhone unzipped us from the bags, helped us inside the cart, and we were off without anyone suspecting a thing.

"Hey." I hear Talan's voice now, muffled by the heavy tarp and the corpses. "Hungry? I got a full load today. But it'll cost ya . . . "

One wrong move and she could screw up everything. But I hear the beep of the lock, and the wheels of the cart wobble underneath me again as Talan pushes into the building.

I try not to breathe as the corpse beside me lolls against my cheek, matted hair pressed up against my skin like bloody strands of hay. I try not to think about how she died. But I do know why. And I'll do everything in my power to stop it.

I run the plan through in my head. *Talan pushes the cart into the furnace room. When she lifts the tarp, I use Zephyr's gun to shoot out the cameras.*

Sketch creates a diversion so Talan can run.

We have seconds to get inside the air duct.

Tap, tap, tap. Three kicks to the side of the cart. It

means there are no guards at the furnace room door. I hear the lock click-whirr open. Then a clang. The cart begins to move again. My heart slams against my chest.

Zephyr's fingers squeeze mine, and I remember he is here. Sketch, too.

The cart stops again, and I can hear the roar of the furnace, swear I feel the heat of it licking up the sides of the old cart.

Talan lifts the tarp. I hear the whoosh and the heat hits me, searing into me like I'm a marshmallow roasting above the flames.

I tell myself to breathe. When the body is heaved off of me, I start to sit up.

But there is a loud clang. The sound of the furnace room door being opened again. I drop back down. Zephyr and Sketch do, too. Talan looks down at us with wide eyes.

"Talan Banner? 45320?" a gruff voice barks above the noise of the furnace. My heart is pounding in my chest and I know he can see me. One move, even a single breath from any of us, and everything will be over before it even had the chance to begin.

"Uh, yeah," Talan says, and her fingers close over my ankle.

"Your partner isn't with you."

"No skitz, buddy," she says, and I feel a flush of respect for her blatant disrespect.

"You know where he is?"

"Isn't that *your* job?" She snorts. Beautiful and rebellious. Loyal to Zephyr. My insides swell with a nervous joy.

"Then you won't mind if I stick around until he shows up."

"He's not coming, but sure. Stay as long as you want. The scent shouldn't bother you. Essence of Initiative, right?"

I hear the solidity of the slap as his hand meets her face. Her fingers leave my ankle as she staggers back.

"You're a pathetic little homeless slut. Yeah, I've heard about the things you do," he laughs. "Get on with it." He backs away. He's watching, I'm sure. Just waiting for her to screw up.

I slowly open my eyes. Talan is looking down at me. A red splotch marks her pale cheek, and her wicked expression tells me that everything is about to change. I shake my head to stop her, but it is far too late.

"Hey!" she yells over her shoulder. "Hey, can you help me?"

What is she doing? I glance at Zephyr and Sketch, and

their blood-streaked faces are just as panicked as mine must be.

The guard groans loudly. "Oh, I'll help you, all right," he says.

Talan looks at us and winks. Zephyr, Sketch, and I rise to a sitting position in the cart.

And then the guard is standing beside her. "Good for nothing—" His mouth forms a perfect O. He looks directly into my wide eyes. "What the . . ." His hand slides to the weapon attached to his belt. But he's out of time.

Because one of Sketch's knives meets his throat.

Blood splatters. The metallic scent surges up my nostrils as Talan opens the door of the furnace and the flames lick out at us. The guard staggers forward and she steps to the side, a wicked grin spreading across her face.

"Go, Meadow, go!" Zephyr grabs my arm and pulls me out of the cart. All I can hear is the roar of the furnace, the sputtering, choking coughs of the guard as blood fountains from his throat.

Zephyr tosses me the gun, remembering the plan although it is already too late.

I turn in a fast circle, letting bullets soar from the barrel into every last camera in the room. It's silent for one moment and we stand here, frozen. In seconds, everything has gone wrong.

The alarms begin to wail.

The last thing I see before we hoist ourselves into the air duct is the door of the furnace room flying open. Guards race in. Zephyr slides the vent panel closed before they can get a glimpse of us. We stare through the slits in silence.

The guards close in on Talan. Sketch fights off two others. Talan falls to the floor, laughing hysterically, as they beat her with their clubs.

"Arden!" she screams. "Arden!" They bludgeon her skull in with a club, and they drag her limp body to the furnace.

I hear Sketch yell, see her knives flashing, but there is nothing she can do.

I hold in my own scream as Zephyr pulls me back into the darkness.

CHAPTER 76

ZEPHYR

The grief hits me like a rogue wave.

My friend. My best friend.

"Dead. She's dead because of *me*."

"We have to keep going, Zephyr," Meadow whispers behind me. "It's what she'd want us to do. Sketch is buying us time. We have to do this. For Talan. Go left."

We crawl, sliding on our bellies, through the cool metal.

They must be searching for us. But they won't find us. We're invisible until we decide we don't want to be, and then we'll drop from the sky and destroy them all.

Their blood is going to stain the floors, but no matter how much we spill, it's never going to bring back Talan. The anger starts rising in me like fire, the flames licking through me so hot I want to scream.

CHAPTER 77

MEADOW

We are painfully slow.

The worst part is the sirens. The wails travel through the metal like the moans of dead spirits, echoing and ringing so that my eardrums feel like they are going to explode.

They could find us at any moment. They could start sending bullets through the ceiling, and we would have nowhere to run. Every so often I think I hear a scream. I think it is Sketch, that they are torturing her, that she will be dead soon.

Finally, a man's voice comes over some sort of loud speaker, crackling throughout the air ducts. "We have your friend," he says. "If you come peacefully, we won't kill her."

Sketch.

"They're going to kill her anyway," Zephyr whispers. "Even if we do come to them."

I nod. Everything has gone wrong so fast. "What now?"

Zephyr shrugs. I can barely see his face, but the darkness cannot hide the pain in his voice. "We can't go back."

We come to a fork. I know that left will take us past the Equipment room. Right leads past the SPC room. All the ducts lead in zigzags, but eventually, we'll get to the back of the building. To the Motherboard. To the cells, where my family is. We should go left. It is the faster way. But there are secrets I want to discover.

So I make the choice. "Right," I whisper.

It is what my father would want me to do.

CHAPTER 78

ZEPHYR

I don't want to look.

But when Meadow gently lifts one of the slats of the air vent open, there's no other choice. I slide over next to her and look down.

At first, the room seems totally normal. Plain white walls and tile floors, a row of computer screens embedded in a long silver table. There are a few Leeches sitting on padded chairs, talking in low voices, their fingers flying across the tablets.

I see the glass wall that splits the room in two. On the other side is a small boy.

His head is shaved.

He is surrounded by mirrors.

"Your mom and I were in *this* room. I think your aunt was sitting where those Leeches are now," I whisper to Meadow.

Flux.

The boy sits cross-legged on the floor with his back to the Leeches. He's chained to the wall. A black tattoo marks his bald head, and an X marks the back of his neck.

"What are they doing to him?" I breathe, and I can feel Meadow shrug beside me.

The boy's Catalogue Number puckers as he speaks, and a tiny little squeak of a voice can be heard on the other side of the glass.

"I have to go potty!"

One of the Leeches presses a button. "Just a short while longer, C87," he says. The boy shakes his head.

"But I have to go *now*."

"You're going to have to hold it. We have a very big assignment for you."

I wonder if they still have the red button and the blue button. The boy slumps, and that massive black tattoo makes me flinch. I touch my head. It's like I'm staring down at my own past, and I want to puke.

Meadow shifts beside me.

"My mother had a picture of this room," she whispers. "We should go."

But for some reason I can't move. A memory is calling my name, begging me to let it in. I've got to focus. I turn my attention back to the white room. A Leech produces a key card from around his neck.

"I swear, man, if we would just turn *all* the Wards into Patients, we wouldn't have to go through all this fluxing testing." He swipes his card through a slit in the table before him. And presses a button.

A door opens in front of the boy. Two meaty guards step through, real ChumHeads, and they've got some poor woman with a black blindfold covering her eyes. Crusted blood mats her thin brown hair. She's a walking skeleton.

"Please," she says, and skitz, her voice is desperate. Raspy. She sways as the guards shove her forward and back out of the room. The door slams. "I'll do anything. Anything, I swear."

"Sit down," the Leech demands. The woman twitches, but she does what he tells her to do, staggering forward until she's cross-legged on the floor in front of the boy.

"Hello," the little boy says.

" . . . Aaron?"

"Why are you bleeding?"

The Leech cuts in over the loud speaker. "Because she doesn't follow our rules, C87. Do you understand?"

The little boy nods. "I do." He turns back to the blind-folded woman. She's rocking back and forth on the floor like she's going crazy. "I wish you would've followed the rules. They don't hurt you if you follow the rules."

The woman reaches up to her blindfold, but one of the Leeches barks an order over the speaker. "Not yet!"

She drops her hands. "Aaron . . . baby . . . is that you?"

"I don't know any Aarons," the little boy says. His voice is so honest. He really means what he says.

The woman starts sobbing.

"Don't be scared," the boy says. "The man with the voice is my friend. He says I'm a good boy. Do you think I'm a good boy?"

The woman crawls forward. "Aaron . . ." Her hands fall on his smooth cheeks.

"Would you tell me a story about him?" he says, and the woman gasps, moves away.

"What have you done with my son?" She rips off the blindfold. She starts to scream.

"You said he was dead!" She crawls to the boy and pulls him into her arms and starts rocking him back and forth.

"You said my son was *dead*!" She sobs over and over again. The boy just sits there, blinking slowly.

"Let him go!" She yells up at the ceiling, and I realize she can't see through the glass.

I look down at the Leeches. They're just sitting there, observing.

"All right, get it over with, man," one of them says.

Oh, skitz, I know what's about to happen. I watch in horror as the woman pulls away and stares right into her son's eyes.

The second she does, he changes. His eyes turn to snakelike slits. He bares his teeth like some crazy feral dog.

"Do not resist," he says, and the voice is horrible and deep. The woman's mouth parts in shock.

The boy starts to scream. This is what I did to Meadow? She grabs my hand and squeezes it tight while we watch the boy twitch and writhe against his chains, struggling to break free.

The chains drop away. They slither back into the walls like snakes.

I want to scream. Tell her to snap out of it, turn and *run*. But she just sits there. She has no place to go.

The boy dives at her.

For a second, it doesn't seem real. All I can hear are her screams. She and her son are tangled up on the floor. The glass wall starts darkening, going to black, but just before it turns totally solid, a splatter of crimson blood hits the glass. It drips like wet paint, down to the floor.

"You owe me five Creds," one Leech says to the other. He leans back in his chair and kicks his feet up on the metal table. "I told you Natural-Borns would work just the same as the Test-Tubers."

"I still say it's a stupid plan. Let's go eat. I'm starving."

They leave the room, totally unfazed, like they haven't both just watched a stolen son murder his own mother. As soon as they're gone, their words hit me.

Test-Tubers.

They're creating Wards in the lab.

CHAPTER 79
MEADOW

We move from the air vent as quickly as we can. All I can hear is Zephyr's ragged breathing behind me. Horrified. Shocked. Disgusted. Once we get far enough away we stop and lean into each other in the cramped space.

"The boy . . . he . . . ," Zephyr says.

"I know."

"His mother. It was his own mother. And he didn't even know. . . . "

I have nothing to say. I never should've let him see what we just saw. So instead of speaking, we continue to crawl. We come across another air vent, and this time I am the only one to look.

There are at least a hundred children lined up in the massive room. Training. Kicking. Fighting with weapons, their fists. Just the way my father taught me. It is exactly as he said. Is this the very room where Zephyr was trained to kill?

We keep going. I peer through another vent and this time it is a medical room of some sort. Rows and rows of clear criblike bins line the walls. Only these are much larger. Each one holds a kid not much younger than us. Tubes run from the bins into the walls.

Everyone is wearing a helmet, silver and polished, with a little screen on the front.

I can see images on each screen. Every image is different.

A child playing on a set of swings that overlook the ocean. A child on the boardwalk, watching the sun go down.

A boy eating ice cream. A girl, building sand castles on the beach.

A woman, singing a song.

So many images, flickering, but all of them like glimpses of a real life. A real past.

"My father was right," I say, and my voice cracks.

"What?" Zephyr whispers. "What is it?"

How can I keep this from him? He deserves to know the truth.

I slide over and let him peer down into the room.

He inhales. A short gasp of recognition.

"Memories," he says. "They're . . . implanting fake memories into their heads."

"Zephyr . . ."

"*Leave* it, Meadow." He turns and crawls away from me. I watch as he settles down and leans his head back against the cool metal.

I picture Zephyr, years ago, lying in one of those bins after they created him in the lab. Getting his own set of memories. And now he is finding out that none of them are really *his*.

None of Zephyr's past is real.

We reach another fork, and this time we go left, following the map in my head. For a while, the only sound is our breathing.

We stop moving once the stench hits us.

It is like rotten eggs or milk gone sour. Like human waste spoiling for days and days under the hot sun. Only it is much worse.

It is coming from the air vent up ahead to our left.

This time Zephyr slides past me and takes the lead. I don't argue, because I am terrified of what I might see.

Zephyr peers down into the room. He cocks his head, as if he is confused. Then he motions for me to join him. "It's all right," he mouths, and he wraps his arm around my waist and pulls me close. "It isn't them."

I press my eye to the slat and look down. My breath catches in my throat and I force myself to *breathe* again. It is not my father. It isn't Koi or Peri. It is a woman.

She is so frail. Gaunt, like a skeleton, her body reduced to skin and bones. Her skin is green, almost as if it is rotting, and she is covered in a thick film of dirt and filth, her hair dulled to a pale gray in the dim light of the cell. I do not have to be a doctor to realize that they are starving her to death.

There are three guards with her, sitting against the far wall.

The woman turns her head just in the slightest way, and for a moment I am scared it will fall off of her neck and roll across the floor. It's almost as if she knows there is someone looking down on her. She freezes, and she is so thin I can see the pulse in her neck. I exhale when her shoulders relax.

But then she wheels around faster than I thought

possible. She looks up at the air vent high on the wall. At us.

Our eyes meet for one fleeting second before Zephyr and I duck down.

Hers are gray. Like the ocean.

Like mine.

My fingers claw at my thighs. As if they will help hold me in place when it seems like nothing else can. Not even Zephyr matters anymore.

Nothing does.

Because I know the dying woman with the silver hair.

"She is my mother."

CHAPTER 80

ZEPHYR

The only thing I feel is this awful, paralyzing shock.

Meadow turns to me. "We have to get her out."

"What?" my mouth falls open. "Meadow . . . "

"She is my *mother*," she says.

"But she's . . ."

I can see the shadowed outline of Meadow's face, staring back at me like I'm the enemy.

"Meadow," I say again.

Meadow isn't even listening to me. She checks her gun. Three bullets. There's only five arrows left on her bow. She stops and sits totally still. "Are you coming?"

When I speak, my voice is just a whisper.

"Please don't make me choose."

She makes the decision for me.

Darkness swallows me up as she snaps off the metal vent and drops into the cell.

CHAPTER 81

MEADOW

I roll to my feet inside the small room.

I take out the first camera. Glass shatters and the guards scramble as my bullet hits the second one.

"The girl! It's the girl!" one of them yells, and then I am on top of him.

I knock him face-first into the ground. Behind me I hear the other guards coming, but I slash with my dagger and am rewarded with the gushing sounds as blood splatters from the neck of one of the guards.

The third guard lunges for me, but I am too quick. My mind and body are two weapons that have melded together as one. He stumbles, and I take the chance. I wrap my arms around his neck the way my father taught me. And then I pull.

I feel the pop. It is satisfying, like removing the cork from the top of a bottle. He goes slack in my grip and I let his body fall to the floor.

Something hits me from behind. I crumple to the ground. Reinforcements. They collapse on top of me and I cannot move. I look across the room. My mother is pressed up against the bars of her cell, and I know this is how she will watch me die.

But then she smiles.

There is a gunshot, so close to my ears that the shock causes me to scream. Everything is ringing, swirling around me. Another shot. A guard's face slumps against mine. A bullet hole stares back at me from his forehead, and the blood starts to trickle like a stream.

Someone heaves the bodies off.

Zephyr scowls down at me. For a second, everything is silent.

But there is another gunshot, from the doorway.

"I'm hit," Zephyr moans, just once. He grabs his head.

He slumps to the floor.

I drown in my own screams.

CHAPTER 82

ZEPHYR

The pain doesn't come for a second.

There's this tingling, tickling sensation that runs through my body, kind of like someone's shocked me with a small volt of electricity.

And then it hits me in one solid wave.

Fire. White-hot fire.

I can't hear anything. I can't feel anything. Only fire.

I touch my head, and when I pull my hand away, it's bleeding.

The Leech shot me in the *ear*.

I feel around, and it's not there anymore. The ChumHead shot my ear off.

I roll over and see Meadow sprinting toward me with a fury I've never seen before. At the last minute she leaps, her body crashing into the Leech guard that shot me. She pulls a feathered arrow from her crossbow. She thrusts the thing right through his eye and he falls to the floor, broken, like me.

CHAPTER 83

MEADOW

I have dreamt of this moment for as long as I can remember.

Sometimes I picture my mother and me walking to each other across the sand. When we meet, the sky erupts into color. The sounds are electrified. We are together, and alive.

Other times, I stand by the train tracks, waiting for her to arrive. I wait for hours, and when she comes, she is as beautiful as I always knew she would be.

"Meadow," she says. I don't recognize the ragged voice that comes out of her mouth. "You look so grown up . . . you have no idea what I'd give to see you again."

She thinks I am not real.

A hallucination.

"Mother . . . ," I say. "I *am* real. I'm right here. Look at me."

Her hands tremble as they find my bloodstained shirt. She gasps as she touches me, lifts her hands to my face, my lips, runs her fingers through my hair. There are tears in her pale eyes. "I knew you would find me," she whispers, and she pulls me close. Zephyr gasps. He stands up and tries to move. He wobbles, off balance, then falls against the wall.

My mother pushes away from me when she notices him. Her head is cocked, like a dog's. Her eyes sparkle like she's looking at a drug she has longed to taste for years. She reaches for a fallen gun and hands it to me. "Patient Zero," she says. "He was always strong, but this won't do. Put him out of his misery."

I stagger back. "You . . . he . . . he's with me . . . "

"You do as I say, Meadow. This boy needs to die. It's strange, isn't it—pain?" my mother says.

She is insane. She wants him dead. I don't know what else to do. I stand and point the gun at her chest. "He's fine. Can't you see that? I'll pull the trigger if you so much as look at him. I swear on your life I will."

She laughs, a cold, steely cackle that sounds nothing like I remember. "You don't have the guts to do it, my darling."

She's right. I would never shoot my own mother. Instead I swing the gun across her jaw. She tumbles to the floor. "You're sick."

"You were always stubborn," she says as she wipes blood from her face. Her teeth are black. Rotting. "If you only knew what I've done for you. I've saved your life more times than I can remember."

She has never done anything for me but open up a world full of conspiracies, a world full of pain and lies and loss. I want to go back to the beginning. This woman is not my mother.

"He will only slow us down," she snorts. "He's dead weight."

"They have Peri and Koi . . . and Dad . . . "

My mother flinches. "I see . . . my God, what have I done? What have I *done*?" She starts pacing. Tearing at her hair.

And then, as the alarms begin to wail overhead, she regains control of herself. She stands up straight. She looks at the door. She could run now, run away from me. But she turns and our eyes meet. She is so frail. Her eyes

373

watch me with a hunger that makes me squirm.

"You will do exactly as I say," she says. "You're still my daughter. So you do what we trained you to do. You leave no man alive."

She crosses to a metal cabinet outside the cell and flings it open. There are guns. Rifles. Throwing knives. Clubs. I discard my crossbow, pick up a club and strap it over my shoulder. My mother tosses me a black handgun. I slide out the magazine. Fully loaded. I snap it back in place, grab another full magazine, and tuck them both into my waistband.

She turns to me when she's done strapping a rifle over her shoulder. "Ready?"

I feel like I am watching five different versions of my mother. Pain. Sorrow. Horror. Love. Evil.

"Meadow," she says, chewing on her lip.

"One second," I say, and go back for Zephyr. "I'm so sorry," I whisper, but as I bend down to help him stand, his eyes open.

"No," he says, and I back away as he clenches his teeth and rises to his feet. He sways a little, but I let him stand strong. "I'm fine now. I was just . . . in shock."

I hand him the club.

I draw my blade in one hand, my gun in the other,

and hold them firmly. They are my sanity along with Zephyr. For one fleeting moment, I remind myself that my instincts should be my guide. Not my mother.

But when she steps out into the hallway and starts to miraculously run, I follow.

CHAPTER 84

ZEPHYR

It happens when we're only halfway down the hall.

One second I'm running along behind Meadow, trying to keep myself upright, trying to keep things in focus.

Then it comes.

It hits me like a fire poker inside my skull. I let out a piercing scream that bounces off the walls. I crumple to the floor. Flux, it's too much.

Meadow rushes to my side. "Zephyr! What's happening to him?"

I can hear the fear in her voice. I want to tell her I'm fine, that everything's okay. But she feels like she's a thousand miles away.

I writhe in agony while emotions run their course through me. First there's pain. Then the loss of my mom and dad, the emptiness that came after I realized what I did.

Next, I feel like I'm floating in the stars, happier than I've ever been.

"When did he last activate?" I hear Lark's voice.

"About a week ago," Meadow says.

"It's an aftershock," she says. There isn't even a drip of sympathy in her voice. "They rebooted him."

"What the hell are you talking about?"

"He was flawed, now he's not. They've healed him."

"He's not healed! *Look* at him!"

"They've been torturing me, trying to get me to reboot the system. Yesterday, I caved. Gave them all the codes, all the control."

"You did *what*?"

I hear a whimper. "I'm so sorry. My god, darling, I've made a mess of things." A deep breath. A trembling whisper. "Meadow . . . when Patient Zero was just a boy, something in him was so *strong,* so good, to his very core, that he was able to fight the Murder Complex. That was his flaw. I guess they've figured it out. We're all good until we're not strong enough to be anymore. He's healed. He's going to change now. Kill him while you still have the chance."

I'm crying. I can't stop. All I feel is sorrow, for every death I've ever experienced, every life I've stolen. Meadow screams something, but I can't hear the words.

I look at her. She turns to me, everything in slow motion. I see her wave of hair. Her eyelashes. Her gray eyes when she looks right at me.

"Welcome back to the Murder Complex, Patient Zero. Initiate Termin—"

Meadow.

Love.

"Kill.

Destroy.

No escaping.

No turning back.

This is your duty.

Purge the Earth.

This is the Murder Complex."

Meadow.

Love.

I grit my teeth. I open my eyes and stare right at her.

"NO!"

I refuse to obey the system. The effort is so much that the world goes black around me.

CHAPTER 85

MEADOW

The smile never leaves his face.

When he wakes a moment later, I pull him to me and crush my lips against his.

"Meadow." He is weak as he pulls away. Breathless. "I fought it. I fought it."

"I know," I say. "I told you you were strong."

"Fascinating," my mother says. "Fascinating, just as he always has been."

Zephyr pulls himself upright, wincing. "Lark. *She's* the voice. The voice I hear in my mind."

I look away from him, to where my mother stands over two dead guards. Where did they come from? Their throats are slit. She stares down at them as if they are beautiful. She points the gun at one of them. He is already dead, but I hear the squelching sound as the bullet penetrates his flesh. She smiles. "Let's move."

The halls are strangely empty. No guards come rushing for us, no alarms sound. There is a chill that snakes its way up and down my spine. This feels wrong, like the way the ocean is always calm just before a massive storm hits.

"We have a job to do before we get my family," I say, pointing down the hall. There's only one way to go.

"*Your* family?" My mother raises an eyebrow at me, a look she used to give me when she was about to scold me.

"Yes. *My* family would never abandon me," I say. "Let's go."

"I can't take you there, Meadow. I know what you plan to do."

"You have to take us," Zephyr says, gritting his teeth. "Or we'll kill you."

"My daughter is strong, Patient Zero. But she is not strong enough to kill her own mother."

"I wasn't talking about Meadow," Zephyr says. He takes the gun from my waistband and points it at her face.

"The apple doesn't fall far from the tree, I guess," my mother says, nodding her head. "I trained you well. This way." She turns on her heel and marches down the hall.

CHAPTER 86

ZEPHYR

There are two Leeches outside of the Motherboard Room.

And on the floor in front of them, lying in a pool of blood, is Sketch.

"Something isn't right about that," Meadow whispers in my ear, and I agree. So far it's been way too easy. It's like they want us to walk right into a trap.

"There's a code to get inside the room," Lark says.

"74B87K23H9," Meadow whispers. "We didn't come here unprepared."

"The Resistance is helping you. But they're foolish, all of them. The code alone won't get you in. There's a catalogue scanner. A retinal scanner. A voice scanner."

"Programmed for who?" Meadow asks.

We both already know the answer.

"The Commander," Lark says. "And me, of course. He thinks I deleted my entry codes. But I installed a back door, as anyone with a brain would." She coughs into her sleeve. "But I won't let you in. Not unless I get something in return."

Meadow tenses. She pulls out her gun, polishes the barrel on her shirt. "What do you want, Lark?"

Lark. She doesn't even call her Mother. Skitz, it's great, and I want to smile, but I hold it back for her sake.

"Let me leave," Lark says. "Let me out of here alive, and you'll never see me again. They got what they needed. I reset the system, gave them full control. They'll kill me now, the first chance they get. I have . . . collateral." She steps closer to Meadow. "They seem to think time has changed me." Her eyes glaze over for a second, and she does that strange wobbling thing on her feet again. "Sweet girl . . . would you let your own mother die?"

"My mother died a long time ago," Meadow says. "You have your deal. Now get us inside so we can shut this thing down."

The guards pace back and forth, waiting, like spiders on a web.

Lark points at Meadow's gun. *Shoot them,* she mouths.

Meadow nods. She lets two bullets fly, one right after the other.

The guards drop. I run to Sketch, drop to her side, and untie her while Meadow pulls the bag from her head. She's still alive.

"'Bout time, assholes," she says. She looks over my shoulder at Lark.

"Not yet, Sketch," I warn her. "We need her."

"Like skitz we do," she groans. Her leg's dripping blood, so Meadow takes the bag that was over her head, rips it, and bandages Sketch's wound. "Lost too much blood. They got me good, with some kind of red knife."

"I designed that myself." Lark smiles, a look of wonder on her face. "It reverses the nanite's healing process. You'll probably die soon." She enters the codes on a massive panel embedded in the door.

The room opens with a hiss. A red glow pours out.

Meadow and I haul Sketch inside.

"You good?" I ask her.

She grunts. "Better than you, Zero. You look like hell."

The door slides shut behind us. The room is circular,

with enough empty seats to hold a hundred people, at least. Sketch collapses into a chair, breathing hard. "What the flux is that thing?" She points at the far wall.

It's lit up a dark, bleeding red. Barcodes soar across it. They're constantly moving, changing places. In the center is the Initiative eye. Beneath it, at the bottom of the wall, is a line that wavers up and down, up and down.

"It's measuring a heartbeat," I say. "Look at it. It's connected to someone!"

But Meadow's too focused on her mom to listen to me.

"I created her a long time ago," Lark says. *Her*, like the Murder Complex is a fluxing human being. I sway, and slide down into the chair next to Sketch.

"How do we shut it down?" Meadow asks. She walks across the room, taps the massive computer screen. The barcodes keep soaring and sliding and changing. They never stop. Skitz, I wonder how many citizens this thing's killed, how many like me it's controlled.

Meadow pulls out her gun, loads another clip from her belt, and shoots.

The bullet hits the eye, but evaporates instantly. It's gone. Just *gone*, in a puff of smoke. Meadow gasps.

"She has an impenetrable protection system," Lark says. "Bullets don't work. Water or fire won't stop her. You cannot unplug her, or shatter her, or shut her down. She's my greatest creation, Meadow. And my greatest regret."

"You regret nothing," Meadow snarls. "You love the Murder Complex. You're staring at it like it's your *child*."

Lark shifts. Looks down at her toes. "A mother always loves her child, even if she becomes a monster."

"You never loved me." Meadow sinks down to the floor and puts her head between her knees.

"They said there would be a Protector," Sketch growls beside me.

"There *is* a Protector," Lark says, shaking her head. "And that's the worst part about all of it."

Meadow stands up. "Who is it?" she asks.

I can see it all clicking into place. I can see the answer.

Lark looks at Meadow. Meadow looks back at her, and when Lark speaks, there are tears in her eyes.

"You're the Protector, Meadow. In order for the Motherboard to be shut down, in order to stop the Murder Complex . . . you have to die."

CHAPTER 87

MEADOW

I have survived this long because of my father. He taught me that in a world full of death, living was a beautiful thing.

I fought for each day because of him. I always did what I had to do to stay alive.

And now, as I stare at the Motherboard and realize that its destruction lies within *me,* I want to die.

"You're sick," I hear Zephyr say.

"You deserve to rot in hell for eternity," says Sketch.

I have a gun in my hand, and a bullet lodged in the chamber.

"How did you do it?" I ask my mother. "How did you link it to . . . me?"

"Your brain," she says. "When you were a baby, I pro-grammed your brain to the Murder Complex. When you die, the system does, too. I've been implanted, too. It's brilliant, really. If the Initiative kills me, the system will throw all of them in. The lottery will choose them, and they will all die."

"Why?" I ask. "How could you do this to me?"

"I did it to *both* of us, Meadow. We've always been in this together, you and me. But for you, especially, I did it because I knew that someday I might feel regret or even guilt. I might want to undo everything . . . shut it down. But it is the only way to keep it all alive, Meadow. Don't you see?" She rubs her hands together, lets out a crazed giggle. "Someday, the Initiative is going to take the Murder Complex *everywhere*. I'll save the earth, and not just our little piece of it."

She sways. "You have to understand, some days, I want-ed to destroy it all. But you," she says, reaching out to touch my cheek. I flinch away. "You, I could never regret. You I could *never* destroy."

I am strangely calm, as her words settle in. This is why the Initiative hasn't tried to kill me. This is why they let me come to them on my own terms.

"My father told me that someone keeps trying to put

me into the system. Someone wants me dead. Is this why? Because they know what you did to me?"

My mother nods, a strange, haunting look on her face. "I kept it secret for as long as I could so you could live a normal life."

"*Normal?*" I can't help but laugh. "Nothing is *normal* in the Shallows."

"It's your sister, isn't it?" Zephyr asks. "Your sister is the person who wants Meadow to die. She's the good one. Not you."

"Don't talk about my sister!" my mother screams at Zephyr.

I wonder how they'll keep me alive after the Cure fails me. Will they take out my brain and keep it sealed inside of a jar?

"Let me kill Lark," I hear Sketch say. "Let me cut her eyes out!" She staggers toward my mother but only makes it halfway. She falls to the floor, unconscious.

Everything is ruined. "It's over," I say.

"Meadow." Zephyr's voice is so full of pain. He looks at me, and I look back at him, and I know what he is thinking.

"I'm sorry," I say. I want to die. I want it more than I have ever wanted anything.

I turn to him and press the gun to his sweaty palm. "You do it," I say. "Please. I'm begging you."

"No." The gun falls to the floor. "Never."

"I want it to be you," I say. "It has to be you."

My mother is standing in the corner, watching us. "Don't do it, Meadow," she says. "Think about your little sister. Think about your brother. They need you."

"It's not worth it!" Zephyr says. He is trembling now, pressing his hands to my cheeks, holding me too tight. "Let the world die. You don't have a choice."

"I have *always* had a choice, Zephyr," I say.

I bend down and pick up the gun. He moves for it, but I turn it around and point it at him. "Stay back," I say through tears. He keeps coming for me anyway, until the gun is pressed against his chest. "Zephyr, please. I want this. I have to do this." I stare into his eyes, will them to memory, and hope that in the afterlife, I will remember their soft green color. As I turn the gun toward myself, ready to fix what my mother broke, I hear the one sound in the world that can stop me right now.

Peri's scream.

We race outside, across the hall. I shoot the door handle, kick it open, run down a long, winding hall. There are guards at every turn, and I take them all out. "There it is!" my mother screams, and finally, I see two doors at the end of the hallway. We slam through. My mother uses the rifle, shoots with an effortless grace, taking down one guard, then another, then two with a single deadly shot.

There are cells lining the room. I scream at the prisoners, "Where is she? Where?" They shake their heads and stare back, frail and skeletal, as if they don't know how to speak anymore.

Peri screams again. She's close, somewhere inside.

The scent of human waste and death fills my lungs, burns through me like hot acid, and suddenly I hear the beep of a keypad. I round the corner past a cell, where the room ends. There's another door. It slams shut just before I reach it.

I shoot the lock and yank it open.

And there is light. Outside. I see the Perimeter in the distance.

Thick bars block my exit.

"Peri!"

I can't get through. I can't get to her. A guard drags her across the grass. She's kicking and screaming. Rage surges through me.

Because I am too late.

Her pale eyes meet mine just before the guard reaches an armored truck and throws her inside. The sun appears from behind a cloud and for a moment I am blinded.

"It's over, Meadow. She's too far away," my mother says beside me. I lower my dagger.

The truck door slams shut. A door in the Perimeter slides open, and for one second, I see the outside world.

Everything is green. Alive.

The truck hurtles through.

The Perimeter closes.

"No!"

Peri is gone.

CHAPTER 88

ZEPHYR

The only way out is to go back the way we came in.

Meadow rounds on her mother once we're back in the main hall.

"Where did they take her? Tell me!"

"To the Ridge," she says. "Up north."

"North, where?" Meadow screams. She points her dagger at her mother. A drop of blood drips from its tip and splatters onto the floor like a raindrop.

"We aren't the only testing site, Meadow. There are two others, one for genetic mutation and the other for breeding. The Ridge is a good place. Peri will be happy there."

"How can you say that?" Meadow snarls. "She's your *daughter*."

Lark sighs. Deep wrinkles line her filthy face. "You will never understand, Meadow, so don't ask me to explain it to you. You're not smart enough, dear."

I stumble toward Meadow and put my hand on her shoulder. She flinches like she's been hit. I pull her into my arms. I kiss her head, tell her I'm sorry, tell her it's going to be fine.

"We can't stay here," her mother says. "They'll have sent the Patients by now."

"You make me sick. You're pathetic. You deserve to die," Meadow says.

"There is nothing we can do for her now, Meadow. But pray, maybe . . . "

"Pray?" Meadow throws her arms into the air. "You don't have a soul!"

Her mom sighs.

"I never should've wasted my time saving you, you bitch! You're already dead to me."

"Meadow."

"Get the hell away from me."

The sirens start wailing again.

"Let's go." I pull Meadow with me. She sways and I use the club to hold us both up. My shoulder screams and my head spins. I've lost too much blood.

We turn and walk down the hall.

CHAPTER 89

MEADOW

We walk in silence.

Zephyr staggers, but he won't let me help him. My mother walks ahead of us, never looking back.

I decide that today, I will not take my life.

I will get my revenge on the Initiative. I will die killing every last one of them. If they run and hide, I will find them. If they beg for mercy, I will slit their throats.

I focus on putting one foot in front of the other. Walking with Zephyr. I will get him out of here, safe, before I do anything else. We say nothing, following my mother. I do not know where we are going. I don't think I even care.

They finally come at us from all sides.

An army of the mindless. The good soldiers of the Murder Complex. They fill the hallway like rushing water.

"Don't look in their eyes, Meadow," my mother says. "We'll be okay if you don't look in their eyes."

I don't want to obey her. But I do.

We press against the walls and I keep my head down.

I squeeze Zephyr's hand, will him to hold himself together.

"I'm alright, Meadow. Keep going," he says.

I pull my strength from somewhere deep within. I listen to my father.

"Silent strength, that's what you were born with, Meadow."

The hallway is blocked by a gate that has dropped down from the ceiling.

"What now?" I ask, and my mother shakes her head.

"That door," she gasps, pointing to our left. "Open the door!"

It's some kind of supply closet. I flip the light switch and a dim light fills the space. I grab a broom and shove it under the door, like a stopper. It will buy us some time, maybe.

Zephyr settles down on the floor, his head in his hands. I crouch near him and whisper, "We'll be okay." I am surprised how easy it is to lie.

But he knows. He has always known this is how it would end.

I turn to my mother. "What now?" I ask. "Where are we?"

"It's over, Meadow."

I sink to the floor and let my head fall back against the door. "You don't know that."

She smiles. "Don't I, dear? They'll never stop until they have you. You're *special,* Meadow. Very, very special. You have me to thank for that."

"Why did you do it?"

"I wanted more," she says.

She offers no apology. No acknowledgement that she loves me or wants what's right for me. She closes her eyes. Zephyr moans. "I can't fight it twice in one day," he whispers. "Not when you're so close, Meadow."

My mother slumps down beside me. "The creation takes the creator," she says. "Marvelous. I always knew it would end this way."

She watches Zephyr in silence. I watch her. I can almost imagine a trickle of sunlight spilling across her face, the gentle rock of the houseboat. I can almost taste the sea breeze, and I wonder how many years she has longed for it it as well. I wonder if she feels anything at all, or if her heart is too dead to have wants and desires.

Her head lifts. She tilts her chin upward. "Can you feel it?"

"Feel what?" I ask, but she is right. The air in the closet has grown cooler.

"Behind me," Zephyr chokes out.

I pull him gently to the side, and clear off the shelf as fast as I can. Paint cans. Old rags. A tornado of dust.

And a breeze, like the taste of cool freedom on my lips. I shove aside a roll of wire and that is when I see a vent leading directly outside.

"Zephyr! Zephyr, give me your club!"

I swing hard into the metal grate. It puckers, so I do it again. Again and again and again, until the bolts pop loose and a small window to the outside is staring back at us.

Freedom.

The door splinters. They're pounding on it.

My mother stumbles past me and drops to her hands and knees.

She turns, just before she crawls through. Our eyes meet.

"Zephyr, let's go," I say. I turn to him. When I look back, my mother is gone.

The pounding on the door grows louder.

"You first," he says. He reaches his hand out to help me. Instead of taking it, I place my gun in his palm and close his fingertips around the cool metal.

"Meadow!"

I lean down and hold his face with shaking hands. "You'll find my family, won't you, Zephyr? You'll find a way out, and you'll go to them?"

"Of course," he says. "Now let's go, Meadow, we need to go now!"

"Be fearless, Zephyr James." I kiss him once. "Go on."

He crawls through. It takes all my strength not to follow him.

As soon as his feet disappear, I fit the vent grate in place. I lever the club across it, then the shelf, and everything else heavy enough. I can hear Zephyr's fists pounding the metal, hear him screaming my name.

I unsheathe my dagger and face the door. I imagine Peri running up to me on the beach. I imagine Koi, his focus and his love. I remember the one thing I have always known all along. I am not my mother's daughter. I do not run from fear, but dive into it headfirst, the way my father taught me.

The door splinters. I close my eyes.

Count to three. Relax your mind. Now survive.

Acknowledgments

I never thought I'd be a real author, and there are so many people who helped me get here. You deserve a million wonderful, beautiful thanks. And puppies.

First, to my Lord and Savior Jesus Christ, for helping me through my illness. You gave me books, and they saved my life.

My agent, Louise Fury, who championed this series and fought like Meadow to get it a home. You are amazing for making my dreams come true! Thank you for dealing with my crazy self, and for always e-mailing back no matter the hour.

My editor, Virginia Duncan at Greenwillow, who pushed me hard, and made this book a thousand times better than I ever could have on my own. Thank you for giving me and this book a chance. You changed my life when you said YES.

The team at Epic Reads and everyone at HarperCollins, for being so excited about this series, and helping promote it like a boss. The cover gods, Matt Roeser and Paul Zakris, who gave *TMC* a face and made it fierce and RED.

Team Fury, especially Kristin Smith, for helping me edit behind the scenes, and giving me magical, amazing ideas.

My parents, Don and Karen Cummings, and my sister, Lauren, for helping keep me sane during this entire process, and for believing in me.

My husband, Josh Price, for always pulling me out of the internal writing cave, and giving me the gentle love and care that Zephyr gives Meadow.

My best friend, Cherie Stewart, for loving books almost as much as I do. My cousins Abby Haxel and Landon Davies, for loving books and inspiring me. My first friend-turned-fan, Jen Gray, for being so sweet and supportive and loving this book.

To all of the Murder Complex fanpages on Instagram, you rock! Sasha Alsberg, for pimping me like a pro. My Superfan, Sama Aziz, for being amazing.

The ladies at my Tuesday morning Bible study, for years of prayers.

My team of #booknerdigans, for having faith in me and my work. You are the BEST book nerds EVER. The YA Valentines, for helping me get through the craziness of debut author life! All the TX book hangout peeps, for all the fun times!

Authors Patrick Carman, Lauren Oliver, Veronica Roth, Marie Lu, Beth Revis, Suzanne Collins, and J.K. Rowling, for inspiring the heck out of me. You guys made me believe the writing dream would come true.

READ ON FOR A PREVIEW OF

THE
DEATH
CODE

CHAPTER I

ZEPHYR

It's going to be a dark night.

Weeks ago, the darkest nights were the worst. Bodies dropped like flies around the Shallows, and blood dried in rivers all over the streets. The Dark Time meant dread. It meant the Murder Complex and its Patients came out to play.

That hasn't changed. If anything, the deaths have gotten worse.

But something good will happen tonight.

It's a new moon, and black clouds are gathering over the tops of the crumbling buildings. The thunder and lightning and the Dark Time combined make for the perfect distraction, the perfect storm.

And that means Lark Woodson will come out of hiding.

I've been tracking her for weeks, but every time I'm about to find her, she disappears. Like the wind.

Not tonight. Tonight, I'm going to catch her.

As I run, I see Meadow's face in my head. Her gray eyes, determined and cold as steel. Her dagger in her hand, slicing Patients and Leeches as she fights her way through the Leech Headquarters from the inside out.

It's been three weeks. She *has* to be alive. I'd know it if she were dead, wouldn't I?

Maybe not. Maybe she *is* dead. Like Talan.

Oh, god, Talan. My best friend. Dead, because of me. I try to shove the guilt away, but it's too strong.

"Damn it!" I growl and sprint harder, faster, down the streets of the Shallows. The gun sheathed at my thigh bobs with every step. I skid around the corner of an alleyway and stop. Fade into the mass of people heading for safety before the Dark Time takes over.

The Leeches are out in packs, searching, but they won't find me easily.

I pull a baseball cap low over my eyes. My arms are covered in temporary tattoos, drawn on just this morning.

Hiding in plain sight is exactly what the Leeches

wouldn't expect me to do.

The crowd moves along, and I walk with them. I keep my head on a swivel, searching. Always searching, for the woman who created me. Turned me into a monster.

Five minutes, and the Night Siren will go off.

There's a crackle in my left ear, the only good ear I have left, where a stolen Leech earpiece sits. *Take the alley directly across the street. And hurry up. My little sister runs faster than you.*

It's Rhone, the guy from the Resistance who was so interested in sending Meadow into the Leech Headquarters in the first place. Now she's gone, stuck inside. And I can't reach her.

Zero, move! Now.

I do what he says, shove my way through way too many people. Running is still hard since losing my ear, and my balance isn't quite right. But I can't stop now. I wobble on my feet before I leap over the train tracks, then dive into the alley to my left. The setting sun disappears, and suddenly it's dark.

And quiet. Too quiet, almost like it's the Silent Hour.

I stop and look around.

There's a Leech lying all bent and broken up against the brick building to my right. His rifle lies on the concrete at his side, and there are empty bullet casings all over the place. But no other body, which means if Lark was here . . . she's gone. I take a step closer to him. Fresh blood drips from a slit in his throat, a perfect line of red, like a smile. The Leech chokes, lifts a hand for help that he's not going to get.

"She was just here," I say into my wrist mic. "Slit throat, like all the others."

We'll get her next time, Zero, Rhone says, and I want to believe him, but he's been saying the same thing for weeks. 21 days, and 7 hours, to be exact. *I'm on my way.*

I sigh and run a hand through my hair. I have to find Lark. When I do, I'll take her to the Leeches, knock down their front door, and hand her over in exchange for Meadow. I've thought about killing Lark instead. But in the chaos that will come afterward, I might not get to my moonlit girl.

Trading Lark for Meadow is best. We'll be together again, and we'll find some way, *any* way, to leave the Shallows behind. Find where the Leeches have taken her family, set them free.

I promised her I'd rescue them.

But I won't leave without her. I refuse.

The Leech groans, one last time. He takes a rattling

breath and dies.

"You deserved it," I say to his body. I lean down to grab his rifle, and that's when I see it.

A bloody footprint, just a few feet away from him.

And then another, and another, heading out of the alley, toward the exit that leads to the beach. The footprints are small, but not small enough to be a child's. They could be Lark's.

I lift my wrist to my mouth. "Rhone, I think she's hurt. She couldn't have gone far from—"

The Night Siren goes off.

It starts as a whoop, dipping low, and then goes so high it's like a piercing scream. I cover my ears and drop to my knees. My whole body shakes, all the way to my fingers and toes. I hear a voice in my head. Lark's voice, welcoming me to the Murder Complex.

And suddenly I want to *kill, destroy*, give in to the pull of the system in my mind. I feel myself slipping away, feel my heart turning cold and solid as stone, see a victim in my head, their Catalogue Number, 65098, in bright red numbers.

But I think of Meadow. I think of one word, with four letters, and it's stupid as hell but I don't care.

Because love is what saves me and sets me free. It's still

working, for now, but each night it's becoming harder. If I don't save Meadow soon, I'm afraid of what I'll become.

I shake the Murder Complex from my mind and sprint into the darkness.